IV

(handwritten signature: "To the C-man Woodall")

Need

The Landrys Book One

Mandy L Woodall

Need

Need Copyright @ Mandy L Woodall 2017

Woodall Publishing

All rights reserved.

ISBN-13: 978-1542904568

ISBN-10: 1542904560

Cover photo and design by: Sara Eirew

Cover Model: Mike Chabot

Mandy L Woodall

Tobale of Contents

Need

Dedication

This book is dedicated to my Woodall Squad. My husband's support makes me strong enough to do this. My three babies' belief in me pushed me forward.

Introduction

Bailey

The things I've seen, the things I've lived through, left me with scars, both physical and mental. I was closed off to people, not wanting to make attachments that I knew would break. I had friends and someone I considered family, but I didn't let myself need anyone. Then, there he was. I felt high when I was with him and like nothing could touch me. It was a crazy, insane, have me committed type of situation.

Ryker

Growing up with five siblings and awesome parents, I knew what love and support was. I was surrounded in it. I listened to my mom explain to us that we would find the one, and I believed her. I believed in love. I just didn't realize it would happen so soon. Then, there she was. I knew right away she was my one. I needed her, but would she let herself need me?

Chapter One
Bailey

"Yes," I breathed. I was on sensory overload, or was it sensual overload, sexual overload? I didn't fucking know. The only thing I knew was that all my senses were on high alert with my vision taken. With the sliver of moonlight shining through around the edges of the curtain, the room was cast in shadows.

I was on my back laid across a big bed with soft sheets, cool against my overheated naked skin. He had his hands and mouth on me, and his body was under my hands. Music streamed through the speakers, and our moans and groans surrounded us.

"Fuck," I moaned as he assaulted my breasts in the best way possible.

One of his hands cupped my breast playing with my nipple while his mouth sucked and licked the other. When he moaned against my chest, my center clinched, the vibration traveling straight to my core.

"Your skin is so fucking soft," he said rubbing his stubble covered jaw against my skin.

I shivered and moaned from the sensation. My breasts were already sensitive from all the lip and tongue action he was giving them, so adding the roughness of his prickly facial hair made me wild. My body writhed and twisted. My eyes fell shut. My breathing became heavy.

My chest tightened as he sucked my nipple deep in his mouth. My back arched from the bed.

I felt like a live wire waiting to go off. I moaned and groaned shamelessly. *Could I come just from him playing with my tits? Should I be embarrassed if I did?* When his teeth were added into play, I decided I didn't care and moaned low in my throat. It felt so good. He felt so good.

My hands rubbed against his naked chest and around to his back trying to feel as much of his skin as I could reach. His body was fucking amazing, hard muscle covered by soft skin under my hands. His abdomen was defined, and I could feel the indention of each of his abs. I ran my hands along his arms picturing the tattoos I saw back at the party, the muscles in his forearms and biceps tightening at my touch. My hands wandered up his neck to his hair. My nails scraped lightly along his scalp before latching onto the longer pieces on top.

He let my nipple go with a pop and moved his lips down my torso. His hands moved down my back and around to my hips where he squeezed. He unbuttoned my jeans and slowly dragged the zipper down. His tongue made a circle around my navel before dipping in the indention causing my stomach to quiver. He trailed his lips to the waistband of my panties where he ran his tongue under the elastic skimming my pelvic bone. He sat back to drag the denim down my legs leaving me squirming from the slow and steady pace he set.

He licked each new section of skin he uncovered causing me to shiver and moan. His fingertips skimmed my skin in a barely there caress that I felt in my core. I felt frenzied with need. My panties were soaked. My nipples were pebbled to hard points. My hips rocked up and down looking for friction.

He gripped my ankles with firm hands creating a trail of heat as his hands moved up my legs. He cupped behind my knees opening my legs slightly. That small movement caused me to gasp at the feel of my swollen folds rubbing against the cotton of my panties. His hands traveled along the back of my thighs to grab handfuls of my butt.

He squeezed and groaned. "Your ass is so fucking right."

His hands glided around my hips straight to my mound where he made a triangle with his fingers, and his thumbs brushed the lips of my sex through my panties. My body jumped as though I was shocked with an electrical current.

"Ohhh," I uttered while my fingers clenched on his shoulders.

"You are so wet for me," he moaned sliding his hands up to my breasts.

He cupped them with his big hands engulfing them. My B cup chest never felt so fucking good. He rolled my nipples between his forefingers and thumbs. His hands were sure and steady slowly moving over my body like he was memorizing every inch of me. I felt almost cherished, and even if it was for just one night, I would enjoy it and keep the memory tucked close.

His hands sank into my hair tilting my head up to him. His lips devoured mine. I gasped in shock from the demanding kiss. It was rougher than the gentleness he just showed my body. He took advantage of my open mouth, and his tongue dove in to tangle with my own. He nipped my bottom lip with his teeth and sucked it into his mouth causing me to moan. He licked his tongue across his assault causing a warm tingle to flutter in my stomach.

He dragged his tongue across my jaw to my neck where he ran his nose along my skin inhaling deeply. His teeth sank into the spot behind my ear that made my toes curl. The pain turned to pleasure with the flick of his tongue soothing the bite. His lips ran down my neck causing me to shiver. One hand gripped his short brown hair, and the other clutched at his back, my nails biting into hard muscle. He ground his erection against my center. The rough denim of his jeans and his big erection hit my clit with enough friction to make my eyes roll back in my head.

His hands glided around my back bringing my chest to his. I moaned at the feeling of skin on skin contact with him. His chest hair rubbed against my sensitive nipples and, my thighs clenched around his waist. My back arched off the bed seeking more of his skin.

He groaned when I pushed harder against him. I could feel his dick twitch in his jeans when he slid his hands down to my ass slipping under my panties to grab both cheeks tilting my hips up. My clit dragged along his bulge roughly.

"Fuck!" I was so going to come from dry humping! Well, not really dry considering moisture soaked my panties.

He slid my panties down my legs breaking away from me. I moaned in disappointment as my body turned cold without his heat. I stared up at his shadow watching him moving back toward me. His hard body came down on me, pushing me into the soft blankets.

"Ryker," I gasped hitching my knee around his hips pulling him into me further with a calf against his butt.

His lips took mine in a searing kiss. He bit my lower lip causing me to suck in a harsh breath. His tongue delved into my mouth taking possession of my tongue quickly. This kiss was frenzied. He ran one hand along my torso while his other hand gathered my hair into his tight fist exposing my neck.

His hand tightened on my ribs before sliding under my body to curl around the back of my shoulders bringing my chest up to his mouth. He sucked one nipple into his mouth causing me to groan and throw my head back. My nipple beaded tightly with his suction. His teeth caught my hard point, and his tongue swiped over the bite; pain then pleasure. Holy shit! That felt so fucking good. *He rocks at this pain to pleasure thing!*

He switched breasts, nibbling and licking around my nipple before latching on. With every pull on my breasts, I could feel my core clench. I was throbbing with need. It was excruciating and exhilarating to need someone like this.

I was in pain, and it hurt so fucking good.

"Please," I begged.

His fingers glided down my torso going straight to my core. As soon as his finger entered me, my pussy locked tight around him, and my body came off the bed with an orgasm so unsuspected I felt out of control. I didn't even know I was that close to the edge. Brilliant light flashed behind my closed eyelids, my breath stuck in my chest, my fingers locked tight in the blanket.

"You with me, Bailey?" His husky voice sent chills down my spine. His hands were high on my thighs opening me for him.

"Yes," I responded slowly as I released the blanket from between my stiff and tingling fingers.

Damn! That was the best orgasm I've ever had including self-induced ones, and we didn't even get to the best part yet. *How was I going to survive this?*

"Good," he said.

That's it, just one word. That was the only warning I got before he dropped his head between my legs. He ran his tongue from the bottom of my slit to the top, circling my clit before plunging his tongue in my core.

"Ryker!" I screamed. I could hear the sucking sounds he made drinking up my essence, and that turned me on even more knowing that he ate me out like he was starved, like he needed me for his survival.

I've never let anyone go down on me before. It was so personal and intimate. I felt too open and vulnerable. My hands went to his hair with the intention to pull him off, but I felt myself pulling him closer instead. He growled sending vibrations to my pussy that made me lift my hips and grind on his face. I should have felt embarrassed by my actions, but I couldn't. I was so far gone. All that registered with me was Ryker.

He consumed me.

He possessed me.

In that moment, he fucking owned me.

Ryker changed everything.

His hands slid beneath me grasping my ass lifting me up against his face even more. My hands tangled in his dark brown hair pulling slightly causing him to groan again. His groans vibrated through me better than any vibrator I ever used. Nothing could ever compare to this.

I gasped as my pussy tightened around his tongue. He squeezed my ass before his hands moved to my hips and pushed me back down to the bed. His grip on my hips was gentle but restrictive, not allowing me to move, keeping me right where he wanted me. His tongue made another swipe along my slit teasing my clit before returning to my core. His thrusts were shallow, but strong and on point. He was on a mission, and I wanted nothing more than for him to be mission accomplished.

His tongue left my channel, and I moaned in protest. The protest died on my lips quickly when my body jerked, and my breath rushed out in a groan so deep it felt like it came from my very soul. He had latched onto my clit with his lips sucking the hard nub in between his teeth while slipping his finger through my wetness spreading it across my lips before opening them. He thrust his finger inside of me shocking me at first with the sudden intrusion. That one finger turned into two as he nipped my clit causing my hips to lift searching for more. His free hand laid flat on my abdomen anchoring me to the bed, and I groaned in frustration. I gripped his biceps, my nails digging into his skin. His muscles flexed in my grasp while thrusting his fingers in and out of me faster, and his tongue flicked my clit back and forth furiously. I was at the edge and didn't know how to go over. I pulsed and throbbed.

"Please," I begged not exactly sure what I was begging for, but I knew Ryker could give it to me.

I had never felt like that before. I'd never felt that overwhelming need for anything. I felt alive, not broken, faking it until I make it. This was real. This was raw. My body was tingling, and my heart was pounding. My hands were shaking where they were clutched in his hair. I dropped my hands to the bed when I was seriously in danger of pulling all his hair out by the roots. I needed him inside me. I needed him to make this burning and throbbing stop. I needed him to put out this flame he ignited in me. All I could do was whimper, my body shaking.

"Shhh," Ryker said as his lips brushed mine. "I've got you."

His hot breath against my wet flesh sent shivers down my spine. I shifted my hips moaning. His hand tightened on my belly where I quivered as he growled into me. My fingers dug into the comforter so hard, I was afraid I would tear the fabric.

"Let go," he rasped before his teeth locked on my clit and two fingers thrust into me hard and fast.

I lost it.

I fucking lost it.

I screamed out his name and other stuff that I couldn't understand. I squeezed my eyes shut, my neck arched. I was shattered, not sure if all the pieces of me could be found. My pussy squeezed his fingers as he continuously hit my g-spot. He replaced his mouth with his thumb, keeping pressure on my clit. He licked up my juices as though it was the best thing he had ever tasted. My hands curled into fists in the blankets as the aftershocks ran through me. That orgasm made me see flipping stars!

"You taste so fucking good," he rasped breathing heavily.

Slowly he moved back up my body. My body laid limp while my breathing slowly returned to normal. My limp body came alive with the feel of his body on top of mine, but it wasn't from fear which is what I would have expected. His weight showed how much stronger he was than me, but I knew he wouldn't hurt me. I don't know how I knew that. I met him a few hours before at a frat party, but I trusted him to not hurt me, which was really fucking ridiculous considering my past experiences.

With a growl, low in his throat, his lips slammed down on mine. I could still taste myself on him, surprisingly causing more wetness to form and a fire to spark alive again. We were in a battle with our mouths. Our teeth clashed, our tongues licked every crevice they could, our lips moved desperately against each other.

When we broke apart to catch our breath, I was on fire again. His chest lay against my sensitive nipples, and his hard cock behind his jeans was pressed against my core. My hands glided along any of his skin I could reach. I shifted my hips and rubbed against the rough denim, a moan moving past my lips. This may be the one and only time I would have to experience a passion like this, and I couldn't miss a minute of it.

He broke our embrace and rocked back on his knees. He undid his belt, the metal clanking loudly where it fell next to his hips. I shifted on the bed at the sound of his zipper lowering. He stood at the end of the bed, and then his jeans and everything else was gone. I could see the outline of his hard cock bounce against his stomach before he wrapped his hand around the base. I groaned. Fuck, he was hot even in the dark.

"I need you now," he gritted out between his teeth. He was about to lose his shit, and I shivered in anticipation. I was surprised I wasn't scared of the way Ryker was acting. I could see the strength in his body, but I also saw his tight control. I don't know why, but I trusted him to not hurt me. He just wanted me.

He grabbed something on the bed and brought it up to his mouth. By the sound of the crinkling, I assumed it was a condom he opened with his teeth. Not sure when that got there, but I was glad he thought of protection because I wasn't thinking about anything but getting him inside me. His hand moved up and down on his erection. I watched his shadows as he rolled the condom down and into place, pinching the tip.

His body came back over mine holding himself up with his elbows. His hand wrapped around my neck to pull me into his kiss. Our tongues met as his cock slid into my core to the hilt in one thrust. My body tensed up with the initial pain I felt. His body froze, and the hand on the nape of my neck tightened slightly.

"Bailey?" he ground out with concern and lust battling in his voice. He was worried he hurt me and was holding himself back waiting for me to answer his unasked question. Tears stung the back of my eyes, not from pain but something else. I closed my eyes and cleared my throat of the emotions balled into a tight knot. Now was not the time for this emotional bullshit. I'm getting laid for fucks sake! I needed to get this back to where it was going. I moved my hips in small, slow circles. Now that I adjusted to his size, I needed more.

"I want you now," I said, voice trembling.

He must have heard the truth of my words in my voice because he started to move, slowly at first which made both of us groan. Smooth strokes in and out that dragged against the walls of my pussy. I wrapped my arms around his neck and spread my legs further around his waist. I locked my ankles across the top of his ass and angled my hips upward causing him to go deeper.

"Bailey," he groaned burying his face in my neck, his hands in my hair. "Your pussy is so fucking tight, gripping my dick so fucking good."

I moaned at his words. His honest dirty talk with his gravelly voice was going to make me come. His breath was coming out harshly against my neck, his fingers dug in my scalp. Every part of him was against every part of me. I started moving my hips in circles, grinding against his pelvis hitting my clit with every pass. My eyes were rolling to the back of my head with the unreal pleasure that movement evoked.

His fingers tightened in my hair causing a slight sting against my scalp pulling a gasp from my lips. The burn in my scalp traveled down to my pussy causing me to throb deep in my core where his dick jumped in reaction.

He reared back, his hands banded around my hips as he started thrusting in and out of me faster. He was done holding back, and I loved it. My hands fell above my head as my back arched. My eyes squeezed shut as my impending orgasm gathered strength. I thought the other two orgasms were amazing, but this one was going to be fucking epic.

My eyes flew open when his mouth latched onto one breast while his other hand squeezed my other breast, pinching my nipple between his thumb and forefinger. My hands curled into fists around the pillow underneath my head, and my legs tightened around his hips.

"Bailey," he growled lifting his head, and I could feel his eyes on me as he pulled himself almost completely out of me before slamming back in causing my breasts to bounce with the force. My hands released the pillow moving up his arms to his shoulders. Before they could get there, he had them in each of his hands interlocking our fingers above my head. His body hovered above mine. With his nose almost touching mine, his tongue glided across my bottom lip. He thrust in and out of me in a steady hard rhythm.

My breaths were sawing in and out of my chest. The pressure was building fast. His lips sealed around mine as he slammed into me with an angle that reached that special spot deep inside while putting the perfect amount of pressure on my clit at the same time.

My orgasm overtook me.

I detonated.

I fucking exploded.

My eyes closed, and all I could see were bright spots. All I could hear was my blood pounding furiously in my ears drowning out all other sound. His mouth absorbed all my screams as my pussy clutched his cock squeezing tightly. I drew a deep breath when his lips released mine.

His thrusts became erratic as he pushed through my still convulsing channel. His hips pounded into mine prolonging my orgasm. My hips lifted and fell in sync with his thrusts. There was not a rhythm anymore. He unleashed the chain on his self-control, and it was amazing to witness. Watching this guy with cut muscles and fierce looking ink losing his mind because of me was the greatest high I would ever hope to achieve.

I felt his dick thicken with each thrust. His swollen cock caused me to come again screaming out his name. My pussy clamped down on his growing member trying to milk him dry.

"Bailey," he growled in my ear in a husky, sexy voice as he came, his hot release filling up the condom.

The combination of his voice and the stubble on his jaw rubbing the spot under my ear caused aftershocks to course through my body making me gasp and him to groan with the pressure on his cock.

When the aftershocks stopped, he collapsed on top of me pushing me further into the mattress. His fingers loosened on mine but didn't release them. His breaths matched mine in harsh spurts. We both recovered without saying a word. I had no idea what to say to what just happened. That was so much more than a one-night stand.

Wait! What?

Of course, it was a one-night stand. I had just met him a few hours before. I had to get out of here before I did something stupid like fall in love with him. I was a grown up. I had to know the difference between sex and love. I had to stop those thoughts before they took root in my brain.

"I'll be right back," he whispered in my ear. He dropped a light kiss on my lips as he gently slid out of me causing us both to groan with sensitivity. He cupped my jaw and rested his forehead against mine. I couldn't understand what the tenderness in the gesture meant. He placed a kiss on my forehead and inhaled deeply.

What was that?

I had no fucking clue what was happening, and I couldn't think straight enough to figure it out at that moment. My body was still humming, and my mind was a swirling mess. All I could do was lay there and watch him move away from me.

He walked across the room and opened another door which I assumed was the bathroom. I caught a glimpse of his naked backside when the light turned on. His ass cheeks flexed with each stride he made. His butt was so fucking tight, I wanted to latch onto it with both hands and bite the cheeks leaving my mark on him.

Oh, my god! I had to get out of there fast!

My fight or flight instincts were on high alert. The life I had lived up to that point gave me only those two choices. I had honed them to perfection knowing which one was the best in any situation. That situation called for flight.

As soon as I felt like my legs would hold me, I got out of the bed. I was light headed at first, so I steadied myself with a hand on the wall. I took a deep breath and slowly released it. My thoughts were a jumbled mess, and I didn't have time to try to decipher it. I had to get my shit together and get gone.

He emerged from the bathroom as I slid my panties up my legs and into place. I grabbed my jeans and started wiggling back into them. My breasts bounced softly with the motions.

"Where are you going?" he asked with his eyes fixed on my chest causing me to shiver.

"Home," I answered surprised my voice didn't waver. My hands were shaking when I zipped and buttoned my pants. I grabbed my bra and slid it on covering my breasts to his gaze causing his eyes to move to mine.

"Why?" he asked with a frown as he walked closer to me not at all uncomfortable with his naked state.

I grabbed my tank and pulled it down over my head before he reached me. "I have to work early," I lied avoiding his gaze.

I tried to shake the tangles out of my hair. I was never going to fix this mess without a brush. Instead, I gathered up the long strands and made a sloppy bun on top of my head securing it with the pony tail holder I wore around my wrist.

Once I finished that, I started looking for my flannel and purse. I really needed to get out of this room and away from Ryker. I had no problem when the night started, but at that moment I was a nervous wreck. I was looking for a one-night stand that could temporarily take away the lonely ache I felt inside. I lost my virginity to some guy I picked up in a bar after getting drunk. Although I wasn't wasted tonight, I had the same feeling I had that night. I just wanted to connect with someone on a basic level, but I got way more than I expected. Hell, I got way more than I wanted. I really didn't know what to do with any of it.

What I had just experienced was way too intense for a little fun at a college keg party. The connection was way more than just pleasure of the moment between two naked, horny people. I swear the connection between us was so real I could almost see the wire linking us together. My mind was a jumbled mess, and I couldn't get a grip on what the fuck was happening. I was so confused and couldn't decipher what the more was.

My air froze in my lungs when he put his hands against the wall on each side of my head, his body pushed into mine, so we were touching from chest to thigh my back against the wall. My eyes stayed focused on the tribal that ran around his shoulder and down his arm. I tried to steady my breathing as I traced the thick black lines that twisted on his body with my eyes.

"What's wrong?" he asked while nuzzling the spot right below my ear. My whole body shivered from his hot breath against my skin.

"Nothing," I mumbled tilting my head slightly to give him better access to my neck with no permission from my brain.

He placed a kiss on my neck before moving back to look at my face. I felt his stare silently telling me to look at him. My skin flushed hotly under his scrutiny causing a blush to redden up my neck to my cheeks.

One strong hand cupped my face. His thumb brushed back and forth along my jaw. His fingertips dug into my scalp along my hairline. He tilted my head until our eyes locked. "What's wrong?" he repeated. His voice was soft and soothing willing me to confide in him what was running through my mind.

What was I supposed to say? Nothing in my mind made any sense to me. I didn't have anything in my past to give a definition of what sex with Ryker felt like. The pull he had on me was something I couldn't define, and that scared the shit out of me. I would sound like a fucking idiot if I told him I didn't know what the fuck I was doing there. I was the one that asked him to take me home with him. We had talked for a couple hours at the party that took place at the frat house on campus. We laughed and goofed off flirting back and forth. We both felt the chemistry between us. It was undeniable, so I figured he would be a great one-night stand. I could tell he wanted me as much as I wanted him, but he was holding back. I couldn't wait so I asked him if he was ready to leave. He grabbed my hand, and we rushed back to his apartment.

His grip tightened on my face bringing me back to the moment. I wanted to look away from his stare, the one I was afraid saw too much, but I couldn't stop staring into his eyes. I was drowning in his warm brown irises. I was frozen, too scared to move or even breath. He was looking at me intently searching for something.

I'm not sure what my expression was telling him, but his eyes flashed with awareness. His grip on my chin eased as he swept his thumb across my bottom lip, and his fingers moved along the nape of my neck.

"Don't go," he whispered against my lips as he gave me the gentlest, softest kiss I had ever had. "I still need you." His breath fluttered against my lips as his tongue traced first my bottom lip and then my top lip. "Stay with me."

I moaned parting my lips slightly giving his tongue access. My arms slipped around his waist and up his back until my hands curled around his shoulders. All my scrambled thoughts ceased. I couldn't think anymore feeling his warm skin on me through my clothes.

I had never experienced a desire like this. I wanted him like I never wanted another. Those were not the feelings I thought I would be experiencing when the night started at a frat party. I fiercely wanted his hands on my skin, his lips tasting me, his cock deep in me making us one. I started the night wanting a one-night stand to break my dry spell. I ended up with something so much more, I didn't have the words to explain it and that would scare me later. Not now though. Not when I was surrounded by him.

He groaned and slid his arm around my waist pulling my body closer against his, my breasts pressed firmly against his hard chest. His hand landed on my ass and squeezed pushing my pelvis up into his erection where my clit rubbed roughly against the cotton and denim I wore. I groaned into his mouth. His arms gripped around my thighs lifting me off the ground. I wrapped my legs around his waist as he brought me back to the bed.

I stopped thinking for the night. I would have to deal with reality the next day, but that night I let go. I let my body take over and surrendered to the sensations coursing through me. I needed to hold onto that feeling for as long as I could because I didn't know if I would ever find it again.

I was so fucked.

Chapter Two
Ryker

I should have been amped up for the party. We had just won a big game against our rivals. The frat party was for us. A lot of the guys on the team were members of the fraternity. It was a big deal, and since I was friends with almost everyone, I felt like it would be rude to not show up. I was seriously considering getting back in my truck and going home, but I would feel like shit if I didn't at least make an appearance.

I heaved a heavy sigh as I walked along the mile-long line of cars crowding the sides of the street leading to the house. I could hear the music thumping loudly along with loud voices coming from the front and back yard. Luckily, all the neighbors were college kids and of the party life or this party would be shut down with a noise complaint to the police.

I dodged groping couples and the arms that were flailing wildly by a blonde girl giving the drunk "I love you" speech to a girl with short black hair who was bent over laughing hysterically. I nodded at the guys watching the girls with humor on their faces.

I went through the open front door and made my way down the crowded hallway. I had to shrug off several pairs of grabby hands from some very intoxicated girls. They all had on tight skirts or dresses with strappy sandals with skinny, tall heels. There were a lot of chicks on the prowl.

Too bad I wasn't interested. I blew out a heavy breath. I should be all over a sure thing right now, but I wasn't feeling it which was fucking crazy. I was always up for a party. College was kicking my ass. I pushed myself physically and mentally every day. Between my classes demanding intense all-night study sessions and football pushing me to be faster and harder, I needed to blow off some steam, find a release. Too bad I wasn't interested in any of the girls on display. Only one girl was all up in my head that made my dick hard just by picturing her face.

I groaned and shook my head to try to get out of this funk. This wasn't me, the normal fun-loving guy. I was always up for a laugh and enjoyed hanging out with my friends. Watching people drinking themselves stupid for a few hours was always hilarious and entertaining.

I didn't drink much, just a couple of beers every now and then at parties like these since I wasn't legally able to drink. I liked to be in control and aware of what was going on around me. I also tried to watch out for people getting behind the wheel of their cars when they shouldn't. My dad pounded no drinking and driving into my head since I hit puberty. I knew what could happen if people drove drunk. It was dangerous for them and everyone else on the roads.

I will need a designated driver tonight, though. Tonight, I needed a few alcoholic beverages to try to stop thinking about her.

Bailey.

I don't even know her last name, and she was fucking with me. I didn't really know her at all. It had been three weeks since we hooked up, and she was still stuck in my head. I showed up at the parties these last few weeks in hopes of seeing her again just to leave disappointed. I knew she didn't go to the university, but she was neighbors with Lyla Gautreaux who was a regular at the parties because she was dating Cody Blanchard, a frat member who lived in this house. I was hoping she would show up with her again, but it hadn't happened.

The night I met Bailey we had won the first game of the season, and the team was celebrating. I was in the kitchen mixing up some killer drinks for some of the party goers when I felt the hair on the back of my neck stand up. I lifted my gaze from the liquor bottles cluttering the countertop and locked eyes with the greenest eyes I'd ever seen.

I was shocked stupid, literally. I couldn't pull my eyes away from her. She was fucking hot, fucking beautiful. I trailed my gaze along her face taking in the cheeks tinged in pink to her plump lips. She ran her tongue along her full bottom lip leaving it shiny with moisture. I couldn't look away. I wanted my tongue on her. I wanted my hands in all her long wavy blonde hair. I trailed the length of her hair to where it laid over her shoulder and curled into the top of her tight black tank top she wore under a flannel shirt. The ends of her hair tickled the tops of her high breasts showing an amazing cleavage.

Logan smacking me on the back was the only thing saving me from major embarrassment. My dick was so hard in my jeans I thought it was a strong possibility I would pop the zipper. Not to mention the drool I was sure leaked out of my open mouth.

After Lyla made the introductions, I knew I wanted to spend the night with Bailey. We spent hours talking about nonsense, random, everyday stuff. We talked music and movies. She loved action movies and wanted to puke during romantic comedies which made me laugh because I felt the same way. She loved any music that got to her. She wasn't picky, but she swayed between bluesy soulful sounds to hard rock depending on her mood. She had lived in the same apartment complex as Lyla for about a year. We debated different bands and lyrics. We joked around about the cheesy lines guys used on girls. When she laughed, it was the most beautiful sight I've ever seen. Her green eyes sparkled with golden sparks, and the sound went straight to my dick.

That's all I really knew though. Anytime I would ask something more personal, she would retreat and change the subject. She would deflect the attention off herself and ask something else about me. She knew my whole life story, and I didn't even know where she worked or what she did with her time. The only reason I knew where she lived was because Lyla introduced her as her neighbor. I had a feeling she didn't want that information disclosed. I also felt her tense up when I drove us to my apartment that happened to be the complex next to Lyla's.

I've had one night stands before. I've hooked up with girls sticking to first names, and I've never regretted it. I treated every girl with respect, but I kept a barrier up between us. I was honest letting them know it was only physical and for one night. I was nineteen years old and a sophomore in college. I wasn't ready for the real thing with anyone. At least I wasn't until I met Bailey.

I never felt the overwhelming need to find a girl before. Bailey was so different, so much more than just a hook up. She was someone worth exploring. The connection I felt with her needed to be defined to me. I needed to see what it meant.

My momma always told me when I met *the one* I would know. I had a feeling Bailey was it. If I couldn't find her, she would become *the one that got away*. I didn't want that shit to happen.

I believed in the one my momma was talking about. I knew she was out there. I knew it made me sound like a sappy pussy, but I didn't care. The girls in high school wanted me because I was on the football team, and it was fun and easy. There was never any pressure to please the girls. Some of them wanted bragging rights; others wanted the popularity being friends with me brought. None of them wanted me just for me. None of them wanted to be with me for the long term. In college, things weren't much different. Looking at the girls dancing around in barely any clothes brought home that fact. Those girls wanted fun with the winners of the moment.

The emotions swirling around me were too thick. I couldn't decipher all of it, and I'm not sure if I even wanted to. I just knew that I wanted to at least see her again. There was a reason she snuck away, and I really wanted to find out what that was. I knew she felt the same intensity I did. When I felt her move from underneath my arm, I was waiting to see what she would do. I had stopped her the first time she tried to bolt, but I didn't want to have to beg her to stay. But I sure as fuck didn't like the situation.

I wasn't ready to let her go. I wanted to move with her all night, to feel her soft against my roughness. I wanted to breathe her in, inhale the coconut scent that clung to her. Fuck! I just wanted her next to me. I wanted to yell that she was mine. I had never had that possessive need before. It scared the shit out of me, but it also excited me. I was in unknown territory, but I was always up for an adventure. I already knew Bailey was the biggest adrenaline rush I've ever had. I had done a bunch of thrill seeking shit with my brothers, and sometimes even with my sister. But nothing compared to just being near her.

After I filled my cup with beer from the keg set up in the kitchen, I walked around the bar to come to an abrupt stop when a small hand landed on my chest. My eyes met seductive blue ones, and I groaned. I really didn't feel like dealing with Crystal Thibodaux tonight.

We had sex one night after a football game in high school. She was the head cheerleader, and we had won the championship game, so we were celebrating at a big block party. We ended up naked in my truck. I regretted it as soon as it happened. I knew I wouldn't date her, and that's what her end game was. I told her I wasn't interested in anything with her, and she agreed. I knew better, but my dick led the way that night. She was a cheerleader at the university and was still convinced we should have been together. I had made myself clear over and over, but she won't give up. She is a manipulative, mean girl. I've seen some of her handiwork, and I wanted no part of it.

"Hey, Ryker," she said in a voice that I was guessing was supposed to be sexy, but it made me cringe.

I backed up a step to put distance between us, and her hand fell to her side. "Excuse me," I said deciding to just walk around her. We weren't friends. I didn't want to talk to her. It would only encourage her.

She put her hands on her hips that were wrapped in a black miniskirt and pouted red, shiny lips at me. I wanted to roll my eyes at her immature ways. I have spelled out my feelings that don't exist with her. She just won't back off. I figured I could start ignoring and avoiding.

She grabbed my arm when I stepped past her and dug her fingernails in a little bit. "Come on, baby. We could celebrate privately tonight." She pushed her chest out making her tits bounce in the low cut red halter top she had on. I'm a guy. I glanced. How could I not when they were trying to get to my face? I quickly looked back to her face.

I shook her hand off and noticed the fingernail marks. I scowled at her. "I'm not interested."

I didn't give her the chance to say anything else. I walked out of the kitchen and followed the hallway to the back of the house. I looked around the crowded room until I spotted Logan leaning against the wall staring in the direction of the make-shift dance floor set up in the middle of the living room with all the furniture pushed against the walls. I followed his gaze and wasn't surprised to see he had his eyes locked on Riley. My sister was his best friend, but I thought there was more to it. He just wouldn't admit it. He insisted they were just friends, and he would never cross that line with her. I already had my brotherly duty talk with him about hurting Riley before I had my best friend talk where I told him I had his back. She was my sister, but he was my best friend and like a brother to me. I didn't want to see either one hurt.

I just shook my head and made my way over to him. I didn't have the brain cells to help navigate their issues when they were all wrapped up in my own issues. I fist bumped and back slapped friends and teammates as I winded my way around the edge of the living room. I threw my hand up in acknowledgement from my name being called from across the room.

"What's up?" I thumped him on the shoulder causing him to jump and the liquid in his cup sloshed over the rim onto the back of his hand.

"Asshole," he grumbled shaking out his hand flinging wet drops on my shirt.

I laughed at him. He was so intent on staring at my little sister he didn't even notice when I approached. I looked down at my shirt and wiped the drops off as best as I could. I shrugged my shoulders. It would dry.

I quirked an eyebrow and took a sip from my cup. "People were yelling my name over the music, and I still managed to spook you. What's going on?"

"Nothing," he grumbled bringing his cup up to his mouth.

"Right," I said sarcastically looking over the dancing bodies.

Standing against the wall watching the growing crowd, I knew I didn't want to be here. This week had been brutal. Who the fuck was I kidding? The last three weeks had been brutal. I've been in a foul ass mood, and everybody was questioning me.

Crystal had made it to the dance floor and was moving her body while looking at me. I broke eye contact with her quickly before she got any ideas and kept scanning the crowd. I sucked in a sharp breath when I saw who had walked through the door. There was a crowded room of people separating us, but I still felt the pull.

Bailey. My mind chanted her name. Bailey.

There she stood in all her sexiness. Even in a hoodie and sweat pants, she was sexier than any other girl in the room. She was looking around as though she was trying to find somebody. Was she meeting someone here? Who the fuck was she looking for?

I couldn't stop my thoughts from spinning. I wanted her to be looking for me. I wanted to be walking next to her. Shit, this is so fucked up. I'm acting like a freaking idiot, but I couldn't seem to stop.

She took a few steps into the room scanning the people dancing. She had a worried look on her face. There was a wrinkle in between her eyebrows, and her mouth was pulled down in a frown.

She had a blow pop in her mouth, and my dick twitched in my pants at the sight. As her tongue rolled around the sucker, I remembered the taste of her tongue. My mouth watered to taste that candy on her tongue again. I wasn't the only one that was enjoying the sight of her plump lips wrapped around that stick. I saw several guys inching closer to her with their eyes on her mouth. This overwhelming urge to throat punch every one of those mother fuckers was almost too much to ignore. This is the shit that was fucking with my head. I was a laid-back kind of guy that liked to relax and have fun. I loved to laugh and joke around. I was like a different person when I was around her, and I wasn't convinced that it was a good thing.

"Are you going to go talk to her?" Logan asked.

I had talked to Logan about Bailey and the confusing feelings I was dealing with. I wasn't a pussy that went around talking about my feelings and shit with everyone, but I needed to vent a little bit. He didn't say much. He just listened while I got it all out. The way that one night felt so different than any hook up before. The way she looked at me that had me feeling all possessive over her. The way I felt when I woke up alone. When I was done, he asked if I wanted a beer. I laughed and grabbed the beer he offered, and that was that.

I shrugged my shoulders a little hesitant to do anything. Would she want to talk to me? Would she be happy to see me?

"I'm not sure."

What the fuck is wrong with me? I never hesitated to do anything before. If I wanted it, I went after it until I had it. I wanted Bailey. I wanted her to be mine. Something was holding me back, and for the first time I questioned if I would get what I wanted.

She didn't look like she was here to party. Her sweats were hot as fuck on her showing her amazing body, but they weren't going out clothes. She turned her head in my direction, and our eyes locked. I saw her chest heave as she took a deep breath. Yeah, the connection was real. She felt it. I felt it.

"Damn," Logan muttered letting me know even he felt it.

Fuck it. I had to try. I wasn't a quitter. She would be mine. I needed her to be mine.

I took a step in her direction when she turned around to a guy standing behind her talking. I found out how amazingly she worked sweat pants. The black material molded to her body making me groan from the sight of her perfect ass and thick thighs. Her sexy calves were visible from where the pants were pushed up from her ankles to below her knees. Her hair was in a messy ponytail exposing the nape of her neck and the three stars behind her left ear that I enjoyed licking with my tongue.

The guy put his hand on her shoulder and bent down to talk to her. She angled her head away from him as she tried to put distance between them. Drew Morrison was in her space, and I didn't like it. I liked Drew. He was good people. We were on the team together and both sophomores. He started working at the gym with me a couple of years ago. He was a player, but he wasn't mean about it. He flirted with everyone, but he didn't cause any harm. He was friends with most of the girls I've seen taking the walk of shame after a night with him. He wasn't a bad dude, but I knew it was a possibility that he was too drunk to realize how uncomfortable he was making her. I didn't like seeing her uncomfortable, but I really didn't like seeing him touching her.

He was too fucking close to her, and I felt a possessive anger build up. I started weaving through the crowd on a mission to get his hand off my girl. I knew if I stopped and thought about it, I was being irrational. He wouldn't do anything to hurt her, but I didn't like the way her body stiffened up when he got in her personal space. It brought protective instincts in me that I've only ever had with Riley, but this didn't feel anything like brotherly love.

I didn't stop to think though. I just acted. I walked up to her back and curled my right arm around her waist pulling her back to my front. Drew's hand fell from her shoulder, and his gaze snapped to mine. I glared at him daring him to say something. Her whole body tensed, and I looked down into her eyes when she turned her head to look up at me. Her eyes had widened with a flash of fear crossing her face. Shit! I didn't want her to fear me. Before I could do anything, her body relaxed into mine and the fear disappeared. However, when she saw my satisfied grin, she stiffened again and tried to pull away from me. My hand held her left hip tightly not allowing her to escape. Now that I knew I didn't freak her out, I wasn't letting her go.

"What's going on?" I asked directly in Bailey's ear making her shiver. I groaned softly when her ass rubbed against my dick that was already hard.

She gasped and went to pull away. I just moved with her, my thighs rubbing against the back of hers. She sighed and melted back into me, surrendering to me. The back of her head rested against my collarbone. I rubbed my cheek against the top of her head. Her breath feathered across my neck when she turned her head into me, and I had to close my eyes. Her nose rubbed against my neck where my pulse was thumping furiously.

"Lyla called for a ride," her voice was low and raspy.

The position we were in was so intimate, I had to take a minute and breathe. Her body leaned into mine with trust. She laced her fingers through mine against her hip. Her other hand was resting on my forearm, her fingers rubbing against my tattoo. I inhaled a deep breath of her coconut scent and kissed the crown of her head before lifting my head to look at her face.

For a minute, I almost forgot we weren't alone. The people, the noise, the music, everything had just faded away. I looked down into lust filled eyes, and I had to stifle a groan. She ran her tongue along her bottom lip when her eyes landed on my mouth. My fingers tightened around hers at the sight of her eyes darkening with desire and the flush working up her neck to her cheeks. She looked so right, and satisfaction ran through me knowing that I was the one who made her look like this. She wanted me.

That look was too much, and after three weeks of constant thoughts of her, I was ready to get her alone and naked. Since she was here to pick up Lyla, I don't think she would appreciate it if I took off with her somewhere. I looked around the room noticing that Drew had disappeared, and a few people were looking at us curiously. Crystal had a glare aimed at Bailey that pissed me off, so I turned us with my back to Crystal blocking her view of Bailey.

She cleared her throat, and her eyes widened before she turned around to face me. I didn't let her go so my arm banded around her back. I pressed my hand firmly in the indention of her spine pulling her into me. Her hands flattened on my chest, but she didn't push me away. My fingers rubbed lightly along the slip of silky, warm skin exposed from the space between the bottom of her hoodie and the top of the sweats hanging low on her hips.

She shivered slightly in my arms, and I felt goose bumps pop up across her skin where my fingers trailed from side to side. Her eyes darkened to this beautiful deep green, the gold specks glowing. Her nose flared as her breaths quickened which made me groan when her hardened nipples rubbed against my chest. My hand stopped on her hip giving her a tight squeeze pulling her into my painful erection.

She closed her eyes and took a deep breath before pushing on my chest. I had no choice to loosen my hold on her, but I couldn't let go of her completely. I kept my hand on her hip as I took a sip of my beer. I made a face in distaste. It was warm, and I didn't feel the need to drink anymore. Bailey was better than alcohol any day. The buzz she gave me was something nothing ever gave me before. The high that thrummed in my head I knew I could never get from any drug, not that I've tried drugs before. Well, I've smoked pot a few times, but that's it.

When her eyes opened, I was disappointed to see the walls up. When we were locked up tight together, she let me see her for a minute. I want to see more. I want her to lose the walls for me. It didn't matter how long it took, I would demolish those walls.

"I'm looking for Lyla," her voice came out husky, and she had to clear her throat while she licked her bottom lip. "She called me to come get her."

I kissed her. I couldn't help it. Her lips were right there, plump and inviting. I didn't know yet if licking her lip was something she did when she was nervous or not, but it was going to be the death of me. I wanted to capture the wetness her tongue left behind. The kiss was chaste compared to what I really wanted to do. I wanted to devour her, but this was not the time or place. I was marking her as mine right now. Drew and every other guy in this house needed to get the message. I moved my lips across hers before dragging my tongue slowly along her bottom lip.

Fuck, she tasted good, like candy. Her skin was so soft along her hip.

"Bailey," my voice was low and raspy.

Her eyes fluttered open, and I sucked in a deep breath. Her eyes were glassy and dazed looking like she wanted to eat me up. My hand tightened on her hip as I tried to calm the fuck down.

Lyla.

She was here for Lyla.

Help her find Lyla.

"Bailey," I warned. She had to get that look off her face now before I threw her over my shoulder and found the first secluded spot.

Shit! She had me by the balls and didn't even know it.

"I haven't seen her around yet," I said. I had to clear my throat and shift my legs to give my erection some room. "She might be with Cody."

"Yeah," she said slowly looking at me in confusion before her eyes cleared. She stood up straight and tried to step back from me as she looked around the room. I didn't release her hip though. I couldn't.

"Why did she call you to pick her up?" I asked. "She didn't have her car?"

"No," she answered. "Sometimes when she stays here, she leaves her car at the apartment. Cody picks her up from her place. Plus, if I need to use a car, I can use hers."

"You don't have a car?" I asked. I didn't mean anything by the question. I just wanted to know everything about her.

"No," she said stiffly trying to back up even more. She was in defense mode.

Back to searching for Lyla. I didn't mean to offend her, but that's what I had done. I figured the best thing to do was to let it go.

"I don't see her in here," I told her scanning the room we were in. "Do you know why she wanted to leave?"

"No, but she didn't really sound too good when she called," she said looking up at me with a little wrinkle in between her eyebrows showing her concern.

"Let's go look around," I told Bailey, grabbing her hand.

We waded through the hall to the back-sliding glass doors that led to the outdoor patio. She didn't try to pull her hand back, surprising me. She just laced her fingers through mine, and I had to take a breath of relief. I realized then that my hesitation stemmed from my fear of rejection. For the first time, ever, I was scared to be turned down by a girl. I knew her body wanted me, but I needed all of her to want me.

I was turning into a fucking girl! I shook my head and walked through the open doors. I scanned the people and saw my brother, Ryder, talking to Lyla. Ryder looked pissed and ready to go to war while Lyla just kept shaking her head looking at the ground. His shoulders slumped slightly when he put his fingers under her chin making her lift her eyes to his. I could see a tear trail down her face and her lip quivered. He leaned in until his forehead rested against hers.

What the fuck? I've never heard Ryder ever say anything about Lyla, not even in a casual sense. We've known her forever, so we saw her regularly. We all had the same group of friends, but he's never said her name. Not to mention that she's been with Cody since high school, so she's never been single. Looking at them now, I couldn't help but wonder how long he's been in love with her. That's what it was, I had no doubt.

I walked over to them, and I heard Ryder tell Lyla, "Let me take you home."

She shook her head, "No, I called Bailey."

Ryder growled and moved his body closer to her making her head jerk up as she glared at him. Her hands balled into fists where she had them propped on her hips. She was giving all kinds of attitude when she said, "Don't you fucking growl at me!"

I decided it was best to interrupt this even though I was enjoying the show. Nobody ever gave Ryder shit, and I had to give Lyla props. However, Bailey came to get her friend, and I needed to let her deal with this if I hoped of having my turn with Bailey tonight. That sounds insensitive to Lyla even with the tears down her face. I'm an asshole.

"Hey, bro," I put my hand on Ryder's shoulder and felt his bunched muscles twitching. I don't know what happened, but he was extremely worked up.

He turned his glare to me, and I held up my free hand like I was surrendering. His gaze snapped to the hand that still held Bailey's securely. His eyes rose to mine with his eyebrow cocked in question. I shook my head slightly letting him know now was not the time.

He looked at Bailey curiously. When his eyes met mine, I saw the question in them. I nodded my head slightly in answer. I knew what he was asking. I told him about Bailey the day after she left. Yeah, bro. This is her.

"Bailey!" Lyla exclaimed pushing in front of Ryder to hug Bailey.

Her hand tightened in mine but didn't let go when she hugged Lyla back with one arm. "Hey, are you good?"

"Yeah," she replied. "I'm just ready to get the fuck out of here."

"Bailey," I said looking down at her. "This is my brother, Ryder."

She looked from Ryder to me a couple times before nodding. "Hey."

Ryder smiled at her and stuck his fist out to her. She looked down at it and smiled before she tapped it with her own fist.

"Let's go around the back. I don't want to go through the house." Lyla interrupted looking down as if she were ashamed.

I raised my eyebrow at Ryder. He just shook his head slightly letting me know he didn't want to get into it right now.

We all headed off in that the direction when we heard, "Lyla! Get your ass back here! I'm not done with you!" being yelled from the backdoor.

I pushed Bailey behind me as I turned toward the voice. Cody was storming through the now silent backyard. Everyone moved to the sides, out of his way. His face was twisted in rage, and he was barreling straight to Lyla. Ryder shifted her behind him, and she curled her hands in his shirt on his lower back. Her shoulders sagged in defeat as she pressed her forehead into the back of Ryder's shoulder. One of his hands was holding her hip, and the other was curled in a fist.

"Get your hand off my girl!" Cody yelled as he got closer to us.

This dude was either drunk or really stupid. He was stepping right up to Ryder. Ryder didn't move. He didn't say anything. He just glared at him. That's how Ryder was though. He didn't say much, but his look could convey so much. The look he was giving now was pure murder. He was holding himself in check barely. I think his control was hanging by a thread that Lyla was holding. She meant something to him.

"I said get your hand off my girl, asshole!" Cody was toe to toe with Ryder now. "Come here now, Lyla!"

"Back the fuck up," Ryder growled.

"Fuck you," Cody spat. "I'm not going anywhere without her. I need to talk to her."

"I said we were done, Cody," Lyla said with her head still down.

Everyone was quietly watching. Someone even turned off the music.

"We are not done. I say when we are done, not you, and we are not done. Now get the fuck over here, you who..." he didn't get to finish that sentence because Ryder's fist was in his face.

I heard Cody's jaw snap as his head turned sharply with the hit. Ryder had moved away from Lyla pushing Cody farther away from her. I moved up with him. With a deathly low voice, so only we could hear, Ryder said, "Stay the fuck away from her. She said y'all are done, y'all are fucking done. If I so much as see you anywhere near her, I will fuck you up repeatedly. You understand me?"

I heard a gasp and looked over my shoulder to see Lyla walking forward. She didn't look sad and defeated anymore. She looked pissed. She walked forward. Ryder tried to block her with his body, but she sidestepped him and stood toe to toe with Cody.

"Cody," Lyla stated in a determined voice. "I need you to listen and hear me right now."

"I," Cody began.

Lyla put her hand up and shook her head. "No. I said I was done up there," she pointed in the direction of the second floor of the house where the fraternity brothers had their bedrooms. "You followed me down here making this big fucking scene because you didn't get the last word. Well, let's finish this scene. Five years we've been together, so many happy memories, fun memories. Things were awesome, fucking amazing until two years ago."

"Lyla," Cody growled shifting forward.

"No, let me say what I need to say," she demanded. "Let's get this done."

"Get back upstairs," Cody snarled bending to get almost nose to nose with her.

Ryder had a hand on her hip ready to move her back at any sign of a threat from Cody.

"Step the fuck back and listen to what I have to say," Lyla glared at Cody. "And you are going to hear me this time!"

He backed up a step looking unsure.

"Two years ago, a terrible accident changed our lives," she continued. "You decided to drive drunk, and I couldn't stop you. You went to jail, lost your scholarship, and fucked up your knee to the point you couldn't play football anymore. I have stayed by your side to help you get through your pain, your anger, your grief. You won't let go though. You are so pissed off at the world because it's easier than being pissed off at yourself. You place the blame on me and let me know what a disappointment I am on the fucking daily. I am done being your crutch. I am done trying to help you heal because you must do it. It's time I work on healing myself. I blamed myself for the longest time, but it's not my fault. You made the choices you made. I hope you get to a place where you can be happy. I know I'm going to try."

She turned her back on Cody and started to walk away. He took a step forward only to be stopped by Ryder. He got chest to chest with him. His whole body was strung tight with tension and restraint. Ryder was on a full scholarship, and I'm not too sure what would happen if he got arrested.

I didn't say anything to him though. I wasn't going to hold him back. I knew this is what he had to do. For some reason, he needed to be the one to protect Lyla.

"So, what? You're fucking her now?" Cody snarled.

Fuck! That was not the right thing to say. This fucker really was an idiot. One minute he was standing up nose to nose with Ryder, and the next he was on the ground with his nose bleeding all over the fucking place.

I saw Lyla's hands land on Ryder's back twisting his shirt in her fists. I felt Bailey move against my back. I looked back at her as she reached for Lyla. Lyla looked at Bailey and nodded her head. They both turned to leave with Bailey wrapping her arm around Lyla's shoulders. Bailey looked back at me and nodded her head.

I looked back at Cody still on the ground. "Bro, let's go." I said. Ryder looked like he was going to blow, and nothing would ever be the same. He looked capable of anything at that moment, so I knew Lyla meant something to him if he would risk his scholarship.

"I'll take care of him, Ryder," Logan said stepping in front of us.

Ryder nodded his head at Logan taking deep breaths trying to calm the shit swirling in him. We turned around and headed the way the girls went. We reached them as Bailey pressed a button on a key ring unlocking the doors to a newer model Honda Accord.

"Bailey," I called causing her to turn around as she reached the driver's side door.

I walked straight up to her and slipped an arm around her waist pulling her into me, my hand curving around the rise of her backside. I put my lips on her forehead savoring her warmth. Her breasts were smashed against my chest bouncing slightly with her breathing. I could feel her nipples harden causing my dick to jump against her belly.

She moaned blowing her warm breath against my neck. I tightened my arm around her waist and buried my face in her neck breathing her coconut smell deep in my lungs. My hand gripped her hair where I was probably destroying her ponytail, but she didn't pull away right away. Her arms were wrapped around my waist, and her hands knotted in the back of my shirt like she did back at the party.

We stood like that for a while. I'm not sure how long, but I could have stayed that way all night long.

"Bailey," Lyla broke our moment.

Baily jumped back from me like she was scared. Her eyes met mine for a brief moment before she looked at Lyla on the other side of the car.

"You ready to go?" Bailey cleared her throat. Her cheeks reddened, and she blew out a breath.

"Yeah," Lyla answered with a small smile tinged with sadness. "You drive."

She opened the driver's side door and slid into the car without another word to me. She didn't even spare me a glance. As soon as Lyla closed the passenger side door, she put the car in gear and took off down the street.

I stood there and stared until I couldn't see the tail lights anymore. This whole situation felt insane. I've had two encounters with her. That's twice she ran out on me. We have barely spoken to each other. I don't know anything about her, but I needed to know everything about her.

In the brief glance, she gave me, I could see the fear in her eyes. When I had my hands on her, she let her body guide her. She curled into me like she's done it forever, like we've been together forever. When we separate, and reality comes to invade our space, the fear is visible. I think she believes she hides the fear, but I see it. Why? Why was she scared of me? Why did she have these walls built around her? I was going to get the answers I needed so I could demolish those walls. There wasn't another option. She was mine. I had to clear the course for me to become hers.

I was so fucked.

Chapter Three
Bailey

Waking up to the sound of sirens made me shove my face in my pillow and groan. I didn't groan because the cops were going to swarm my place in a raid. I groaned because those sirens meant I had to get my ass up and moving. I had gone through every alarm setting on my phone before I found the sirens were the only thing to get me awake. I probably should have known that considering the way I grew up, but I tried to forget the different homes and shady neighborhoods I traveled from.

I had an hour to get ready and be at work for the lunch shift. Normally, this wouldn't be a problem. I'd be ready with time to spare. I didn't spend a lot of time on my hair and make-up. I never saw the point in doing all that if I wasn't trying to impress anyone or gain any attention.

This morning it would be a problem though. I woke up slowly even with the noise coming from my phone. I felt like shit. My eyes burned and felt gritty when I tried to open them. I rubbed the palms of my hands against my eyelids with a groan. There was a slight thumping in my skull. I had an emotional hangover. When I stopped drinking and doing the drug scene, I was sure I was never going to see a hangover again. I was wrong.

I spent hours with Lyla last night, and I'm not sure how I feel about that. I have a rule about getting close to anyone. I don't do it. I had Carter, and that was enough. Most people suck and float in and out of your life. Attachments are stupid and pointless. I learned that lesson a while ago. For the last few years, I haven't gotten close to many people. Well, a lot longer than that, but it has become worse in the last few years. My point is that I didn't have friends. In my experience, friends would always let you down. So, it came as a shock to me how quickly I became friends with Lyla.

Seeing Lyla break last night, it hurt me to watch. It was like I felt a portion of her pain. I knew I couldn't just leave her. She was good people and deserved to have people there for her. I met her when I moved into the apartment across the hall from her about a year ago. She was carrying one too many boxes piled on top of each other in her arms to see where she was going. She tripped on one of the steps and was going down. I was walking up the stairs behind her. I quickly closed the space between us and grabbed ahold of her shoulders to keep her upright. She had dropped the boxes spilling photographs across the landing. She hurriedly shoved them back in the box before she turned around to face me and introduced herself with a blush of embarrassment. She called herself clumsy and laughed, but the humor didn't reach her eyes. There was this sadness in her eyes, sadness that I recognized. I lived with the same sadness every day. It was the kind that didn't leave, and you didn't move on from.

I dropped my arms and opened my eyes. I had to blink several times before my vision cleared, and the sun coming in from around the edges of my curtains covering the windows was slightly bearable. I grabbed my phone from my nightstand and silenced the alarm. I dropped my phone back down. A hot shower and a good cup of coffee would hopefully clear my brain enough to be productive today.

I jumped out of bed and almost face planted in my thick, gray carpet when I became light headed from my fast movements. Damn emotional hangovers were the worst kind of hangovers. Believe me, I knew several types of hangovers. I slammed my hands on my bed and took deep breaths until I felt steadier. I slowly stood up and was relieved when I remained standing.

Slowly, I walked across the hall from my bedroom to the bathroom I shared with Carter. I closed the door before I went to the shower. I pushed the clear shower curtain aside and turned the lever up that made water rain down from the showerhead. While the water heated, I opened the medicine cabinet above the sink. I rummaged around until I found something to calm this raging war in my head. I put the two pills in my mouth and stuck my head under the faucet to swallow the pills with cold water. I turned the water off and removed the big t-shirt I wore to bed and took my panties off. I stepped inside of the bathtub and stood directly under the hot spray, moaning in relief. That felt so good.

Hanging my head under the stream of water, I rotated my neck on my shoulders. I slept hard for only a few hours, and my muscles were all tense and stiff. Last night was brutal, and I was so sure I would have a nightmare. I guessed that was why I was so achy. I was waiting for the nightmare to make an appearance and kept my body locked in anticipation.

Lyla was quiet the whole ride home from the party, just staring out her window with a blank expression. She seemed to snap out of it when I pulled into her designated spot. I was driving her car since I didn't have a car. She gave me the extra key to her car about six months ago, after an incident where she needed me to get her, but I had to ask Carter to leave work to go get her. It made her so uncomfortable since she seemed to spend a lot of effort on avoiding him that she gave me the extra key as soon as she made it back to the apartment.

She jumped out of the car before I had even put it fully in park. She was practically running to the entry way. She ran up the stairs so fast I was afraid she would trip and bust her head open on the cement steps. By the time, I caught up with her, she was frantically trying to shove her key into her apartment door. I calmly took her keys and let us in the apartment. I didn't really know how to do the whole friend thing, but I figured I should stay close.

She went into her bathroom without a backwards glance at me and slammed the door shut. I heard the shower turn on, but it wasn't loud enough to drown out her sobs. The sounds of her agony will be with me forever. The heartbreak was real and raw. My eyes had tears in them just listening to her pain. She emerged out of the bathroom about an hour after she went in with bloodshot eyes and a red nose.

When she told me she was going to bed, her voice was hoarse and scratchy. I followed her into her room and stretched out on the bed next to her. I knew nothing I could say would make this better for her. It happened, and she would have to grieve in her own way. I wasn't entirely sure that she knew I was there or not since she didn't acknowledge me. I was reluctant to leave her on her own, so I stayed.

She stood her ground at the party, and it cost her. She told me before that her and Cody had been together since high school, and there was an accident their senior year. I never pushed for details, but I gathered some of it. The accident cost Cody a football scholarship, and he hadn't dealt with it well. I knew he was an angry person, and he wasn't nice to Lyla. I never said anything to Lyla because I didn't really feel like I could judge a situation without knowing that much about it, but I didn't like the things I had seen when they were together.

The sun was starting to rise when her breaths became even with a hiccup every now and then. She had sobbed herself to sleep. When I was sure she was sleeping soundly, I covered her with her comforter and left her apartment quietly locking the door behind me with the extra key she gave me. I had been so exhausted, I'm sure I looked like a zombie making my way to my room in my own apartment. I changed into one of Carter's old t-shirts and fell face down on my bed. My last conscious thought was of Ryker and that lingering forehead kiss.

As I started lathering my hair, Ryker's face popped up in my head. It was the last image I had of him from the quick glance in the rearview mirror as I drove away from the party. He just stood there watching the car speed away. His hands were shoved in the pockets of his jeans with a half-smile on his face. That quick glance told me something I had to listen to. When I realized how hard it was to look away, I knew I had to stay away from him.

I had never had a relationship with anyone, nor was I looking to. Speaking of relationships, I wondered what it would be like in a relationship with Ryker.

What?! Relationship?!

This is exactly what I was talking about. This was exactly why I had to stay far away from him. He had my head in a place that wasn't safe. We had sex once and saw each other twice. Why did I let him kiss me like that in front of a room full of people? All my walls came down in that moment and that scared the shit out of me. I was always aware of the things happening around me, but I couldn't even tell you who was all around when we were kissing and holding on to each other. It felt so natural to melt into him.

I couldn't do normal, and he was normal. I mean he kissed my forehead for goodness sake! What was up with the forehead kiss? A forehead kiss usually means you are friends, but it could also mean the person has deep affection for the other. I read another article that stated a forehead kiss meant protection, respect, and possession. And yes, I did Google it. While Lyla locked herself in her bathroom last night, I grabbed my phone and read several definitions of forehead kisses. How fucked up was that? I had to look something like that up because I had no idea what it meant. My life had been so fucked up that I didn't know how to act with the affection Ryker gave me.

As I started washing up, I tried to come up with a game plan of avoiding him, but I couldn't focus enough for a solid idea to take root. I thought about the way his brown eyes darkened when they landed on me. I thought about the way his rough hands glided across my skin. I thought about how I felt at peace wrapped in his arms. I thought about how his warm breath on my neck made me shiver.

Not to mention the way he blocked me from Cody when I wasn't even his target like he was protecting me. Nobody has ever stepped in front of me like that except for Carter. It was very confusing and frustrating. He acted almost possessive of me which was something that I usually hated. I didn't hate it when it came from Ryker. Hell, it turned me on, and I wanted to be mad at myself for being weak. Giving over to someone else made you weak but being weak was not an option. I had to stay away from him.

I hated when I didn't have control over any situation. This situation was too complex for me to figure out. I was out of my league so today I would make sure I stayed away from Ryker from now on. I didn't have enough pieces of myself left to risk losing it all over someone like Ryker. That would be the outcome. I knew this. We fucked. That's it. It may sound harsh and a little slutty, but it was what it was.

I grabbed the towel from the hook on the wall and ran it jerkily over my body. I had to stop thinking about him and move the fuck on. I needed my mask in place and my indifference surrounding me.

After wrapping a towel around my hair and one around my body, I yanked open the door and let out a loud squeak when I came face to face with a naked chest.

"Shit!" I gasped for breath. "Give me some fucking notice when you want to scare the shit out of me."

I gave him a firm shove, my hand flat against his chest to get him out of the doorway. He didn't move an inch. Carter was over six feet tall packed with solid muscle. His skin was slightly sweaty making me angry for missing my work out this morning. I would have to work out in the morning. I usually took Sundays off to run errands and take care of the overflowing basket of laundry if I didn't have to work. However, those things would have to wait until after I ran.

With a sigh, I walked around Carter into my room shutting the door behind me.

"Coffee's ready," he said through the door.

"Fix my cup," I demanded dropping the towel around my body to the floor. "It's the least you could do for trying to kill me."

He didn't respond, but I didn't expect him to. He wasn't big on talking which worked for me because I wasn't either. We could spend hours in silence comfortably. We didn't waste time with sharing useless information.

I heard his heavy footsteps as he made his way down the hallway towards the kitchen. I should have heard him stop outside of the bathroom door, but I was so stuck in my head that everything else faded away. I go to the gym to make myself strong enough to protect myself against anyone. I have spent years learning to always take in my surroundings, so I don't get caught by surprise.

I shook my head in annoyance as I grabbed my work uniform out of my closet. I worked at *Left Turners*, a sports bar and grill that was located downtown. It had a NASCAR theme, but there was always a game of whatever sport playing on the television screens hanging on the walls. I loved working there because it didn't matter what day of the week or what shift it was, we were always busy. Staying busy was safe for me. My mind would be occupied, not to mention the nice tips I would make.

I saved every penny I made, only spending enough to survive. I didn't own a car, just a bike. I didn't go shopping. I didn't go out drinking. That one had more to do with learning from bad mistakes than anything else, but it was still on the money saving list. I didn't eat out often. I didn't go on any trips or to any concerts. I didn't indulge in anything extra because my future was mine, and I had plans. I wanted to go back to college and pursue my degree in social work. I wanted to help the kids that bounced around the system. I wanted to show them someone cared.

I bent over and unwound the towel wrapped around my hair. I ran the towel over my head roughly soaking as much water out of the long blonde strands as I could. I stood back up and grabbed some black panties and red bra from the top drawer of my dresser.

My uniform consisted of a red shirt with the picture of two black and white flags crossed over each other. I could wear shorts or pants with black converse. I decided to wear my black shorts today. It would probably be hot running around between my tables today. Not to mention, the oppressive heat outside. August in South Louisiana was hot, really fucking hot with heavy humidity.

After throwing on my shorts and shirt, I grabbed a pair of high yellow socks out of my drawer and opened my bedroom door. I walked down the hallway seriously hoping Carter fixed my coffee. The hot shower helped clear the cobwebs from a night of not enough sleep, but I needed my caffeine fix to help me think and function properly. Maybe then I would be able to get the Ryker fantasy out of my head and get back to reality.

I walked into the kitchen and saw Carter leaning against the counter next to the coffee pot. He was staring down at the floor holding a bottle of water loosely in one hand looking lost in thought. He looked up and met my curious gaze.

His lost look disappeared and was replaced by concern when he saw my appearance. After a minute of studying my face, he nodded down to the cup of coffee sitting on the counter next to where he was standing.

"Rough night?" he asked while I walked over to the counter and picked up my favorite coffee cup sporting a picture of Cheech and

Chong. He hated the cup, but I thought it was funny. Those guys were hilarious to watch, I didn't care how old the show was or how much pot they smoked. The show always made me laugh.

"Lyla called me to pick her up from a party last night," I explained knowing that his concern was understandable, but hating the fact I even had to explain myself. "I stayed up with her until six this morning."

"What happened?" he demanded standing up straight.

I shrugged trying to play off the scene from last night as nothing. "She and Cody got in an argument in front of everyone. She was upset and embarrassed, so we left. I didn't think she needed to be alone, so I stayed with her."

I kept my eyes down and blew lightly on my coffee before taking a small sip. I could feel his stare as his eyes burned into the top of my head, but I couldn't meet his eyes. He's always been super protective of me, so I thought it was best if he didn't know that I was almost in the middle of a fight. He would be pissed off and demand names, so he could kick their asses.

After several minutes, I released a heavy sigh when it became obvious he was going to stand there silently staring at me until I told him everything that happened. I should have known better than to try to get out of telling him. I've never could keep stuff from him. If I didn't tell him, he would find someone who would, and I knew from experience it was always best if the story came from me instead of someone else. Other people tend to exaggerate what really went down.

I lifted my head up and met his intense crystal blue eyes. I squared my shoulders and stood up straight. "He wasn't around when I first got there. Once I found Lyla, we were leaving the party through the back door since it was closest when Cody rushed toward us yelling at Lyla and calling her some shitty things. Ryder and Ryker blocked us from him. While Ryder distracted Cody with a fist to the face, we decided to leave. So, we did." I made sure my voice was strong and sure while my insides trembled slightly. I didn't really realize how much seeing the violence shook me up until now.

That's another reason I didn't want to tell Carter anything. Every time I did, my walls came down and my emotions spilled out. He had a way of making me acknowledge events that happened and the way I felt about them. I was scared last night. All the training I had put in over the past year was for nothing I thought as my chin trembled slightly. Tears burned behind my eyes, but I didn't want to release them.

"Shit," Carter grumbled as he slipped his arms around my shoulders pulling me into him. I tucked my head under his chin and rested against his chest as my free hand wrapped around his waist.

I took a deep breath of his familiar scent as I tried to calm down. I practiced the breathing exercises my old social worker, Angie, taught me when I first started having panic attacks when I was fifteen. Deep breath in, slow breath out. Deep breath in, slow breath out.

He ran a hand up and down my back soothingly not saying anything. He knew there was nothing to say. I had to ride it out. I had to beat the panic back and focus on the now. I closed my eyes and concentrated on my breathing letting the steady beat of Carter's heart against my cheek and his steady hands on my back soothe me.

After several minutes, the panic, tears, and trembling were gone. I could step back from Carter and drink the rest of my coffee calmly. I've had a lot of panic attacks over the years, and Carter has witnessed several of them. The ones that he's been there for, he had been able to bring me back. Other people like coworkers or good doers at the grocery store have tried to touch me, and I flipped out. I don't actually remember what I've done while I blacked out from a panic attack, but judging from the ambulances and cop cars, I knew it could be bad. But Carter's different. He has always been my safe place, my comfort zone.

"Did you get hurt?" he asked softly, his hand cupping my cheek.

I shook my head keeping my eyes on his. "No, Ryker and Ryder blocked us from everything. That's when Lyla and I went around the house to the car."

"Who are Ryker and Ryder?" he asked with a lifted eyebrow.

"A couple of Lyla's friends," I shrugged looking down into my cup

I drank the last sip of coffee in my cup and rinsed it out in the sink. "Can you give me a ride to work?" I asked as I turned around to look at him.

His intense stare searched my eyes for a moment before he nodded his head. "Yeah, let me grab a quick shower, and we can head out."

"Hurry up or I'm going to be late," I warned watching him leave the kitchen.

I knew this was just a short reprieve because he wouldn't be able to let this go. When I told him Ryker blocked me from the fight, it was a big deal. To normal people, it would look like Ryker was just a nice guy who didn't want to see a girl hurt. To me, it meant something more, something that I couldn't let myself feel.

While I waited for Carter, I grabbed a yogurt out of the refrigerator and a spoon from the drawer next to the sink. I ate it standing in front of the window above the kitchen sink with a clear view of the parking lot. I saw Ryker's truck in front of the building to the left side of ours. When he pulled into that parking lot that night we were together, I felt a panic attack coming on from the thought of him knowing where I lived without me telling him. He saw my panic and placed his palm on my cheek after he put the truck in park. In my panic, rational thoughts fled so I didn't understand what he was saying at first. When I calmed my breathing, he repeated that he lived in that building. He knew I lived next door because Lyla introduced me as her neighbor.

Once Carter was dressed, we grabbed our stuff and headed out. The ride to work was made with the music turned up to a level that made conversation not possible, which worked great for me. I didn't want to discuss any feelings that I didn't even want to acknowledge in my own head not to mention out loud. Carter still seemed tense, so I knew he was controlling himself from going on a rant. I was glad he had ironclad control especially when it came to me and my fucked-up head.

When he pulled into the parking lot, I turned to him. "Thanks."

"No problem," he answered giving me a kiss on the cheek. "You get off at four?"

"Yep," I answered with a smile. I loved Carter more than anything in the world.

"I'll be here," he smiled back. "I finish at the garage around one."

Opening the door to *Left Turners*, I immediately scanned the area. I spotted a few families seated in the booths lining the walls against the ceiling to floor windows. The blinds were down, but the slats were opened slightly to allow some sunlight in to shine across the dining room. I looked toward the bar and saw Jaxson setting up his station.

Jaxson was working here when I started a year ago. He was taking some classes at the college a few miles away in Thibodaux. He only had a semester left to achieve a bachelor's Degree in business. He was twenty-one years old and smoking hot. He was a playboy and made a great bartender, especially on girls' nights. He had deep blue eyes like the vast ocean water with long, thick eyelashes and dark eyebrows. He had a quick smile and full out laugh that made those eyes glitter like the sun sparkling on the water's surface. He once told me that he spent eighteen years not smiling so he wanted to laugh and embrace the great things with a laugh or smile. On the rare occasion he had a serious moment, his eyes would deepen to the deepest sapphire. His dark brown hair was cropped close to his head giving glimpses of his scalp underneath.

When I first started, he immediately hit on me. Every shift he would come up with some pick up line that he knew I would just fall all over him for. It never happened. The last time I denied his invitation for a date his eyes turned deep sapphire as he stared at me. I'm not sure how long we stared at each other, but he nodded twice. He didn't ask any questions. He didn't probe for more information. He just nodded in understanding and acceptance. Ever since then, he became a friend. We laughed and joked around during our shifts. I've hung out with him outside of work a few times, but always with other people around.

He lifted his head from his work station, and his mouth spread in a friendly smile. "Hey, beautiful." His voice carried across the dining room.

I gave a small smile and a little finger wave before walking to the break room.

I had to train a new girl on waitressing today and let me tell you how excited I am about that. Insert sarcasm. I am so not happy about this. I hated having someone follow me around my whole shift. Some of them flirted with the customers. Some didn't listen to anything I said causing me to have to explain it repeatedly. I really hated repeating myself. Some wouldn't last a fucking week, so they basically wasted my time. Not to mention, I had to share tips. That pissed me off when they ended up quitting or just plain sucked at their jobs that they couldn't get tips on their own. However, when my manager, Jen, told me a few days ago, I would start to train a new hire, she did say she had some experience which I thought was a relief.

I put my bag in my assigned locker. I grabbed my apron and tied it around my waist. I closed the locker and locked it. I turned around the corner with my head down still messing with the strings of the apron and ran directly into a body.

"Shit!" a female voice exclaimed. "I'm so sorry! Are you okay?"

She put her hands on my shoulders when we collided. She didn't remove them, so I took a step back that caused her arms to fall away. I looked up and found a girl I've never seen before staring at me in horror, maybe even fear. Her blue green eyes were very expressive showing me the turmoil going through her. She was a little taller than me, maybe five six or so. She was slim but had great curves. Her hair was deep brown almost black and cut to her shoulders with shorter layers surrounding her face.

"I'm fine," I answered with a reassuring smile. I mean it was probably my fault since I was looking down and not paying attention. "You good?"

She left out a small breath of what I assumed was relief and smiled back. "Yeah. I was looking for my locker, and my mind may have been elsewhere. I'm Evyn." She held her hand out to me.

I took the hand she offered. "I'm Bailey."

"Oh, good! I'm training with you today," she laughed softly. "I know first impressions are crucial, but I would like to pretend I did not try to tackle you to the floor as my first impression. I'm not a complete klutz so I don't want that to be what you think about me. So, I'm going to pick my stuff up and meet you in the hallway where I will have my do over."

"Do over?" I asked.

"Yeah," she nodded. "I definitely need a do over."

I laughed. She had a way about her. Her face was open and honest. She could make fun of herself and laugh about it which was kind of refreshing compared to all the fake bitches in this world.

She scooted around me, found an empty locker, and shoved her stuff in. She looked over at me and smiled. "Go to the hallway. I'll only be a second."

I nodded my head and smiled back. Maybe I was wrong and training her today wouldn't be so bad. She thought her first impression sucked, but I didn't agree. Today may be a good day after all.

When I made it to the hallway, Maya was walking back from the kitchen.

"Hey, girl," she greeted.

Maya was a sweet and shy girl who was working here before I started. When we first spoke to one another, I didn't know how she could be a hostess being that painfully shy. I soon learned she had a mask similar to mine. She could shield herself with a wall of confidence surrounding her even though she didn't have an ounce of actual confidence.

It took a long time for her to look me in the eyes and have a real conversation, but once she did our friendship grew. She was funny and sarcastic. Her personality was as bright as the red curls surrounding her face. I thought it was a shame she hid herself away but could understand her need to protect herself from others.

"Hey," I smiled at her as I leaned my back against the wall. "How are you doing?"

"Good," she answered. "I did awesome at the market this morning!"

She made jewelry that was original and beautiful. She used rocks, beads, and anything else that caught her eye. The first time I went to her apartment and saw her pieces, I was in awe and I didn't even care about jewelry. She was so embarrassed and started putting everything away. It took forever to convince her to sell her pieces. She started going to the flea market that is held downtown every Saturday morning. The more she sold, the more her confidence in her ability grew, and the more pieces she could create.

"Awesome," I held my hand up for a high five which she returned with enthusiasm and her cute girly giggle.

"Don't y'all have work to do?" someone snapped cutting off Maya's giggle and caused her body to stiffen, her mask coming down.

I turned towards her voice with a glare. Crystal was standing there with her hands on her hips and scowl on her face. Crystal was a waitress and the biggest bitch I've ever met. I try to avoid her as much as possible. She was a mean, nasty person who got off on other people's unhappiness. I've seen her at the few frat parties I've attended and always stayed away.

"Don't you?" I asked in return with a scowl of my own.

I didn't know who the fuck she thought she was, but she didn't run shit. I wasn't going to answer to her.

"Hey!" a cheery voice broke our stare down.

Evyn was smiling at me reaching her hand out towards me. "I'm Evyn." She had a great smile that showed pretty white teeth and included laugh lines at the corners of her mouth. Her voice was chipper and slightly high pitched making me think she was a cheerleader at one point in her life. She seemed like she was happy with life in general, but her eyes sang a different song. They were sad and haunted, maybe even lost. The weird thing was she wasn't trying to hide it. I think the smile and happy voice was to try to be cheerful because she wanted to be that. She didn't hide behind a wall. She didn't seem to care what people saw when they looked at her.

I smiled back trying not to laugh about her "do-over" and took her hand. "I'm Bailey. You ready to get started?"

"Yes," she nodded her head and smiled bigger.

The hours flew by. Working with Evyn was a lot of fun, and she soaked up everything I taught her. She asked questions and listened intently to the answers. She was friendly with all the customers even the rude ones. She took a copy of the menu to study on her break and made small talk with Jaxson when we needed to go to the bar for orders. She was a genuinely nice person. Jaxson tried some lines on her that she just laughed off without taking them seriously. I didn't think Jaxson knew what to do with that which just made me laugh my ass off.

She even managed to get Maya to have a conversation with her. She found out more about Maya than I even knew. She made people feel so comfortable to talk with her. She stayed away from Crystal like she was toxic which I thought showed she had good instincts about people.

We had about an hour left to our shift when we walked up to the bar to fill a drink order. Evyn handed the order to Jaxson while I looked around the bar and noticed most of the stools taken. I spotted a blonde that looked familiar. He turned his head and caught my eyes.

He got off his stool and started walking my way when Crystal latched onto his arm.

"Hey, Drew!" she exclaimed in her annoyingly high-pitched voice.

He stopped and turned his head toward her. "Hey," he responded with a small smile and slid her hand gently from him.

He walked to me. "Hey," he greeted. "Bailey, right?"

He was tall and lean looking. He had the definition of muscles in his arms and legs which showed with the work out gear of a sleeveless shirt and basketball shorts on. His hair was sandy blond cut close to his scalp. His eyes were a striking sea green that contrasted nicely to the tan he had going on.

Recognition caught me as I remembered him from the night before. He was the guy that was all in my space before Ryker pulled me back. I straightened and nodded stiffly.

"I'm Drew," he stuck his hand out to shake mine.

I took his hand warily. His hand was warm and smooth. He gave my hand a gentle shake and let go making me let out a soft breath in relief. I didn't like it when people touched me which was really fucking ironic since I let Ryker touch whatever he wanted.

"I'm sorry," he blurted in a rush wincing slightly.

"For?" I asked raising an eyebrow. I wasn't sure what he was apologizing for.

"For my behavior last night," he said shaking his head slightly, a frown pulling down the edges of his mouth as he looked away from me for a second before making eye contact again. "I was way too drunk, and that's no excuse for the way I was hitting on you. I didn't mean to make you feel uncomfortable."

I could see the sincerity in his eyes and hear the deep regret in his voice. I didn't think he was a bad guy. I could understand the way alcohol made people stupid.

"It's okay," I replied with a small smile, my body relaxing.

He sighed with relief and smiled a smile that reached his eyes showing the cute dimples in his cheeks which caused me to smile bigger. He really was a cutie.

"Is Ryker meeting y'all here?" Crystal asked as she slid close to Drew.

He glanced at her and then quickly back at me. I shrugged my shoulders, not sure what the look was for.

He looked back at Crystal and shook his head. "No."

She pouted in what I was guessing she thought was a cute look but was pathetic and fake. I didn't think there was anything real about this bitch.

"He texted me and said he was coming in," she said.

I narrowed my eyes as I looked at her. My heart stopped beating for a second and then sunk into my stomach where a hard knot formed. I was pissed when I realized this feeling was jealously. I had no right to be jealous, and I seriously shouldn't be jealous of this bitch. I believed her words until I saw her little smirk that she tried to hide. If I wasn't looking so closely, I would have missed it and the evil glint in her eyes.

Suddenly, it made sense. She was at the party last night. I remembered seeing her for a second while Ryker and I were in the middle of the living room, but then Ryker was kissing me and touching me, and I forgot all about her.

She obviously wanted me to believe Ryker and she were tight, and maybe that was true. I didn't know, but I did know that he didn't text her. The look on her face combined with her question to Drew confirmed that. If he texted her to tell her he was coming to the bar, she wouldn't have had to ask Drew.

Drew was looking really confused and uncomfortable. I couldn't really blame him. She was asking about a guy that was all over me last night and saying he was texting her. I could see the wheels turning in his head. He wasn't stupid. He would probably figure out her game, but I was done. I didn't spend time on useless shit. And Crystal was under the category of useless shit.

"Alright," I said to Drew. "Thanks for that, but I got to get back to work."

He smiled at me. "See you around, Bailey." He turned around and went back to his stool ignoring Crystal which made me want to laugh when her forehead wrinkled with confusion over the blow off.

I didn't spare Crystal another glance. I turned and started my end of shift work. I was so ready to go home and go to bed.

Chapter Four
Ryker

The next morning, I woke up with determination and anticipation flowing through my body. I had to make Bailey mine. Last night proved that all the shit I had been imagining for the last three weeks was real. I was beginning to question my sanity a little bit. I almost convinced myself that the connection I felt from my one night with Bailey was something I made up. That thought went out the fucking window when she walked into that party, and my dick rocked up immediately. That right there let me know she was mine. I've hooked up with girls before, but I've never had an erection because of someone across a crowded room before. I couldn't feel her, smell her, or taste her, but just knowing we occupied the same space excited me. I recognized her as mine. I just had to convince her of that fact. As much as I felt she was mine, I was hers, too.

I rolled over in my bed and grabbed my phone from the table beside my bed. After sliding my finger across the screen, I saw I had a few missed calls from Logan but no texts which had me frowning in confusion. Usually, if I missed his call, I would have a text letting me know what the call was about. It was a little past noon, and he tried calling a couple of hours earlier. I didn't get to sleep until after four. After the girls left, me and Ryder got into my truck and went home. He was super quiet. I tried to ask him about Lyla, but he wouldn't answer me. Finally, he said to let it go. So, I let it go. For now, that is.

My mind was on Bailey and how to fix the situation anyway. She ran from me twice, and I had to find out why. I wanted to be with her. In order to do that, I had to break down her walls to have her. I was a patient guy, but I had a fierce determination when it came to something I really wanted.

I wanted Bailey. I would crush the bricks one by one until they were pebbles. I would stomp on the pebbles until they were ash. I didn't care how long it took. It didn't matter. She was worth it. I just needed to find a way to see her.

Since Lyla introduced her as her neighbor, I knew what apartment building she lived in. I wanted to go knock on every door to see which she answered, but I didn't really want her to see me as a stalker and if she was already scary about me, I didn't want to give her a reason to be.

I got out of bed and headed into the living room to see Ryder sitting on the sofa staring into a cup of coffee. He must have been thinking hard because he didn't even look up when I entered the room.

"Morning, bro," I called walking into the kitchen.

His head snapped up. "You missed morning, bro." He gave me a half smile.

"I noticed. How long you been up?" I asked. I knew he was still awake when I went to bed. After staring at his phone the whole way home, he went to his room and put his stereo on.

"A couple of hours," he answered. "You talked to Logan?"

"No," I looked at him. "I had a couple of missed calls from him. Is he home?"

We all shared a three-bedroom apartment. Logan was Ryder's age, but since we were just a year apart, we were all close growing up. Logan lived in the house next to us, but he was at our house more than his. His parents travelled a lot, and he stayed at our place. He was there so much we called him Landry number seven.

"No," Ryder answered with a frown. "He said he gave Riley a ride home from the party and ended up crashing at her place."

"What's up with the frown?" I asked.

It wasn't unusual for Logan to stay at Riley's apartment. She lived in Thibodaux which was about thirty minutes away from our place in Houma. She wasn't a morning person. She wanted to be closer to campus, so she didn't have to get up so early every day for class.

"I don't know," he shook his head. "Logan sounded off. When I asked if everything was cool, it took a minute for him to answer."

We all knew the feelings between Logan and Riley. You could see the love they had for each other just by watching how they interacted. They were always together, except for when Riley dated Jacob Ledet. There was a riff that caused them both pain, and it sucked to witness. They wouldn't listen to anything we had to say, so we had to step back.

"If anything was wrong, he would tell us." I walked into the kitchen to grab something to eat. "What time you going to the gym?"

We both worked at Heavy Bags that our dad owned. Ryder taught some boxing and self-defense classes while I mostly handled all the paperwork like schedules, inventory, and memberships. We could make our own hours around our classes at school.

"Soon," he answered walking into the kitchen. "I want to get a workout in before my classes start."

"Alright," I said taking a bite of my toast. "Give me about twenty minutes, and we'll ride in together."

"Okay," he answered standing up and heading into the kitchen. He rinsed his mug out before putting it into the dishwasher. "Want to talk about it?"

He sighed and dropped his head down leaning over the counter. Without looking up he said, "I'm worried about Lyla. I've seen the way Cody has been with her for a while now, but every day I tried to talk to her she would run off. Last night before y'all showed up he had grabbed her upper arm and dragged her upstairs. By the time, I made it up there, she was running down. I followed her back down when I really wanted to beat the fuck out of him. I wanted to get her out of there, but she said she called Bailey already. She wouldn't talk to me. She would barely look at me."

"I'm glad you got those hits in, man," I said. "Once she calms down from the situation, try to talk to her again."

He nodded, "I will."

I finished up my toast and drained my orange juice. I rinsed off the dishes and put them in the dishwasher.

"I'll be ready in a sec," I told him.

Twenty minutes later, we climbed into Ryder's white truck and headed to the gym. I turned the music up and rolled the windows down.

Opening the door to the gym, the bell sounded throughout the open area. Looking around, I couldn't help but smile. The gym was my second home growing up and still was. The smell of sweat and leather lingered in the air. The sounds of flesh against heavy bags, the constant motion of the speed bags being hammered, and the men sparring in the ring echoed around the room. My dad opened *Heavy Bags*, a boxing gym, a little over twenty years ago. My brother, Rian, was a toddler, and my brother, Rylan, was a newborn. My dad came up with a plan he felt good about supporting his family and gave it his all. Not long after, my mom found out she was pregnant for Ryder. He put in a lot of hours at the gym to get it up and running. At first, he didn't have employees, so he did everything himself, staying at the gym from opening to closing. My mom helped where she could, mostly did some paperwork from home, but sometimes she would take us into the gym and work next to my dad. My parents were and always have been a united front. They loved each other deeply and thoroughly, and that never changed.

The look of the gym was old school, but all the equipment was kept up to date. The walls were a worn brown wood covered with pictures of some of the greatest boxers in history along with the boxers that came and went from the gym. Some went on to be pro while others stayed local. It was one big open space filled with heavy bags spread out, speed bags hanging from beams along the edges of the room and a ring in the middle of the floor. In the far-right corner was a weight bench along with a shelf of weights against the wall. There were three treadmills in the left corner of the room. Jump ropes, extra gloves, and other equipment were put up on shelves set up along the back wall. There was a staircase to the left of the front door that led to some rooms upstairs. My dad's office was up there with an open glass window, so he could keep an eye on things when he had to go up there.

Kole and Kason were sparring in the ring while my dad yelled out commands. Kole and Kason Gaudet are brothers. They both showed up one day looking for work. They looked bad off, so my dad put them on the payroll. At first, they cleaned up around the place, wiping down the equipment, washing towels, and keeping everything picked up. They worked hard but kept to themselves. We were sure they didn't have a place to stay, but we couldn't get them to talk. My dad didn't let that go on for long though. He got them to talk enough to know they were staying in shelters when they could and alleys other times. My dad cleaned out one of the rooms upstairs, got a couple of beds, and put them in it. They didn't want to take it, but my dad made sure they did. Once they were settled, my dad asked them if they wanted to give boxing a shot. My dad never boxed, but he was passionate about the sport. He studied books and observed tapes. He attended so many matches. He was able to talk to a few professional boxers along with some trainers. They started training and doing some local amateur fights.

"Hey, guys," Lorelei called from the front desk.

Lorelei Guidry worked the front desk and trained here. She's had a few amateur fights that she dominated. She was fierce and trained hard. She was a knockout with long brown hair and beautiful hazel eyes. Her smile lit up her whole face which didn't happen often. She's had it rough growing up. I didn't know her whole story, but I can see the shadows fade a little more each time I saw her.

"Hey, Lo," I greeted walking up to the counter. "How's it going today?"

"Good," she nodded. "We had a few new members sign up, and this afternoon's classes look like they will be full."

"That's great," Ryder replied standing next to me. "Are you training today?"

"Yeah," she looked back at the ring with a frown. "I'm waiting for my turn in the ring."

I looked over to the ring to see Kole's eyes on Lo while Kason was listening intently to what my dad was telling him. There always seemed to be a weird tension when Lorelei and Kole were in the same space, and I couldn't figure it out. The looks that passed between them were heavy with something. I tried to get one of them to talk to me, but neither would say a fucking word.

When Lo turned back to us, her eyes were shadowed again. The phone rang, and she picked it up with the traditional greeting. We took that as our cue to continue in. A few of the guys called out greetings to us as we made our way to the ring. My dad looked down at us, nodding before turning back to Kason.

"Keep your gloves up, arms close to your body," he told Kason. "Alright, that's good for today."

Kole glared at me as he passed, but he didn't say anything. I was sure it was about Lo even though nothing ever happened between me and her. Whatever. My head was so far gone with Bailey I didn't want to deal with shit from Kole.

"Hey, boys," Dad greeted jumping down from the ring.

"How's it going, old man?" I threw a fake jab to his shoulder as he dodged it like I knew he would.

He laughed. "I'm not old, boy."

I laughed and asked, "Mind if I go up to the office and get my shit sorted?"

"You know you don't have to ask, Ryker," he frowned at me. "That's as much your office as it is mine."

I followed him up the steps to the first door on the left. He walked up to the big wooden desk and gathered up the papers strewn over the top.

"So, how's school going?" he asked moving the papers into one pile off to the side of the desk.

"Good," I replied looking out of the glass making up one wall watching the activity on the gym floor.

I saw Lorelei step in the ring with Kason and wondered what it would be like to get in the ring with Bailey. Would she like this gym? Would she want to work out here, train here? Did she even like boxing? I knew she did something physical because her body was toned and in shape. I wondered what she did. Did she go to another gym?

"What's with the look?" he asked snapping my attention back to him.

"What look?" I asked back already knowing I would not get out of this. He could always read us. He knew something was up.

He raised an eyebrow and just stared at me. Looking into the same brown eyes I saw every day in the mirror, I could see what I would look like in twenty years. His brown hair was cut shorter than mine and his build had more weight to it than mine, but our features were the same.

"I met a girl," I said with a sigh running my hand through my hair in frustration.

"And," he prompted when I didn't say anymore.

"And she keeps running off," I admitted. I knew that's what she was doing, running. We saw each other twice, and each time she walked away without giving me any information.

My dad laughed. He fucking laughed. I scowled at him. I did not find this situation amusing. I was getting ready to leave the office when his hand landed on my shoulder.

"I'm sorry, son," he tried to get his laughter under control by coughing and clearing his throat. "It's just that you sounded like a disgruntled kindergarten kid."

I shook my head, my mouth pulled down in a frown. "It's not that. She runs away. She didn't give me a number or anything to reach here. When I look into her eyes, there are walls guarding her. I want to break through, but I'm not sure how yet."

His expression turned serious. "What do you mean walls?"

"I mean like how Lo used to look when she first got here but more," I answered. "I want her. I have to find her and talk to her, but I have to figure a way to get in behind the walls."

He slapped my shoulder and leveled his eyes on mine. "Proceed with caution, Ryker. Walls like that were built for a reason. You make sure this is what you want before going forward. I know you son, and you would never want to hurt someone. Sounds to me if you managed to get behind her walls, she would be very vulnerable to you."

My hands turned to fists, and my jaw locked tight. I understood where he was coming from, but I was dead serious about Bailey. I would never intentionally hurt her. I wanted her as mine. I wanted her to talk to me. I wanted her to lean on me. I wanted to show her happy.

Need

"I am serious, Dad," I gritted through clenched teeth. "She's the one for me."

His eyes widened in surprise. I never said that about anyone before, but I was only nineteen, so it shouldn't be that shocking. "Ok, then. Let me know if you need anything, son. I'm always here."

I nodded. I knew that. He always had our backs. "I will." My jaw loosened, and my fists opened.

"I love you," Dad said walking to the door of the office.

"I love you, too," I replied watching him walk out of the office to the stairs.

I shook my head to try to clear it and got to work.

About two hours after going into the office, I sat back in the chair and moved my head side to side to try to get the kinks out of my neck. Paperwork around the gym wasn't too bad. It just needed to be done carefully. Orders for equipment, payroll, scheduling, it all took time and needed to be handled

"What's up, man?" someone called from behind me. I turned around and saw Drew walking in.

I was glad he came in today. I really needed to talk to him about getting in Bailey's space. I was claiming her, and I couldn't let that shit slide. This would only be a warning, but he would only get one.

Once he locked eyes with me, he threw his hands out in front of him, palms facing me in surrender. I'm not sure what my face looked like, but I knew I was still mad about him being all up in Bailey's face the other night. I could feel my muscles tighten, my hands formed fists by my sides, and jaw lock.

"I know. I was an asshole last night," he stated honestly. "I already apologized to her."

My gut clenched hearing him say he talked to her when I wasn't around, but, "Where?"

He looked confused. "Where? Where what?"

"Where did you apologize to her?" I asked my fists clenched at my sides.

"Left Turners," he answered. "I went there to watch a game with some guys, and she was working. I just came from there."

Left Turners? She worked there? That was useful information to have. I would have to use this to my advantage.

"Is she still working?" I asked. I was ready to jump in my truck and get to her.

"No. She was finishing up after I talked to her," he said slowly tilting his head to the side.

I could see the questions he wanted to ask, so I prepared myself.

"Are y'all together?" Drew asked.

"Not yet," I answered truthfully.

"Yeah, well," he shuffled nervously making my eyes narrow.

"Well, what?" I prompted when he didn't elaborate.

"Crystal was there when I talked to Bailey," he started.

"And?" I snapped. What the fuck did she have anything to do with anything?

He let a big breath and his eyes nailed me to the spot with anger. "She asked me if you were meeting me."

His voice was hard, and I saw his fists clench. What the fuck?

I just stared at him waiting for whatever the fuck he was trying to say.

"She said you texted her and told her you were going to stop by," he bit out.

"That's bullshit," I responded immediately. "I don't have her number, nor do I want it."

He unclenched his fists and his shoulders relaxed. What the fuck?

"What the fuck is your problem?" I gritted out.

"Nothing, man," he responded quietly. "I just don't want to see Bailey get played. I don't know her like talking about, but I can see she's good people. I figured Crystal was playing bullshit games, but I had to make sure."

My first reaction was to punch him for trying to protect my girl because Bailey was my fucking girl. I checked that reaction because I knew Drew was a good dude. He was coming from a good place, and I couldn't really blame him. Something about Bailey made it hard not to protect her.

"I appreciate your concern about Bailey. I really do," I let him see my sincerity. "But you don't have to protect her. I want that responsibility. I want her to be mine."

He smiled and nodded his head. "I got you, but I will kick your ass if you hurt her."

"I'd like to see you try," I laughed as I went to the weights and started my work out.

I did my reps with the weights before I moved on to the heavy bag. I wasn't a boxer, but I loved the heavy bag. It was a great work out and was a great release. I was in the zone watching my fists connect with the bag, the power of the punch travelled up my arm.

Once I was done, I sat heavily on the bench and started removing the gloves on my hands. Logan walked over and sat down next to me. Looking over at him, I was shocked to see how haggard he looked.

"Rough night?" I joked, but he didn't crack a smile. He just stared at me a second, his eyes conflicted before he looked away.

"What is it?" I asked with concern. I could see something was seriously wrong.

"Look," he started blowing out a heavy breath still not making eye contact with me.

As I waited for him to continue, a bunch of scenarios filled my head. Did something happen to Riley? Did something happen between Logan and Riley that ended badly? Did something happen with his parents? They had a shitty relationship, but he loved them. It would kill him if something happened to them.

"Logan," I barked impatiently.

He looked at me nodding seemingly coming to a decision. "After y'all left last night, I had Cody hauled up to his room. I was preoccupied with him that I lost track of Riley. When I found her, something went down with her and Jacob." His hands clenched into fists and his jaw started ticking. "I dealt with him and took her home. I stayed with her, but she wanted me to leave this morning."

I could see the pain he was in, and I could feel his anger like it was living thing. It made me tense, and I was straining to keep my shit on lock. Riley and Jacob dated a few months before she found him fucking a frat groupie at a party. She ended their relationship and stopped speaking to him. I saw him trying to talk to her a few times, and I always intervened. My sister did not need the shit he brought with him. In fact, we all had talks with him, but he was a dumb fuck who thought he could do whatever he wanted.

"What did he do?" I gritted out between clenched teeth.

He hung his head, running his hand through his hair making the blonde locks stand up. "I can't tell you."

"What the fuck you mean you can't tell me?" I demanded standing up.

He looked up at me. "I told her I wouldn't tell you, but she promised she would tell y'all. She said she needed today alone and would talk to y'all tomorrow at your parents' place."

I looked away from him. That's bullshit. I knew they were best friends, but he was also my best friend and we were talking about my sister here. I understood and even respected his loyalty to her, but I wanted to put my fist through his fucking face at that moment. I had a bad feeling that whatever happened didn't involve just words. I wanted to hurt him so many times, but Riley asked me to leave it alone. I listened to her because I didn't want to upset her. She was determined to get through her first breakup on her own. She acted like it didn't bother her, but I knew her self-confidence took a hit. After a few months, I had finally seen Riley come back. Now, the dickhead fucked with her, and I was afraid she would retreat again. I felt helpless when she was hurt.

Logan stood up in front of me and put his hands on my shoulders. "Give her today, man."

I just stared at him. I didn't have words. Worry and guilt warred in my gut. I was so focused on getting Bailey out of there that I didn't even stop to think about Riley. I should have been there. I should have protected her. I failed her.

"Stop, bro," Logan stated sharply. "I was there. I should have been able to stop it."

I could see the same guilt I felt in his eyes. He loved Riley fiercely, and I knew he would keep the blame on himself. That snapped me out of my own head. It wasn't our fault. Yes, we should have been there for her and watched out, but this was on Jacob.

"It's Jacob's fault," I stated. "We will talk to her tomorrow and help her."

"What's going on?" Ryder asked walking up to us.

We both turned to him. He was looking back and forth between us curiously with worry in his eyes.

"Something happened between Jacob and Riley." I held my hand up when he went to push past me. "She wanted today, and then she'll fill us in tomorrow."

"Fuck that," he spit out going to move.

I put a hand in the middle of his chest to hold him back. "Bro, we need to give her a minute. If we don't, then she will lock up and not tell us anything."

He growled and swung at the closest heavy bag making it jerk back on its chain. "Fuck!"

"Boys," my dad approached.

"It's cool, Dad," I assured trying to sound honest.

He looked like he wanted to argue but decided to let it go. "Let me know." He stated simply and walked away.

"Let's get out of here," I told them.

They both nodded in agreement, so we headed back to our place, all of us stuck in our own thoughts. My siblings and I were super close and knowing one was hurting killed me. Riley was the baby and the only girl. We were all very protective of her and made sure she could handle herself. She tagged along with us everywhere which would bother some brothers to have their little sister trying to do everything they did, but we never minded. We loved having her around, and most of the times we looked at her as one of the boys.

"Y'all want to order a pizza?" I asked once we made it inside the apartment.

"Sounds good, man," Ryder replied. "I'm going shower."

I nodded picking up my phone to place the order. After that was done, I sat on the sofa where Logan already was watching some game on TV.

"Is she going to be okay?" I asked. I knew he wouldn't tell me what happened, but I still needed to know something.

"Yeah, man," he nodded. "Riley's tough. She will bounce back."

I wanted to believe him. I really did, but the worry in his eyes had me uneasy.

We spent the night eating pizza and playing video games trying to get our minds off the girls who were fucking with them.

Chapter Five
Bailey

"Hey, Bailey," Carter called from the other side of my bedroom door as I slipped a fitted tee shirt over my head covering my sports bra.

"Yeah?" I asked opening my door.

"What are your plans today?" he asked.

"Nothing much," I responded. "I'm going for a run right now. What are you doing?"

"I'm going to meet some guys for lunch, and we are going to go on a ride," he answered.

"Okay. I have some errands to take care of. Can I use your truck?" I asked him.

"Bailey," he said sternly. "I told you, you don't have to ask to use the damn truck. It's yours too."

"Whatever," I mumbled. "I'll see you later."

"Bye," he smirked and rubbed his hand over my head loosening my ponytail.

I pushed his hand away with a scowl and tightened my hair. "Bye."

I took a step around him but was stopped when he wrapped his arm around my waist pulling my back into his hard chest. He rested his head on top of mine. I relaxed into his arms reveling in the safe feeling I had in Carter's embrace. He was my safe place, always had been and always would be. We had been together so long I didn't know what I would have done if he wasn't with me. We had been through so much together. He knew everything about me as I did him. He knew when I needed comfort even though I would never ask for it.

He didn't say anything as he held me. He didn't ask what was weighing on my brain. He wouldn't unless he felt it was real heavy. He knew my ticks and tells. He knew whatever it was I would go to him if I needed to. He never pushed me unless I made him with reckless behavior. I went through a year of wilding out before Carter got through to me. He would never let it get as bad as that year was again.

He kissed the top of my head and released me. I looked over my shoulder, gave him a small smile, and walked out of the apartment. I slipped my ear buds in my ears as I jogged down the stairs. I pulled up the Pandora app on my phone and switched it to Three Days Grace Radio putting the volume at maximum level.

I hit the parking lot at a good jog warming up my muscles. I liked the location of our apartment because it was in the middle of a neighborhood with sidewalks. I wouldn't run along a highway. People were stupid especially operating vehicles, so I wouldn't trust I wouldn't get ran the fuck over on the side of a busy road. Running had been my outlet for a long time. I ran to make my body stronger and my mind focused. It was how I coped. It was how I survived. The more time passed, and years turned into more years, I used running as my release. Release from the world and feelings and emotions that I didn't have the capacity to handle.

Growing up in the system, you learned a lot about survival, about how to get to the next day with as little hurt as possible. I started running when I was a little kid and didn't know how to get rid of everything inside of me. I never dreamed of princesses and white knights climbing towers. I was never a little girl in pretty dresses and stars in my eyes. I knew what the world was about at an age I should have been having tea parties with my stuffed animals. The only dreams I ever had were to be strong enough to run away from my reality.

I cleared my mind and concentrated on the rhythm of my feet slapping against the sidewalk and listened to the music blaring in my ears. I emptied all the shitty life lessons I had to learn the hard way over the years. I couldn't get Ryker out of my head, though. It scared the fuck out of me how much I felt with him. I was clogged with emotion. I was comfortable and tense around him. I was drawn to him with my walls up high. I was happy and angry to see him. I was a mess of contradictions where he was concerned.

I focused on my breathing, in and out slowly. I counted my steps as my heels met the hard concrete. I kept my arms stiff and close to my body. I could feel the sweat gather along my hairline and slip down the middle of my back soaking through my tee shirt.

I felt my chest loosen as I got into a steady rhythm. I tried to run every day, but with my work schedule, it wasn't always possible, so I took advantage on my days off. My muscles relaxed until I was loose and limber. The oppressive heat made breathing a little more difficult, but I liked the challenge because I was able to concentrate harder on getting oxygen into my body and not think about anything else.

Of course, nothing could make Ryker leave my head completely. I didn't know what it was that drew me to him, but I needed to let him go. I needed to push him away before my heart was invested too much into him. I couldn't depend on anyone, but Carter. I knew what it felt like when someone you were close to left and never came back. What happened when Ryker left my life? What would I do then? I didn't know, and I didn't want to find out.

After about an hour or so of running, I realized I wouldn't be able to run Ryker out of my brain. I turned around to make the lap back to the apartment. I needed to do some laundry, cleaning, and grocery shopping. I made a shopping list in my head to distract myself as I pumped my legs harder. There were a few kids out playing in front yards. Parents tended their grass and flower beds. Mini vans and sedans sat under carports. Fishing boats were parked on the side of some of the houses. Basketball goals were standing in driveways while teenagers shot baskets. Bicycles were laid down or propped up on kickstands.

Normal lives. Lives where kids were kids with parents making their childhoods last. A little girl with two blonde pigtails smiled big and waved with enthusiasm as I passed in front of her house. She was around six or seven, her top two front teeth missing. I smiled back and waved as I kept running. I was about her age when my life went from bad to worse.

My mom was beautiful with the same blonde hair and green eyes as me. She had a lot of boyfriends that would come over. Every time they visited I had to go to my room. I would hear her moaning and yelling, and I would get so scared for her. One time I decided to go check on her, and that was the one and only time I did.

Shaking my head to clear the memory away, I ran through the parking lot next to my building. When someone grabbed my arm with a firm grip, I instinctively pulled away. The grip tightened, and I turned around swinging wildly. Another big arm blocked my swing causing pain to shoot down my arm. My breath started to get heavy with panic. I fought to get out of the hold when suddenly the hand let go. I stumbled back almost falling to the hard cement. The familiar looking arms came at me again, but my mind was a muddled mess. I couldn't recognize them.

"You want it. You're nothing but a whore. You will spread them for anyone. Well, now you're going to spread them for me." A hard knee pushed between my legs spreading my thighs.

"No, no, no," I chanted shaking my head, Tears flowing down my face, my eyesight blurry.

He wrapped a hand around my throat cutting off my airway. I started gasping and scratching at his arm. I broke his skin. I could feel his blood.

His free hand grabbed my breast roughly. I wanted to scream in agony, but it was stuck in my throat.

It hurt! It hurt! It hurt!

I heard voices, but I couldn't comprehend what was being said. My mind blocked out everything until I was surrounded in black replaying the past.

I couldn't breathe, my chest burned. My muscles quivered with the need to move, but I was locked up. I couldn't get away.

The voices were getting louder. Then, there was silence. The blackness fully engulfed me, and I welcomed it. There was no past, present, or future in the blackness. There was a comforting nothingness. I didn't feel or think in this hole my brain created for me.

"Bailey," a soothing voice said. "Breathe in, breath out. Nice and slow. Come back, baby."

I felt his breath against my lips, his warm hands rubbing up and down my back, his hard chest under the palms of my hands. I could feel the steady rise and fall of his breath leaving and entering his lungs, the strong and steady beat of his heart. I slowed my breathing to match his and rested my forehead against his chest until my heart beat in time with his.

I lifted my head and opened my eyes to the deep, warm, brown ones of Ryker staring intently at me with a mixture of relief and fear. I felt his hands on my shoulders, his body so close I could feel his heat warming my shivering body.

"I'm so sorry, Bailey," he whispered putting his forehead against mine.

"It's okay," I answered softly with a slight waver in my voice that kind of pissed me off. "I'm fine. You just caught me off guard."

The after effects of a panic attack left me feeling vulnerable and completely exposed. I didn't want him to see me like this. I didn't want him witnessing the crazy that was in my head. My heart kicked up again once the enormity of what just happened registered in my brain. He saw me fucking lose it in the middle of a fucking parking lot where anyone could see. He saw the weakness that lives inside of me.

I lifted my head making him do the same. His eyebrows dipped low on his forehead when his fingertips brushed my pulse throbbing in my neck. His eyes searched mine for answers.

I cleared my throat and tried to sound strong. "Sometimes my mind goes away, and my body locks down. I have panic attacks. It's not your fault."

"I'm going to head over to Mom and Dad's," a voice said behind Ryker making me jump.

I looked to the side of Ryker and saw Ryder looking down at us, his big body blocking the sun. I realized that Ryker and I were on our knees where I assumed I fell during the panic attack. I tried to shift away from Ryker, but he just tightened his hold on me, one hand landed on my ass while the other hand tangled in my hair. Essentially, he had me trapped which would normally cause me to freak but looking at him I knew I was safe. I still didn't know what it was about him that made me feel protected and wasn't sure what to do with it, but I knew I wanted to keep it for as long as I had it.

"Okay, bro," Ryker replied without looking away from me. "I'll be there soon."

I felt the blush work its way up my chest into my face with embarrassment. Not only did I black out in front of Ryker but his brother as well. They probably thought I was a nut case, and I wouldn't have to worry about staying away from Ryker because he would want to stay away from me which made a different kind of panic run through me. What the fuck? This should be a good thing. He should know I was damaged and not relationship or whatever the fuck he wanted with me material.

I felt the prickles behind my eyes and tingling in my nose. I closed my eyes as a tear escaped and dropped down my face. I felt him pull me closer and rest his forehead against mine. I shook my head side to side.

"Hey," he said softly, his lips so close to mine they brushed together with each word.

"Hey," I said without opening my eyes.

Why was he still here? I didn't understand any of this. I tried to move out of his hold again, but he wouldn't let me. I had to escape this emotional bullshit. I took a deep breath to gain some semblance of composure. I put my mask on and slowly lifted my eyelids.

"I'm fine," I snapped. "You can let me go."

He just stared at me without saying anything. He wasn't the least bit concerned with the walls I surrounded myself with. I let out a huff when he didn't move away. I rolled my eyes in annoyance and saw the corners of his mouth tip up. I narrowed my eyes at him making him smile fully.

His lips took mine at that point. I couldn't move to evade it because I would have if I had the chance. I really would have. I moaned when his tongue forced its way in my mouth. Okay, so I probably wouldn't have evaded. My arms snaked around his neck, my fingers delving into his hair clutching tightly. He groaned and his hand on my ass tightened pulling me into his body until we touched from chest to thigh. I felt his dick getting bigger in his jeans, and I wanted to rub myself all over him.

This was a bad idea. This would only end in hurt for me and probably him too. I didn't give a fuck. I wanted him. I wanted this feeling to stay. I didn't care where we were. I just wanted to get naked with him.

When we finally pulled apart, we were both breathing heavily. I could see the lust and desire in his eyes. I could feel it against my stomach which made my core tighten and moisture to flood my panties.

"I have to go to my parents' house," he said hoarsely. "Something happened with my sister, and I need to find out what it was. What are you doing later?"

"I have errands to do," I answered with a pang of sadness.

I didn't want to let him go but I knew I had to. I couldn't become dependent on him. I was stronger than that. I had a lifetime of disappointments to show me that you could only trust yourself to stay.

He brushed his lips softly against mine. "Are you sure you're okay?" I felt his finger trace a pattern along my skin skimming my collar bone.

"Yeah,' I nodded. "I'm good."

"What's this?" he asked as his finger traveled up to my shoulder making me suck in a breath. I didn't know if he was asking about the tattoo or the scar causing me to tense up.

"A dragonfly," I answered giving him the answer I was willing to give.

"Why a dragonfly?" he asked softly staring intently at me.

"I read somewhere that a dragonfly symbolized change, a change in self-realization, a change in mental and emotional maturity, and change in the understanding of the deeper meaning of life," I said softly lost in his warm, brown eyes as they searched mine. He had a little wrinkle in his forehead as he listened to my explanation.

"Do you understand the deeper meaning of life?" he asked quietly, his finger still tracing the wing of the dragonfly that dipped down over my shoulder and ended at my collarbone.

"Not yet," I answered honestly. I was mostly floating along through life. Yeah, I had a goal of going to school and getting a degree, so I could help kids like me that bounced from place to place. That's really all I did, though. I didn't have many friends or people I just kicked it with. Lyla tried to drag me out and about with her on a regular basis, but I rarely let her. I got the dragonfly to help me remember I had to change my mindset to be free. I needed to move past what happened to me and on to my spot in this world.

He nodded and placed a kiss on my forehead before he released me and stood up from the ground. "I'll see you later, Bailey," he said. He held his hand out to me, but I ignored it. I got up on my own, turned around, and walked to my apartment building without a backwards glance. I felt his stare on my back the whole time I concentrated on putting one foot in front of the other. I tried to appear calm on the outside, while my insides were a mess of feelings.

As soon as I made it to the stairwell where I knew he couldn't see me anywhere, I started running. I ran up the flight of stairs and into the apartment as fast as I could. My heart was pounding, and my head was foggy. The remains of the panic attack and the desire I felt for Ryker were battling in my head.

I wanted him, but could I have him? Could I keep him? Would he want to stay? How the fuck was I supposed to put faith in a guy I barely knew? I had so many questions, so many doubts, I didn't know what the fuck to do or think. He made me feel so many foreign emotions that I couldn't name them all. I had never felt this way for anyone, not even Carter.

Carter.

Fuck, I forgot about Carter in this situation. What would this do to Carter? How would Ryker affect my relationship with Carter? I would never let anything come between Carter and me. He has always been the one constant in my life, and I wouldn't let that go. Carter deserved the best I had to give, and I wouldn't stop just because I had strong feelings for somebody else.

Guilt. I felt so much guilt in that moment as I realized that what I felt for Ryker was stronger than what I felt for Carter. I wanted to cling to Ryker and never let go. I wanted him to protect and keep me safe from the world. I wanted him to chase the demons out of my head and hold me close when I broke.

No! I wouldn't go there. Carter was my daily, and he earned his place. I could never, nor would I ever, replace him. He needed me as I needed him, and I wouldn't let him down. Ryker would have to go away. I would have to make him. I would have to push him away. I would have to make him see that we would never work. I would probably have to convince him that I didn't want him which caused tears to fall down my cheeks and my stomach to hollow out.

Good thing I learned to bottle up my feelings and mask my emotions a long time ago and had the experience needed to make Ryker believe me. Lying to him would suck ass, but I knew that's what I had to do. Jeopardizing what Carter and I had wasn't an option. I couldn't do that to him or me. I wouldn't.

I understood I was latching onto Carter as an excuse not to be with Ryker, but it was still a valid point. There had been plenty of girls who tried to come between us, making Carter choose between them and me. He always chose me, but I didn't want to be in a position to have to choose. Anyway, I couldn't open myself up to trust anyone. I couldn't do it, not with the shit I had been through. I'd probably lose all sanity and end up a mental case if I gave everything to Ryker, if he dropped me and left.

With resolve settling in, I dried my tears and vowed to myself I would take care of this fuck up I made. I took a quick shower before getting dressed in comfortable cut off shorts and an old tee shirt. I gathered the laundry that needed to be done and set about taking care of the things I needed to. I was hoping by keeping busy, I would be able to put Ryker out of my mind.

It didn't help, but I already knew it wouldn't. I was grieving for something that could have been, and I knew from experience that I had to grieve. I had to let it out so when the time came, I would be able to make my lie believable, that I didn't want Ryker and wasn't interested in pursuing anything with him.

Chapter Six
Ryker

Sundays were family days spent at my parents' house, the house I grew up in. My mom cooked tons of food, or my dad grilled out depending on the weather. Once we started leaving home, my mom worried we wouldn't take the time to go back and see her, so she made the Family Sunday rule. I didn't mind. A bunch of guys in an apartment did not make meals like my momma.

My mind was on Riley and whatever she had to tell us. I was sick to my stomach with worry for her. I figured if she needed a day and told Logan not to share what had happened, it had to mean it was bad. I was trying to prepare myself for the worst, but it was proving difficult. How do you prepare for your little sister to tell you something bad happened to her when you weren't there to protect her?

When Ryder pointed Bailey out in the parking lot, I felt a calmness come over me. Just the sight of her made my mind quiet down. I wasn't even thinking about scaring her when I grabbed her. I felt like shit when she locked up on me. The blankness, the sadness, the emptiness, the hurt, and the panic all swimming in her eyes made my heart fucking hurt. I felt like a bone snapped within my body, and the jagged edge pierced my flesh leaving me to bleed out.

Why did she look like that? What was going through her mind? What happened to her that caused her to react the way she did? When her beautiful green eyes locked on mine, I wanted to drop to my knees in relief. When my lips met hers, I wanted to devour her to assure myself she was okay.

She ran from me again. Even if she masked it as a calm walk to her apartment building, I knew what it was. She was running from me. I saw the walls come up, and I knew she was retreating. I would just have to keep pushing. I could be very persistent. I didn't get her number or apartment number again which was frustrating. At least now I knew where she worked so that was an option. I didn't want to crowd her at work, but desperate times called for desperate measures.

I watched her until she disappeared into her stairwell. I shook my head as I headed to my truck. I had to have her as mine. I needed to have her as mine. The way I felt around her was serious. I never felt this way, and I needed to keep the feeling.

I started my truck up and pulled out of my spot to head to the highway. About ten minutes later, I was pulling into the neighborhood I grew up in. It was a nice suburban neighborhood where the houses were close together and kids played on the sidewalks. Growing up here, we ran through these streets every day. We were always looking for adventures and usually found them. All the kids played together, and the parents all knew each other. We were always safe here with every parent keeping an eye out.

As I got closer to the house I grew up in, I could see everyone was there except Riley. The driveway was packed with four vehicles and there were two trucks parked in the front yard. I pulled over on the side of the road and parked in the grass next to the ditch getting as far off the road as I could. Once we all started driving and could afford second hand cars, we orchestrated a way to park. It was a pain when someone was blocked in, but we sucked it up. We were lucky to have vehicles, so we just did the car shuffle as often as needed.

I wondered when Riley would get there. She had better show, or I was going to her place. I needed to know what the hell was going on, and I wasn't going to wait another day to get information. I was beyond worried. I knew whatever it was I would have to stay strong and have her back.

I walked in the familiar house and inhaled the familiar scent of food cooking. With a big family like ours, there was always something cooking. My mom was an amazing cook and loved spending time in the kitchen. We usually all ended up in there with her unless she had her *I need space* face on. Then, we would retreat and let her cook in peace. She loved to cook. She always said it was her way of taking care of her family and taking care of her family was the best thing she ever wanted to do.

I walked down the hall passing by all the pictures hanging on the walls. I made my way to the living room to see my dad kicked back in his recliner, remote in one hand clicking through the channels on the TV. Ryder, Ryden, and Rylan were sitting on the sofa while Rian was laid out on the loveseat, his feet hanging over the end of it.

"Hey."

"What's up, bro?"

"What up?"

They all greeted at one time. I went around and tapped knuckles with each one of them in a first bump.

When I went to Rian who stayed silent, he smirked. I lifted my eyebrow at his look. I figured I wouldn't like what was about to come out of his mouth. He was such a shit head.

"How's your girl, Ryker?" he asked.

My eyes immediately snapped to Ryder's. He was the only one who knew about Bailey except for Dad.

He shrugged. "Sorry, man. He asked where you were and why we didn't ride together so I told him you were caught up in Bailey. That's all I said."

I could tell by his expression that he was telling me he didn't say anything about the panic attack which made me relieved. I knew Bailey saw it as weakness, and I didn't want to betray her by having my family know about it. It was bad enough Ryder witnessed it.

Bailey was my girl, but things were so damn complicated. We hadn't had one real conversation, yet I felt we were as together as any couple. I would just have to keep present in her life.

I looked back at Rian and saw him sit up on the sofa. Both of his full sleeve tattoos bright against the white tee shirt he wore. His neck tat rippled when he lifted his head to make eye contact with me. He could see my unease about Bailey and had questions in his eyes, but I couldn't answer him. I didn't know everything I wanted to know about her. I didn't know what we were yet, and I knew I wouldn't be able to give him the answers he wanted.

"She's fine," I said giving him a fist bump.

I walked around the sofa in the direction of the kitchen needing my momma. I didn't care how that made me sound. I needed her familiar face and scent to take me out of my head for a minute. My worry for Bailey and my worry for Riley were boxing in my brain, and I needed to settle the match for now.

"What crawled up your ass today?" I heard Dad ask Ryder as I exited the room.

"Nothing," Ryder lied.

He wasn't going to share anything about Lyla which wasn't surprising. He wouldn't even talk to me about what the fuck was going on. I knew it was more than just protecting a friend, but he was tight lipped about his feelings. I knew he would talk when he was ready, and I would happily listen when the time came.

I walked into the kitchen to see Mom stirring something on the stove, and Logan peeling potatoes at the kitchen table. I smiled at the sight that I had seen so many times. Mom was a mom to Logan too, and he was always trying to make her proud of him. We all had chores growing up, even Logan. He accepted this fact because he felt almost like an equal among us which was the thing he wanted most in the world.

"Hey, Ma," I said walking over to her.

At the sound of my voice, she immediately turned to me with a warm, welcoming smile. "My baby boy!"

I cringed at her nickname, but I couldn't say I hated it. I wasn't the baby of the family, but I was the youngest boy. Once she started calling me baby boy, everyone else followed suit. Of course, I had to beat the shit out of my brothers when they started teasing me with it, but not around my momma. I secretly loved that she called me that. You would never know we had so many in the family because my mom always made sure we each had our special time with her and our own relationship with her. She was awesome like that.

She wrapped her arms around my neck, and I bent slightly to wrap my arms around her waist. She was about a foot shorter than me with a healthy figure that she never lost. She said she was able to keep her shape because she was constantly running around with us. She looked younger than her forty-two years which she credited my dad for keeping her young. I didn't like to think about what exactly that meant.

I squeezed her tight with my chin resting on the top of her head. She pulled back to kiss my cheek and looked into my eyes. A wrinkle formed in between her eyebrows and her eyes filled with worry. I could never keep my thoughts from my mom which sucked growing up, but it sucked even more in that moment.

"What's wrong?" she asked.

"Nothing," I turned around to open the door of the refrigerator.

I grabbed a soda and turned around to lean against the counter. Logan was looking at me knowingly. I could see the worry on his face too.

Mom, being Mom and not missing anything, looked back and forth between us a few times before saying, "What's going on boys?"

Before either one of us could come up with a response, I heard the front door open and immediately walked out of the kitchen with Logan right on my heels. I saw Ryder standing in the middle of the living room, and I walked to him standing at his side. Logan stayed closer to the entrance of the room. We watched Riley walk into the room. Her eyes went to Logan first. Her eyes turned glassy with unshed tears before she stiffened her spine and turned to us.

"What's going on?" Rian asked standing looking between us and Riley.

Riley looked at Logan again, and I saw him give her a nod. She took a deep breath in and slowly let it out. She stood tall and balled her hands into fists. She turned to us and made eye contact with each of us. When she looked at me, I sucked in a sharp breath at the pain I saw swirling in her brown eyes. This was going to be so fucking bad.

"Jacob tried to rape me last night," Riley stated bluntly.

The room went completely silent, still, no movement, no sound. Then, everyone erupted at once, throwing out questions. I didn't speak. I had no words. My mind was moving so fast, I couldn't settle on anything.

"What?"

"What the fuck?"

"Where the fuck is he?"

"Did you call the police?"

"Are you okay?"

She was about to lose it. I could see the struggle. She tried to be so strong around us. She needed to know it was okay to let go. Looking at her pain filled face, I felt like I was sucker punched in the stomach getting all the air knocked out of me. I sat down heavily on the sofa and rubbed my hands roughly through my hair and down my face.

"Enough," Logan barked.

He walked to her, but she backed away.

"Riley," he groaned sounding like he was in pain.

"I'm fine," she stated, the tears falling down her cheeks contradicting her words. "I fought back and managed to get away. Logan beat the fuck out of him, and we called the cops. They showed, I told them what happened, and they arrested him."

I felt such rage, my whole body vibrated with it. The whole room was thick with tension.

"Riley," my mom said softly walking from the mouth of the kitchen through the living room to where Riley stood in the doorway of the living room.

Riley started shaking her head back and forth holding tight to the reins of her emotions refusing to let the unshed tears in her eyes fall. She held her hand up to stop Mom from getting any closer. Mom stood frozen with tears streaming down her face. Dad went to mom and slipped his arm around her waist.

"I'm sorry, Momma, but please don't." The tears started falling down her face, and a sob escaped her throat.

I looked to the ground and took a deep breath squeezing my eyes shut tightly. My hands pulled at the hair on the top of my head stinging my scalp. I looked around at all my brothers, and they were all stuck like me.

"Baby," Dad started.

"No," Riley started shaking her head again, her voice cracking. She cleared her throat and stood up straight. "I'm sorry. I'm so sorry. I will get through this. I promise. I'm a Landry, and y'all taught me everything about what that means. He hurt me. He fucked with my head, but I'm not broken." Her voice wavered. She looked down and took a deep breath. "He dragged me to the woods behind the house of the party I was at the other night. He tore my clothes, bruised my skin, and tried to force me to do something I didn't want to do. He talked shit to me the whole time about how it was my fault. I fought back enough to get away. I ran back toward the party and started yelling. I fell, and Logan was there. He fucked Jacob up before he called the cops. He is handcuffed to a hospital bed drinking out of a straw right now. His football days are over, and his scholarship will probably be revoked. Physically, I will heal. As for emotionally, I'm taking steps to make sure I heal properly. I've already emailed a counselor on campus to talk to. I have an appointment tomorrow."

Her whole body was shaking, and I wanted to put my arms around her so badly. Riley glanced around the room, her eyes landing on mine for a second before she looked away quickly.

"No," I demanded standing up. "Don't shut me out."

We had always been close. She was the baby and the only girl out of us, but she was always my best friend. We hung out, we went to school together, we talked about our plans for the future, and we talked out our problems with each other. She was one of my rocks and one of the strongest people I knew. I couldn't stand it if she distanced herself from me.

"I'm not," she insisted, her eyes snapping back to mine.

"Yes, you are," I gritted out taking a step toward her.

A hand landed in the middle of my chest, and I scowled at Logan. He scowled back and got in my face. I was surprised at the anger I saw in his face directed at me, but I shouldn't have been. He was as close to

Riley as I was, maybe more due to their feelings they had for each other that they never acknowledged.

"Back off," he growled. He looked around the room as he backed away from me. "She told y'all what happened, and the steps she's taking to move forward. Now, she needs some fucking space, and y'all are going to give it to her."

I went to argue, but Mom spoke firmly. "Ryker."

I clamped my lips together. In that moment, I felt helpless watching Riley clinging to Logan. Her face was buried between his shoulder blades, her hands twisted in his shirt at his side. Logan's face was set in stone his jaw clenched tightly, his eyes glassy.

"I love you, Riley," I said softly.

I heard her muffled sobs against Logan's back. Logan turned around and lifted her up. She wound her arms around his neck and her legs around his waist. She had her face in his neck to hide from us. He walked into the hallway and up the stairs.

My mom let out a sob and buried her face in my dad's chest. He wrapped his arms tightly around her and looked around the room. A tear fell from his eye as he made eye contact with each of us. I read the anger in his eyes and knew what to do. I nodded my head at him and looked at my brothers to see the same. We made our way outside quietly. We piled up into my truck since it was the easiest to get out of there and headed to the only hospital in Thibodaux.

Need

The whole ride to the hospital was quiet. I didn't even turn any music on. I couldn't get the look of Riley's ravaged face and the sound of her sobs out of my head. She was hurt, and I didn't protect her. I was at that party. I was fucking there. I made sure Bailey was safe, but not Riley. I had forgotten about her. As soon as I saw Bailey, everything else had faded. How could I make this up to her? I couldn't. There was nothing I could say or do to make this better for her. That killed me. I fucked up, and she suffered because of it.

We arrived at the hospital, and I parked in the first available spot I saw. We all got out of the truck and made our way inside. My brothers knew I had to take point on this one. We all felt this deep, but they knew how close we were. Even though Ryder was at the party too, he knew I took this as a personal failure. I'm sure he carried guilt just like they all did, but I felt it deeper.

I walked straight up to the front desk where an older lady with graying hair sat with a phone in the crook of her neck while her eyes were on the computer in front of her. "What room is Jacob Ledet in?"

My voice came out hoarse and raspy making her jump slightly in her chair. Her head jerked up to look at me. She raised one finger in my direction indicating she would be with me in a minute. I heard her murmuring on the phone as I looked down each of the hallways on either side of the desk I stood in front of. I saw a cop sitting in a chair at the end of the hallway to my left. I jerked my chin in that direction to my brothers and started in that direction.

"Sir, you can't go down there," the nurse at the desk said softly.

I glanced over my shoulder at her and saw sympathy in her eyes. I was sure she knew who the little bitch was that was being watched by the cop. I was also sure she knew what he had done considering she wasn't really trying to stop us. I nodded to her and kept walking.

The cop posted outside of the door stood at our approach. "Who are y'all?" he questioned.

"The Landrys," I answered.

His eyes surveyed each of us as his lip curled slightly at the edges. "I need coffee."

He walked away without looking back. I didn't hesitate in opening the door to Jacob's room. My eyes immediately went to the figure in the bed, and I couldn't help the smile of satisfaction that spread across my face. Logan had really fucked him up. Both of his eyes were black and blue, one almost completely swollen shut, staring at the TV. He had a cut on his lip, and from the look of his jaw, it was wired shut. He had a casted arm resting on the bed, and one of his legs was raised up in a sling attached to the ceiling with a cast from thigh to ankle.

"Hey, bitch!" I said loudly making his body jump causing a groan of pain to pass through his lips.

His eyes widened as we approached his bed, jumping around to each of his. The machine next to his bed started beeping frantically indicating his heart rate jumping up in speed. I saw Rylan out of the corner of my eye approach the bed and remove the thing on Jacob's finger of his uninjured arm, and the beeping stopped.

"We need to talk, motherfucker," I growled looking down at him with all the rage I felt.

He was mumbling something that I couldn't understand with him not being able to move his jaw. I smiled and knew it was evil by the fear on his face. Rylan and Rian stood on one side of the bed while Ryder stood next to me on one side and Ryden was at the foot of the bed. His head jerked around on his pillow as he tried to look at each of us.

"What did I tell you would happen if you fucked with Riley?" I asked not expecting an answer.

I could see his throat working furiously as he tried swallowing convulsively. Tears started leaking out of the little bitch's eyes, and I didn't even put my hands on him yet. I shook my head at this little pussy.

"I told you not to approach her. I told you not to talk to her. I told you not to touch her. I told you not to even utter her fucking name." My voice was rising with each sentence, and I had to take a deep breath to gain some control.

I wanted to fucking kill him. I wanted him to suffer like Riley was. Even though Logan put him in that bed, I wanted to inflict more damage, but I knew I couldn't. I knew I couldn't fuck with an invalid because then I would catch a charge. What Logan did to him was a form of self-defense, and it wouldn't be self-defense if I touched him.

I kept my eyes on him as I breathed through my nose. "I don't like repeating myself. I told you we would fuck you up. Logan already did that, so I'm just here to remind you. You will heal enough for you to get out of this hospital, and then you will sit in a cell for a while. I don't know how long you will be there, but we will be here when you get out. We will be around every fucking corner and in every shadow you see. You fucked with a Landry, and everybody knows that Landrys fuck back harder."

I put my hand on the arm with the cast and leaned on it with all my weight. He started making gurgling noises in his throat, the tears flowed faster down his face, and snot leaked out of his nose. He tried to grab my wrist with his good arm, but Rian wrapped his hand around his wrist and Rylan put his hand on his shoulder, both holding his body down.

I put my face right in his and growled through gritted teeth, "We got us and ours, every day, all mother fucking day. Remember that. We'll be seeing you, bitch."

With that, I let his arm go and stood up. With one last look at the pathetic piece of shit, I turned around and walked to the door. Opening it, I exited the room with my brothers at my back. We strode down the hallway and passed the cop on the way to the elevators. He nodded at us as he sipped his coffee out of the Styrofoam cup in his hand taking up his post once again.

We rode the elevators down to the lobby of the hospital in silence. Once we reached the truck, I stopped and rested my hands against the tailgate. I felt hands on my shoulders as I dropped my head down.

"This is not on you, Ryker," Ryder stated firmly.

I felt the tear fall down my face and the sob catch in my throat. He squeezed my shoulder tightly.

"He's right," Rian voiced. "This is on that pussy assed little bitch."

"He fucked up, bro," Rylan said. "Not you."

"You can't take the blame for this," Ryden said. "Riley would kick your ass if she saw you right now."

That got a shallow laugh out of me. She would kick my ass if she saw me like this. She would be pissed if she knew I felt guilty about what happened to her. She has always been independent and proved she could take care of herself regularly.

Standing up straight, I sucked back my emotions. "Let's get out of here."

We made it back to my parents in slightly better spirits. Confronting Jacob eased our tension slightly. We would help Riley in any capacity we could. We would support her and offer our shoulders for her to cry on. We would have her back always. I hoped she would get to a point where she would accept our help.

Walking into the house the second time that day, I breathed in deeply to capture the familiar scents even more than the first-time I was here. It calmed the storm inside of me a little more. My dad met us in the foyer and looked at each of our faces. I guess he saw what he was looking for because he smiled and started enfolding each of us in a hug that accompanied a pat on the back.

"My boys," he rasped.

"Dinner's ready," Mom called from the kitchen.

We headed in there to help put the food on the table. Riley was setting plates and the utensils at each of the chairs on the big dining room table. She looked up when we entered and kept her gaze locked on mine. Her bottom lip trembled, but she stood up straight.

"Is he alive?" she asked putting her hand on her cocked hip.

I smiled. I actually fucking smiled. My sister was fierce. She was strong. This wouldn't have her down for long. She would deal with it, process it, and move on with her life.

"Yeah," I said grabbing her up in a hug.

I kissed the top of her head and took comfort in her when she wrapped her arms around me. She sighed, "I love you."

"Love you, too, brat," I teased.

She pushed away from me and punched me in the stomach making me grunt. I laughed and mussed up her hair. I walked around the table quickly to put space between us, so she couldn't retaliate. I watched as each of my brothers hugged her and whispered in her ear. I looked behind her and locked eyes with Logan. He had a sad smile on his face, and I nodded at him letting him know I appreciated what he did to Jacob.

He nodded back and looked at Riley again.

"Alright, let's eat," Mom stated dropping platters of food in the middle of the table.

We all got busy and put all the food and drinks out. We all ate and drank, talked and laughed. We carried on knowing that we were all loved and would heal. Riley looked relieved with the normalcy, but I could see the pain and sadness in her eyes too. She rallied through it though. She talked and even laughed at our antics. She took small bites of her food and pushed the rest around her plate.

Chapter Seven
Bailey

Grabbing up all the grocery bags out of the truck, I bumped the door closed with my hip. When I ran into my apartment after the encounter with Ryker, I got myself under control and on to my errands. I washed, dried, folded, and picked up my laundry. I cleaned the apartment which didn't take too long because Carter and I kept it clean. We lived in too many dirty places that we always wanted to have our place organized and free of dirt. Then, I went grocery shopping. That took the most time since we needed just about everything. Plus, I wanted to get stuff to make some good meals for Carter. I had been slacking lately, and it was time to stop. There were a lot of times that we didn't know where our next meal would come from or when. We shared cooking responsibilities because of my work schedule, but I wanted to do more for Carter than I was. He seemed to have shit going on, but I didn't know what. I wouldn't push him to tell me. He would tell me when he was ready, but I wanted him to know that he was a priority to me, and I would always have his back. Good food was one way to let him know he was important to me. I mean, when you didn't know if you would eat at all, you understood the importance of food.

He texted me before I went grocery shopping saying that he and his bike friends decided to stay the night in Baton Rouge. I had made a menu up and decided I could do some prep, so it would be ready to go each day. It would mostly be crock pot meals because I loved that invention. I got so bored standing around the stove stirring and shit. I liked to put it all in the crockpot and do whatever else I needed to.

I trudged through the parking lot with the heavy bags. I could have grabbed a few bags and went back for the rest, but I hated making more than one trip up and down the stairs to the parking lot and back to the apartment. Carter and I had been talking about getting a house for a while now, but we weren't ready yet.

I made it to my landing and came to a standstill when I saw the figure sitting on the ground outside of my door. His knees were bent, and his head was in his hands. At my approach, his head snapped in my direction.

Ryker looked in turmoil. His eyes were swirling with emotions so intense I couldn't decipher them. The edges of his lips were tipped down and his brows were dipped low on his forehead. His hair stood up in messy disarray like he ran his hands through it thousands of times and possibly pulled it in frustration.

"What's wrong?" I asked.

What are you doing here? How did you know which apartment was mine? Those were the questions I should have asked, but that's not what came out. I was worried. He didn't look right.

"I was hoping I could talk to you," he said lifting himself up off the ground.

He blew out a breath and looked away. I studied his profile. His strong jaw was clenched and ground back and forth. His nostrils flared with his deep breaths. His hair fell over one of his eyebrows. He lowered his head to the ground before looking back at me.

I sucked in a breath at the devastation on his face. The emotions swirling in the brown depths of his eyes were intense and bad. Whatever happened affected him deeply. My mind spun with what could have happened. Before he left earlier, he said something had happened to his sister. Was that where the pain on his face came from? If so, it must have been bad.

I took a step toward him, the bags heavy on my arms and stumbled slightly under their weight. He looked down quickly and grabbed the bags out of my hands.

"I'm sorry," he mumbled.

"It's okay," I said quietly. "Let's go inside."

I quickly unlocked my apartment door and led the way inside to the kitchen. "Just drop them on the counter."

He set them down carefully before looking around. I was at a lost as to what to do. We've only had a few encounters, so I didn't really know much about him to know how to proceed. With that being said, I also knew I wanted to be there for him during whatever he was going through. That fact made me nervous, but it also felt right. We had a connection I couldn't lie to myself about.

"What happened, Ryker?" I asked moving toward him.

"I need you," his voice broke as he wrapped his arms around me and buried his face in my neck.

I felt his tears on my neck, his body tremble, and heard the sob in his throat. I wrapped myself around him tight and held him as close as I could. I led him to the couch and pushed him down. He made a sound of protest as he looked at me through his tears. My own eyes watered witnessing his pain. I shushed him and climbed on his lap straddling him. He wrapped his arms around me again, one hand on my ass and one in my hair. I put my arms around his neck, my fingers scraping his scalp softly. Laying my head on his shoulder, I pressed my lips against his neck.

I wasn't sure how long we sat there before his tears stopped and his body calmed. I just waited it out with him and offered him comfort I didn't know I was capable of. All of things about making him think I didn't want him vanished in the face of his pain. I had to make him feel better. I had to take care of him. I needed it. I couldn't handle seeing him like this, and I wanted to take his pain away.

"I'm sorry," he said, his voice hoarse and raspy in my ear sending chills down my spine.

I sat up and stared down into his eyes. I cupped his face in my hands and swiped the remaining moisture underneath his eyes with my thumbs. I figured he would be embarrassed by losing it like he did, but he wasn't. He just smiled softly at me.

"What happened, Ryker?" I asked softly studying his eyes.

"My sister was at that party the other night. She was dancing with some friends when I saw you there. I didn't see her after that. Then, the fight happened, and I left right after you and Lyla did." He swallowed hard and squeezed his eyes shut.

I moved my hands down to his shoulders and waited while he got his thoughts in order. There were lines forming on his forehead, and a vein was throbbing in his neck as he ground his jaw together. Both of his hands flexed on my butt.

He took a deep breath and opened his eyes. "She was almost raped by her ex-boyfriend, Jacob Ledet."

I gasped and closed my eyes against that revelation. I opened my eyes and nodded my head to get him to continue talking. He needed to get this out, and I wanted to be the person he unloaded on. Why? I had no idea because I knew I had enough problems of my own without his, but I needed to be the one there for him.

"She fought back and ran. Logan saw her and found out what happened. He put Jacob in the hospital where he is being watched by the police. He will be going to jail when he is discharged." He lifted a hand to my face and rubbed his thumb along my jaw.

"Who's Logan?" I asked.

"Logan Trosclair. He's one of our best friends. Me, him, and Ryder share the apartment. He lived in the house next to ours but was at our house more than his. He was the one that told Ryder he would take care of Cody." He watched the movement of his thumb on my skin.

"We have Sunday dinners at my parents' place every week. She told us there. It was a rough scene. I didn't know what to do, what to think. I just left that party without thinking about her. I left her there. Then, she didn't want any of us to get close to her. She is one of the strongest people I know." He shook his head before he continued. "She stood straight with her shoulders squared breaking it down to us. She told us what had happened, what steps she was taking, and that she was fine."

"She sounds amazing," I said with a smile.

His lips turned up fully. "She is. She said she already found a counselor on campus she is going to talk to tomorrow."

"That takes a lot of courage to talk to someone about something like that," I said.

I lost count of how many counselors I had seen in my lifetime, but only one knew exactly what had all happened to me. It took years for me to be able to tell her everything. I still saw her once a month, and I struggled every time to give her all my truths.

"Yeah," he agreed looking into my eyes.

"What happened after she told y'all?" I asked feeling a little more exposed after my comment.

"Logan took her up to her old room. Then, my brothers and I took a ride out to the hospital in Thibodaux to have a little talk with Jacob," he answered.

"Brothers?" I asked.

"Yeah," he laughed. "I have four brothers."

"So," I calculated in my head. "There are six of y'all?"

He full on laughed at the disbelief in my voice as well as on my face. "Yeah, from oldest to youngest it's Rian, Rylan, Ryder, Ryden, me, and Riley."

"Wow," I breathed.

I had lived in houses where there were a lot of kids, but none of us were blood related. The foster parents didn't want us. They just wanted the checks they received each month. To have parents who wanted you plus all your siblings, must have been amazing. I wondered how that would have felt, to have all that love growing up.

"You okay?" he asked concerned.

I shook the thoughts off and looked down at him. "Yeah, are you?"

"Can I kiss you?" he asked.

I laughed, "Since when do you ask me for permission to kiss me?"

He smirked, "Good point."

He slid his hand to the back of my head, his fingers tangling in my hair. He pulled me until he could reach my lips, and then we were connected. His lips brushed across mine softly. My tongue snaked out to lick the seam of his lips making him groan and open his mouth. His tongue met mine causing shivers to race down my spine. His hand tightened on my ass, his fingers digging into my flesh. My hips rocked into his, and I could feel the bulge in his jeans.

I groaned loudly. More! I wanted more. My hands tangled in his hair, my fingernails scraping his scalp. He deepened the kiss, licking along my tongue, teeth, and gums. I bit into his bottom lip and felt the hiss of his breath. His hands went to the hem of my shirt and underneath to the skin of my back making me tremble. I lifted my arms up and broke away from the kiss, so he could remove my shirt completely. He threw it somewhere behind me and moved his lips to my neck. He licked and nibbled his way up to my ear where he drew the lobe into his mouth. He sucked before he bit down gently.

I gasped and rocked against his dick causing a delicious friction against my clit. I was so turned on I felt out of control. My breathing escalated, and my heart beat furiously in my chest. I grabbed fistfuls of his shirt to try and rip it out of my way. I wanted my hands on his bare skin. I needed it.

He laughed quietly and helped get rid of the cotton separating us. As soon as the shirt cleared his head, my lips were back on his. He groaned as he grabbed my ass with both hands and pulled me into him hard. I gasped at the contact of his hard bulge against my core. I threw my head back as I rocked into him working my clit on every pass. The denim separating us added a rough edge that felt so fucking good.

He took advantage of my exposed neck and started licking, sucking, and biting his way down to my collarbone. He gripped the back of my neck as he licked down to my breasts. His tongue left a wet trail along the exposed flesh above my bra. His teeth sank down hard into my skin, and his tongue licked the spot to take the sting out of the bite.

"Ryker," I moaned rocking back and forth on his lap harder.

Fuck! It felt so good. I couldn't get enough of him. I was on fire, my body trembled uncontrollable. I was close to the edge, and we weren't even naked yet. Dry humping at its finest. Well, not really dry. My panties were so wet, I knew I would have to throw them away. They were ruined. I didn't care. I would buy more. Fuck, I would buy in stock if this happened all the time. I didn't give a fuck what I had to do. I just needed him.

I looked down at him when I felt his hand cupping my breast, his thumb brushed across my nipple through the cotton bra. My nipple tightened up almost painfully and pushed against the fabric. The black and gray of the tattoo on the back of his hand against my light pink bra was such a stark contrast, my core tightened. The ink traveled to his elbow in swirls and shapes I couldn't make out with my vision so hazy. His other arm was tatted from his wrist up until they disappeared under the sleeve of his shirt. When he pinched my nipple between his thumb and forefinger pulling, my wandering gaze snapped to his. His eyes were dark with desire, almost black. His nostrils flared with his intake of air.

"You have a roommate?" he asked, his hands meeting behind my back on the strap of my bra.

"Yeah," I breathed.

"Is she coming home soon?" he asked looking up at me not moving.

"No," I shook my head.

I should have corrected him on the "she" roommate, but I knew that would be a conversation I wasn't ready to have. I didn't want to explain to Ryker I lived with a guy at that moment. He would have a bunch of questions that I would have to answer exposing a past I didn't want to share with him at that time. Not to mention the fact that I wanted him to keep moving and us to be naked as soon as possible. I didn't want to stop what we were doing to talk.

I felt my bra loosen and the straps fell down my arms. I shivered in anticipation. My nipples were hard peaks and tightened further when the fabric fell completely away. My eyes closed as his rough palms glided across my skin cupping my breasts in his hands licking and sucking my nipple.

"Bailey, open your eyes," he commanded in a voice so rough and raw, I obeyed immediately.

His brown eyes were almost black with his need for me and locked on mine. His stare was possessive and raw. When my eyes met his, I felt a vulnerability I haven't allowed myself to feel for a long time. Vulnerability led to pain so deep, it stayed with you always. My pain was a steady throb in my soul not as strong as it once was, but still there reminding me to be careful always.

"Beautiful," he rasped moving to the other breast, his arms supporting my back with his hands curled over my shoulders.

I was so close to the edge. I moved my hips faster, rubbing myself harder against him. He was driving me fucking insane. His hands gripped my ass, his fingers digging in. His lips surrounded my nipple sucking hard before he closed his teeth around the hard tip. I shivered when his tongue followed his teeth soothing the sting of the bite. I moaned loudly. I wanted his mouth on mine. I gripped his head with both hands and jerked his face up. I slammed my mouth down on his.

He groaned as he wrapped my hair up in his fist deepening the kiss. I was going to come in my shorts. I was going to go over the edge with him not even touching my pussy. I was going to stand up. Wait. What? Why was I standing up?

My hands went to his shoulders to steady myself. I looked down to see a smirk spread across his lips. His hands were spanned on my waist. He pulled me closer to him until my knees hit the edge of the sofa.

"You sure you want this, Bailey?" he asked staring intently at me, his hands traveling down my sides.

"Yes," I said, my voice low and husky.

My eyes closed at the look on his face. He looked like he wanted to devour my whole body, and I was tempted to let him. It was too fucking much. His eyes were so intense when he looked at me, any part of me. It was scary, but I still wanted more. His nostrils were flared, and his cheeks were flushed. His eyes locked on mine. His gaze unnerved me. It was almost too much for me to handle, but there was no way I could look away. I had to witness everything he was giving me.

His hands grasped my ass as his lips caressed my stomach. His tongue swirled around my navel as he unbuttoned my shorts and slid the zipper down. He hooked his thumbs into the waistband and pushed them over my hips and down my legs until they pooled around my ankles.

He groaned when I kicked my shorts completely off and to the side of me. He sat back against the sofa looking at my practically naked body. Black cotton was the only thing separating my trembling core to his hot gaze. He was looking at me as though he could see through the material to every inch of me. His intense stare caused the throbbing to increase making me rub my thighs together for some relief. He licked his lips as his eyes ran over my body and his hands unbuttoned his jeans. His abs tightened as he unzipped and pushed his jeans and boxers down to his knees. His hand grabbed his hard shaft jerking up rolling his thumb over the head and stroked down once before letting go.

My eyes drank up the sight of him. His chest was defined with muscles leading down to a six pack of abs and the V that was so fucking sexy. On the right side of his body, he had *LANDRY* in big block letters starting under his arm and ended right below his hip. I wanted to lick the massive piece from the top of the outline to the bottom. Then, I wanted to suck on all the color filling it up with life.

His cock bounced against his stomach causing him to shut his eyes with a grimace. He wrapped his hand around his shaft and stroked it up and down once before squeezing the base. I moaned at the sight of his own hand wrapped around his dick causing him to open his eyes. I licked my lips at the sight of precum leaking from the tip of his dick. He was long and thick with a throbbing vein running the length. I bit my lip and moaned. I couldn't wait anymore. I wanted him inside me. I was burning up and shivering. My body was on fire and shocks were running through me.

I straddled his lap, my knees digging into the sofa on either side of his hips. His hands landed on my ass and squeezed. My hands landed on his shoulders gliding up his neck to his hair. His eyes were on mine with a possessive intensity that shot straight to my core.

"Bai…," he started to say but I cut him off by slamming my lips down on his.

I shifted until I could feel the tip of his dick at my entrance. I slowly lowered onto him. All I really wanted to do was slam myself down on his dick until I was full of him, but I knew from experience I had to allow time to adjust to him. I like a little pain with my pleasure but not that much pain.

"Bailey," he said with a groan when he was fully seated inside of me, my ass resting on his thighs.

I gasped as he hit the end of me and put my forehead against his. My hair fell around us, our breaths mingled. I lifted myself up slowly and rocked back down. My movements gained speed the more I adjusted to him and, and he glided in and out smoothly. I threw my head back and moaned. Fuck! He felt so fucking good.

He scooted his body down a little making him go even deeper causing us both to groan. He was resting his head on the back of the sofa, his hands digging into my ass urging me to go faster. I started bouncing on his dick slamming my clit against his body. My breasts jiggled up and down with the force of our movements. His eyes watched the movements before looking down to where our bodies were joined.

"So wet and tight," he gritted out through his clenched teeth. "Your pussy feels so good, so fucking right."

"Fuck!" I screamed moving my hips faster.

"Fuck," he rasped out. "Watching your tits bounce as I slam into you makes my dick harder than it's ever been. Seeing my cock going in and out of your pretty, pink pussy covered in your juices is so fucking hot. I'm going to come so fucking hard."

My head flew back. My back arched. I shut my eyes tight and lost my breath. My whole body was on fire as the climax passed through me. I saw white spots behind my eyelids. My whole body trembled as I lost control of all movement. I could feel my nails digging into his skin and his grip tightening on my ass to the point of pain.

"Eyes, Bailey," he gritted out as he pushed through my pulsing channel.

His eyes were focused on mine. His jaw was locked so tight it twitched. A vein was pulsing wildly at his temple. He was losing control. He was losing control because of me. I've caused this. I felt a power I'd never had before. I wanted to watch him explode like I did, him to lose grip on reality like I did. I gasped and grinded down on his lap. Ryker fucked me harder and faster, pushing up as I slammed down. My pussy squeezed his cock. I felt it swell even more right before he filled me with his warm cum. He slowed his movements until the aftershocks passed through both of us.

"Bailey," he breathed, his warm breath hitting my neck where his head was buried.

I rested my forehead against his neck trying to catch my breath. I shivered, and his hand glided down my back in a soothing caress. I was on emotion overload. That was so fucking intense. I felt tears behind my eyelids that I didn't want to fall in front of him. I felt so exposed. I needed space.

I moved to get off his lap, and we both groaned when his still hard dick moved inside my sensitive core. He held me close and tipped his head up to me. As soon as my eyes collided with his, the tear fell.

He wiped it away with his thumb, his lips brushing mine causing more tears. I should have gotten up and put as much distance as possible between us, but I didn't. I slid my hands into his hair and deepened the kiss. I put all of me into that kiss. I rocked my hips slowly back and forth on his lap and felt him harden further.

I broke away from the kiss and shoved my face in his neck. He kept the pace slow and steady. I felt every inch of him glide in out of me. The orgasm took me by surprise, and I tightened my hold on him.

"Ryker," I breathed out.

He groaned my name out when his orgasm hit him. The tears were there and falling down my face landing on his neck. I felt him stiffen and try to pull back to look at me. I shook my head against him. I didn't want him to see my face. I felt so many things, I knew my walls were down, and he would be able to see into me. I couldn't give him that power. I couldn't take the chance of him seeing how much he affected me. I didn't even fucking know him, but I felt so much more for him than I ever felt with anyone before. That scared the fuck out of me, and I didn't know what to do.

"Baby," he whispered in my ear which caused me to shake my head more. "Look at me."

I didn't want to, but I knew I had to. I knew I needed to let him in. I knew he had me, and I wasn't strong enough to fight him. I wanted him in every way. This was so fucking big, and I was on the edge of trusting him with everything. My walls were gone at that moment, and I wanted to give him this. I wanted him to know how he affected me. I wanted him to see the mess he had me in. I wanted him to feel the emotion that was blazing through my body for him.

I slowly raised my head until my eyes were on his. He stared intently at me, his expression softening. He trailed his thumbs down my cheeks wiping away the wetness there. I closed my eyes as his lips brushed slowly against mine. He kissed my closed eyelids before he placed his lips against my forehead.

I let out a soft sigh as his fingers tangled in my hair. "Baby, we need to get cleaned up."

I nodded my head in agreement before I jerked straight up when his words penetrated the Ryker fog I was under. I swiftly stood up almost landing on my ass when my legs refused to cooperate. I felt light headed and weak. Ryker grasped my hips to steady me.

"Whoa, baby," he said. "Be careful."

I felt him leaking down my thighs. I batted his hands away and took a step back. I looked down and saw his cum staining my skin. I was in the middle of a freak out and still turned on. What the fuck was wrong with me?

I lifted my head when I heard Ryker growl. His eyes were where mine were just aimed. His nostrils were flared, and his eyes were narrowed. His arms came up like he was going to grab me again, and I hastily stepped out of his reach.

"We didn't use a condom," I said stupidly. "What the fuck?"

"Baby, calm down," he said softly. "I'm sorry. I tried, but then I was in you and my brain shut down."

"Calm down?" I screeched. "You want me to fucking calm down?"

I started pulling my clothes on hastily. It took three tries for me to hook my bra because my hands were shaking so badly. How could I be so careless? I never forgot about a condom. What the hell was Ryker doing to me?

"Baby," he said standing and walking towards me. "It's okay."

"Stop! Do not fucking touch me right now!" I demanded. "I'm not on the pill, Ryker. We can't fuck without a fucking condom. What the fuck was I thinking?"

I took off to the bathroom. I was losing my shit. How the fuck could I forget the condom? Shit! Shit! Shit! I hurriedly stripped out of my clothes again and jumped in the shower. I put the water to scalding and scrubbed myself clean. Logically, I knew I wouldn't be able to wash away what just happened, but I wasn't thinking logically. I was fucked up in the head over the possibility of being pregnant. I couldn't have a baby. I was way too fucked up to be a mom.

I slid down to my ass on the bottom of the tub, the water washing down over my head. I started sobbing into my knees where my head was resting. I felt the water shut off right before his body wrapped around mine putting his face in my neck. I wasn't strong enough to push him away. I didn't even hear the door open, but his presence didn't surprise me.

"I'm so sorry, baby," he whispered in my ear. "I fucked up."

I looked up at him with blurry eyes and whimpered. "I can't be a mom, Ryker."

"Bailey," he growled sounding tortured. "It won't happen again. I lost my head. I'm sorry. Please, forgive me. I will always be here for you, baby. Please, forgive me."

"It's not only your fault. I was just as responsible for this fuck up as you were," I blew out a breath feeling myself calming.

"It's going to be okay," he tried to reassure me, but the truth was we didn't know what this fuck up could mean yet.

"We should be okay," I said thinking back to my cycle calculating. "I think the timing is right for our situation."

He nodded. "I think you should think about getting on the pill."

"Why?" I asked not knowing what answer I wanted him to give me.

"Because I plan on being inside of you as much as possible, and I think we just proved that we need to rely on more than remembering to put a condom on," he said seriously causing a riot in my belly. "But after feeling you skin to skin without latex, I don't want to use condoms."

I took a deep breath. Did I want that? Did I want that level of intimacy? I know we just had that, but now that I was thinking rationally, I would be committing to something with him. I studied his face, his sincerity showing clearly. He wanted me, I knew that, but how much of me did he want, and how much was I willing to give?

When I felt I had my feelings on lock, I opened my eyes. He was still staring at me like he was reading the thoughts floating around on a loop in my head. I felt like he could see all the feelings that flowed through me as he pushed me closer and closer to the edge. I wanted to break this connection. My brain was trying to tell me this is too much, that I was out of my depth here.

"Baby," he whispered against my forehead where his lips rested.

He sighed before he slowly stood up. He turned and grabbed a towel from the rack hanging on the wall. He leaned over the tub and wrapped the towel around my shoulders. I grasped the edges pulling it tighter around me. He placed his lips on my forehead one more time before he walked out of the door closing it behind him.

I sat there not moving with tears streaming down my face. I knew what I wanted to do. I knew I wanted to be with him no matter what may happen later. I never believed I was going to have a happily ever after, but he gave me hope that I would get that. That hope scared the shit out of me, but I held tight to it.

Chapter Eight
Ryker

I had to go see her. It had been three days since I left her apartment. Three days since the most incredible day of my life. That was so much more than just sex. She referred to it as fucking, and I had to control myself. That pissed me off. I knew it was the most intimate moment of my life, and I didn't want her to lessen it. I knew she was doing it to put distance between us, so I let it go, but that shit wouldn't last for much longer. I could see all her emotions rolling through her emerald gaze. I knew she needed a minute to get her bearings. She was overwhelmed with the intensity of us catching her off guard. She was running scared, but I wasn't letting her get away.

After being inside of her with nothing separating me from her wet heat, I knew I had to have that again. Fuck! I couldn't even believe I forgot about the condom. I never went without a condom. Of course, I did think about it at first. I called her name to stop her, but then she sank all the way down on my cock, and I lost all thought. I let myself feel all of her and the connection between us.

I was going after her. I had to. There wasn't another option. I gave her three days. That was enough. If I gave her too much space, she would be farther away from me, and I couldn't let that happen. I needed to make her see me as hers. I needed her to know she was mine.

After I finished up my last rep with the dumbbell, I sat up and made my way over to the bench against the wall where my water was. I sat down heavily rubbing a towel down my face. I grabbed the water and drank the whole thing down.

"What's up?" Logan asked dropping down on the bench next to me.

"What are you doing tonight?" I asked him.

"Nothing," he replied. "Why?"

"We're going to Left Turners'," I replied.

His eyebrows raised in question. "Does this have something to do with your girl?"

"Yeah," I nodded. "She works there. I need to see her."

He nodded and stood up. "Sounds good, man."

He walked off to do his own workout. We only had about an hour before practice started. I did the free weights and jumped rope for a while my mind on Bailey. The last few days had been brutal. My workouts were harder, I did more paperwork for the gym than I ever had, and I studied until I passed out. I couldn't handle free time. I wanted to give Bailey space, and if I didn't keep busy I would text and call her or even show up at her place.

After another half hour of lifting weights, I headed to the locker room to get ready for practice. I wanted to be done so I could go see Bailey. Just the thought of being near her, my dick got hard. She had me so fucked up, and I fucking loved it.

I was smiling when someone called out, "What's up, man?"

I turned around and saw Drew approaching feeling the smile spread across my face.

"Oh, shit," Drew said with a laugh. "I know that look. It means you got yours."

I smirked. I couldn't help it. I was a dude. I got laid. I was entitled to a little smugness.

"You want to go to Left Turners' after practice?" I asked him.

He shrugged with a knowing look on his face, "Sure."

"I want to go," Avery said walking to his locker. "I love that place."

"Cool," I shrugged.

Avery Duet was a fellow teammate. He was a couple of years older than me and would be graduating next semester. He had a sick sense of humor, and it was always fun hanging out with him.

We walked out of the locker room and onto the field spending the next couple of hours running plays and listening to the coach yelling commands at us. He worked us hard, running up and down the field. Ryder was the focus of coach for most of practice. He looked like he was slacking, and I wanted to know what was up with him. He didn't fuck around with football to protect his scholarship.

I knew he'd been messed up since the shit with Lyla then with Riley went down, but I haven't gotten anything out of him. Every time I had seen him, he ducked me. He shut down conversation if it went to one of them. I gave him that because I wouldn't force him to tell me anything, but now it's affecting his game.

After practice, we all headed to the locker rooms and into the showers. I grabbed the extra clothes out of my locker and got dressed. I was tying up my chucks when Ryder walked to his locker with a towel wrapped around his waist.

"Some of us are going to Left Turners' tonight," I told him. "Are you in?"

"Yeah, sure," he shrugged grabbing his clothes.

I finished tying up my shoes and stuffed all my stuff in my duffel bag. I closed and locked my locker shouldering my bag.

"Are you ready to head out?" Logan asked. We rode to school together a couple times a week because we had the same schedule.

"Yeah," I replied looking over at Ryder. "Do you want to ride with us or meet there?"

"I'll meet y'all there," he answered getting his stuff together.

"Alright," I nodded and headed out of the locker room with Logan.

"So, this girl is the one, huh?" Logan asked as we walked through the parking lot towards my truck.

"Yeah, man, she is," I answered with a smile.

"You are whipped," Logan laughed at the goofy ass look on my face.

He was right. I was whipped behind Bailey, but I didn't give one fuck. I was happy about that. I knew she was the one for me. I just had to convince her to take the risk. I wanted to erase all her fears and know all her secrets. I wanted to be the one to bring her all the way out and let go. I wanted to be the one to make her smile the biggest and laugh the hardest.

I needed her.

We got into my truck throwing our duffels in the back seat. I cranked the engine and pulled out of the parking lot. We made the twenty-minute ride listening to the latest album from Full Moon Posse at high volume.

"That band is dope," Logan said climbing out of the truck once I parked in Left Turners' parking lot.

"I know," I agreed. I fucking loved that band. Their sound was so unique and raw. "You know they're playing in City Park this year, right?"

"I heard that," he nodded. "Do you want to go?"

"Definitely," I replied. "I'm going to see if Bailey is up for that?"

He smirked but didn't say anything else.

"How many?" the hostess asked.

"I think it's going to be five of us, but I'm not sure," I answered. "Can we sit at the bar?"

"Sure," she said waving us over to the bar.

I took a seat on one of the stools, and the bartender came over to take our drink order. I ordered and looked around the place. I had been there a couple of times before, but when Crystal started working there, I stopped going. That girl wouldn't stop. At one point, she seemed to be everywhere I was, and I tried to avoid her as much as possible.

Most of the tables in the big dining area were filled. A few waitresses flitted in between the tables, dropping off food and exchanging words. I saw a body bent over a table distributing drinks, ass pointed in my direction. I bit back a groan at the sight of the most perfect ass I had ever seen.

Bailey.

I sucked in a sharp breath when she straightened and turned around. I felt like I got sucker punched. She had these short black shorts on that hugged her hips and had her ass looking amazing. Her red shirt molded to her body showing her amazing tits and emphasized her small waist. The tall socks she wore made my mouth water at the sight of tanned and toned thighs.

Fuck! My dick twitched with longing. Three days was a long fucking time to go without her wrapped around me. I watched her rest the tray on her hip and smiled at the people sitting at her table. Her mouth moved with her words, and her eyes moved from person to person.

Then, my view was gone, and a bleached blonde with bright red lipstick was in my way. I backed up as much as the bar behind allowed. Crystal reached out a hand toward my chest, but she didn't make contact. I wrapped my hand around her wrist and gently moved her back.

"Do not touch me," I gritted out beyond frustrated with this girl.

Her eyes flared in shock for a second before her mouth turned into a pout that I think she thought was sexy but wasn't at all. I had spelled this shit out to her so many fucking times, and she honestly thought that stupid pout was going to change my mind?

I let go of her wrist, and almost rolled my eyes when she struck a pose, a fucking pose. She put both of her hands on her hips pushing her breasts out further. She already looked like she would bust out of the top of her shirt. I feared the fabric would not be strong enough to hold together against the pressure.

"Why are you denying what's between us, Ryker?" She said my name in a low, husky voice that I assumed she thought was sexy.

The sound of Bailey saying my name in my ear came to mind, and I knew that was the sexiest sound I had ever heard. Crystal was all fake and trying to be sexy, while Bailey just was sexy without doing a damn thing.

Before I could respond, the sexy voice I just heard in my head said, "Crystal, your tables are starting to bitch."

I looked to my right and saw Bailey leaning against the bar. She was trying to go for casual, but her voice was harsh, and her body was tensed all over. One hand gripped the ledge of the bar while the other held tightly to the empty tray she was holding. Both of her hands had white knuckles with the pressure she had on her curled fingers. Her mouth was set in fake half smile while her eyes were guarded as she looked at Crystal.

Crystal turned in Bailey's direction with a glare. Bailey didn't react. She met her glare with a stare of her own. I was about to interrupt the staring contest when Crystal turned to me with a huff.

"We will finish this later," she said softly but still loud enough for Bailey here.

"There is nothing to finish," I said sternly. "I've said all I've had to say."

I wanted to yell at her to leave me the fuck alone and get the fuck over it. I wanted to demand her to never disrespect my girl again. I wanted to let her know that I would never be hers, and she looked like a fool trying to be sexy. However, I couldn't do that. I wasn't an asshole. I couldn't embarrass her or make her feel shitty especially at her job. My momma would have whipped my ass if I did that to anyone, much less a girl.

"We'll see," she responded with a smirk.

She passed by Bailey giving her another glare before making her way into the dining room. I didn't watch her leave, but I knew when she did because Bailey's body relaxed slightly. She made eye contact with me briefly before turning towards the bar putting drinks down on her tray.

She wanted to dismiss me. She wanted me to believe she wasn't affected by the way Crystal was acting with me. She wanted to make this thing between us look like it was nothing. Fuck that! I knew she was aware of me. I knew she felt something for me. I knew she was jealous of Crystal. I knew this thing between us was something. I couldn't make her believe all of that yet. I knew it was too soon to put it all out there. She would probably think I was crazy and moving too fast for her. Normally, I would probably agree, but I trusted my feelings. I knew what I felt was real and too important to fuck this up. I could at least assure her concerning Crystal.

I walked up behind her caging her against the bar with my hands laid flat on the smooth surface on either side of her body not touching her. Her body stiffened, and her hands fell away from the tray she was loading.

I leaned in close and whispered in her ear, "Hey, Bailey."

I saw the goose bumps pop up along her neck, and her chest rose with a sharp breath. Her coconut scent filled my senses, and I closed my eyes to savor it. I opened my eyes to look at her face. Her cheeks were a nice shade of pink, and she was biting the corner of her lip.

"Bailey, you good?" a deep voice asked.

I straightened to my full height without letting go of the bar to see the bartender, Jaxson, scowling at me with his arms folded across his chest. His stance was defensive, and when he looked at Bailey I saw a look I didn't like at all. It was a possessive and protective look. I didn't fucking like that at all. She was my girl, and I'd make the tool understand that. I gave him a glare of my own and curled a hand around Bailey's hip pulling her back into me.

His eyes flicked down to my hand, his eyes narrowed. "Bailey?"

"I'm good, Jax. Thanks," she answered her voice husky. She cleared her throat. "Everything's cool."

After one last, hard stare, he walked back down the bar without another word. I watched him walk up to a few girls seated at the end of the bar. His scowl was replaced with a smile meant to charm. I shook my head. He was smooth, and he had his eye on my girl. I would have to take care of that issue and make sure he understood his eyes had to find a new direction to look in.

My mind returned to Bailey as she squirmed in my arms, her ass brushing against my tightening jeans. Her body was held stiff, but I felt the shiver run through her at the contact she accidently initiated.

I smiled as I ran my nose along her skin. "I don't want Crystal."

I decided that I needed to be blunt with Bailey. She was an observer, so I knew she would analyze the shit out of what she saw, and I didn't want there to be any doubts on my feelings. I never wanted to play games especially with Bailey. I was always going to be honest with her even with things she wouldn't make herself ask. She needed to know that I would always give her the truth.

"Okay," she responded and grabbed the edges of her tray. "I have to get back to my tables."

"I have told her flat out so many times I wasn't interested, but she won't stop with her bullshit," I responded ignoring her hint for me to move. "We went to high school together. After our high school graduation, we were at the same party. I got drunk on keg beer for the first and last time ever. I ended up with her, not my proudest moment. I did let her know it was one night, and that's all it would ever be."

"Why are you telling me this?" she whispered.

"Because I want to be with you, and I want you to know that without a doubt," I answered breathing in her coconut scent. "I only want you, Bailey.

"Okay," she said slowly like she was processing what I said. "I really need to get back on the floor."

She was running, but I didn't mind that time because I would be there watching her. I wasn't going to let her get too far. I backed away from her removing my hands from the bar. She looked at me over her shoulder, her eyes giving me a glimpse of the crack I made in her wall before she turned around and lifted her tray. I watched her walk back in the dining area delivering the drinks as she maneuvered between tables and chairs with an ease that spoke of experience.

"I ordered you a bottle of cold water," Logan laughed. "It looked like you needed it."

"Yeah," I grinned not bothered at all that I was getting shit.

I looked back over my shoulder and caught Bailey's gaze. She looked away quickly, and I couldn't help the shit eating grin on my face.

"What's up?" Ryder asked as he slid onto the empty stool next to me.

My smile slowly faded when I looked over at my brother. His face was drawn down in a slight frown, his eyebrows dipped down in between his eyes. He looked like he hadn't been sleeping well with the dark areas underneath his eyes. He had a lot more stubble on his face than I had ever seen on him before. It looked like he hadn't shaved all week when normally he would shave at least every other day.

"I don't know, bro," I said with a slight edge. "I was hoping you could tell me."

His sharp blue eyes swung my way narrowing slightly. "What?"

"What's been up with you lately?" I asked not backing down from the hard look he threw at me.

"Nothing," he turned away from me.

I clamped a hand down on his shoulder. "Don't lie to me. I need to know you're good, man. Just give me that."

He dropped his head and ran his hands through his hair and down his face roughly, taking a deep breath. When he looked up at me, my hand tightened further on his shoulder. His eyes were so sad and filled with anguish that I felt my jaw lock and my mouth tighten.

"No," he said shaking his head. "But I will be."

I let out a breath of relief at the flicker of determination in his gaze. That would do. His answer was short but honest. That flash of the Ryder I knew made my worries fade. He was right. He would be okay. I nodded my head, squeezed his shoulder one more time before dropping my arm, and grabbed the bottle of water for a drink making me think about the douche bag of a bartender.

"Good thing it's bottled water," I said with a gruff laugh trying to break the serious moment. "Pretty sure bartender boy would spit in my glass if he had the chance."

"Yep," Logan laughed. "I caught that."

"Don't worry about Jaxson," Avery interrupted from his seat on the other side of Logan. "He's protective of all the girls here."

I looked over at him with a frown. "How do you know that?"

He glanced at me before looking away with a shrug. "I come here a lot. I've met him and talked with him. He's the only guy that works here other than some of the kitchen staff, and he takes that role seriously."

Before I could question him further, a coconut scent invaded my senses. I turned around and watched Bailey walk around the end of the bar where Jaxson was now leaning against the cooler. He bent down and spoke quiet words. She nodded a few times and glanced at me before quickly looking away when our eyes connected.

My fists clenched when Jaxson tucked a piece of hair that fell free from her ponytail behind her ear. He gave her a half smile and said something that made her pull back and smack his abdomen with the back her hand, a laugh escaping her lips. That laugh made me scowl. I wanted that. I wanted her to laugh like that with me. I could see the conversation I was going to have with this bartender would probably end in blood loss. I could feel my body tighten with the need to clock this motherfucker.

She's at work.

She's at work.

She's at work.

The chant slowly calmed me. I kept my gaze steady on his when Bailey walked away from the bar, and his landed on me. He had a smirk covering his face that I wanted to remove permanently. He gave a sly wink before moving to replace drinks. He knew he was pissing me off, and he wanted to piss me off.

"You good, bro?" Logan asked.

I nodded jerkily and met his eyes. His were narrowed as he studied me. I took one last deep breath and let the tension run out of me with a concentrated effort. There was nothing I could do about the situation right now. I was going to stick around until the end of Bailey's shift, take her home. I wanted to convince her to take a chance on us, to give us a shot. I figured if I beat the shit out the bartender at her job, that would be a dead conversation. I wouldn't allow myself to fuck up any chance I had with her. The bartender and I would have a damn conversation. I just hoped I could keep my shit on lock.

I nodded at Logan, "Yep."

The rest of the night passed with us watching whatever game was on the screen and passing comments on the different plays. I could honestly tell you that I had no clue what games I had watched. I was sure I commented appropriately and timely, but I was too focused on Bailey.

The end of her shift didn't come fast enough. I just wanted her to myself. I wanted to talk and laugh. I wanted to kiss and lick those full lips of hers. I wanted to wrap her coconut scent around me and bury my face in her hair. I needed to be near her. I needed her.

I knew it was the end of her shift when she started refilling her station making sure all her tables had full salt and pepper shakers along with bottles of ketchup and steak sauce. She stuck the menus into the silver stands on each table before collecting her last tickets.

When she finished dropping the black folders on her tables, she walked to the hallway where she disappeared. I got up from my seat and dropped money on the clean bar. Jaxson had been cleaning and restocking the bar, giving us glances that stated he clearly was ready for us to leave. I slid my wallet back into my back pocket before turning to Logan.

"Can you grab a ride with Ryder?" I asked.

"Sure," Logan said with a grin. He knew what was up.

I clapped his hand in our handshake we developed back in junior high before turning to Ryder and doing the same. I walked out of the restaurant with them following close behind.

"Later, bro," Ryder called as they made the way to his truck.

"Later," I called back walking toward my truck.

I leaned against the driver's side door where I had a clear view of the back door figuring that was where she would most likely come out of. I watched as the remaining customers filed out of the front door and headed to their vehicles. The lights of the building slowly went out before the back door opened.

I groaned when Crystal was the first one out. I looked up at the sky and prayed she would keep walking. I knew it was a futile attempt to rid myself of her, but it was worth a shot. I lowered my head to see her standing in front of me with her hands on her hips, her head tilted to the side, a smile tipping her mouth.

"I'm waiting for Bailey," I said before she had any chance to misunderstand the situation.

"What are you still doing here?"

I looked to my right and saw Bailey standing there with a confused look. She didn't even look at Crystal which made me smile. That reaction may not seem like much, but to me it meant she trusted in what I told her earlier. And that was a huge fucking deal for me.

"Waiting for you," I answered moving closer to her.

"Why?" she asked tilting her to the side as her eyes ran over my face.

"Do you have a ride home?" I asked her.

"That would be me," someone said behind her.

I looked up and saw Jaxson standing behind her with his arms folded across his chest and a scowl set on his face. If I hadn't seen him smiling at the girls at the bar earlier, I would think he never smiled because of the way he kept looking at me.

I narrowed my eyes at him before returning my attention to Bailey. "Let me take you home." I said quietly.

Looking at her, I knew I didn't want the night to end. I wanted to talk to her, to watch her smile, to make her laugh. I just wanted to be with her. That thought caused me to pause, but not in fear. No, I wasn't scared of what I was feeling for her, nor was I shocked. I knew when I would meet my one, I would be all in. I was all in with Bailey, but I knew I had to tread carefully if I wanted her to stay instead of running.

I was not going to waste any of my time with Bailey. I didn't want to spar with Jaxson then and there. I needed to have Bailey alone and fighting with him would not get me there. Staring into Bailey's beautiful, green eyes made everything else fade into the background. So many emotions glided across through her eyes before retreating behind the wall she kept built. The longer she took to answer me, the longer I felt the rejection coming. I didn't want her say no. I needed her to say yes.

After what felt like forever, she nodded her head. Without taking her eyes from mine, she told Jaxson, "I'm going to ride with Ryker."

"You sure?" he asked making me want to growl.

"Yeah, thanks," she turned to him and smiled.

He nodded once before he looked at me with a glare.

I nodded at him. I got the message he was trying to deliver, but I had a bigger message to send to him, so I made it. I may be a dick for it, but I wanted no confusion for anyone. I narrowed my eyes at him before dropping my eyes to Bailey's that was still tilted my way. She licked her lips causing me to bite back a groan. I framed her face in my hands, and I slammed my lips onto hers with a possessiveness nobody would be able to dispute. She opened to me immediately, and I plunged my tongue into her mouth. She moaned into my mouth that had me groaning, and my dick twitched against my zipper.

I gentled the kiss sliding my tongue slowly across her bottom lip before pulling away. Her eyes fluttered open and I wanted to drop to my knees in worship. Her eyes held desire and lust and this intensity I only witnessed from her a few times, all times I was inside of her. Her cheeks were flushed, and her lips were plumped up from mine.

I grabbed her hand and led her to the passenger side of my truck. I opened the door but kept my hold of her hand. I put my other hand on her hip and pressed my lips against hers. I kept the kiss light and teasing. I slid my tongue along the seam of hers, and she opened for me. I touched the tip of my tongue against hers before pulling back.

Her lips tried to follow mine. My grin spread across my face when the flush rose in her cheeks like she was embarrassed.

With one final kiss, I pulled back. "Are you hungry?"

She shrugged, and a small smile lifted the corner of her lips. "I could eat."

I smiled and gave her a light smack on her ass which made her jump. "Let's go."

She turned around, and I had to laugh at the arched eyebrow look she threw me over her shoulder. Then, my eyes followed the line of her back to that ass as she lifted one leg up to step on the running board of my truck. She eased into the passenger seat, and I smothered the groan crawling up my throat when her shorts eased up her thighs and hugged them under that lush ass of hers.

I closed her door, and I walked around the back of the truck, so I could adjust my dick that was throbbing in the confines of my jeans where she couldn't witness it. I had to take a few deep breaths and think about football stats to get it to deflate to a level that wasn't so fucking painful. As soon as I opened the driver's side door and inhaled her coconut smell, I knew I wasted my time trying to calm my dick. There was no calming it when she was around.

Chapter Nine
Bailey

I was struck dumb. That's the only explanation I could come up with. I was sure I looked like an idiot running my finger across my lips that still tingled from his. Every time he touched me, I was done. I couldn't do anything but follow along with him. I wanted him every time he was near.

I watched him from the side mirror as he walked behind the truck to the driver's side where Crystal was waiting not far away with her hands on her hips. He didn't even glance at her which if I wasn't still wrapped up in that kiss I would have smiled with a smug satisfaction I never felt before.

I looked over at his chuckle, raising my eyebrow in question. I didn't understand what was so funny. I couldn't even think much less find humor in anything at that moment. My heart was still beating too fast and my breaths were coming out more like pants which should have been embarrassing, but it wasn't.

I jerked when I felt his arm slide across my chest. I looked down at his tattooed arm against my red shirt before my gaze snapped back to his.

"You need to buckle up, baby," he said sliding the seat belt across me snapping it in place.

I nodded numbly, my mind still on the way he said *baby*. It sounded so natural for him to call me that, like he had done it a thousand times before. My mind went back to the only other time he called me that, the day of my panic attack when he was trying to soothe me.

But what if it sounded natural because he used that term of endearment a lot? What if he called all the girls he'd been with that? My body tensed with that thought. It wasn't fair to hold that against him if it was the case, but I couldn't seem to stop the way I reacted. The jealously was a new and not exciting development I gained when this thing with Ryker started.

When I saw him with Crystal at the bar, I wanted to bitch slap that hoe, but I refrained. I watched their interaction closely and knew he didn't want her even before he told me. The jealously remained though, and apparently extended to the ones that weren't even around anymore. Fucking great. Like I didn't have enough to fucking worry about, now my mind was picturing him with some faceless girl that snagged his attention.

I blew out a deep breath and looked out the window. I felt his hand on my jaw turning me back to face him. I kept my eyes down not wanting to give any more of me away to him. I knew he wouldn't let me hide from him, but I wanted a fucking moment to hide as much as I could. His thumb pushed my chin up to where I had no choice but to look directly into his eyes.

I saw his concern in his eyes and heard it in his question. "What's wrong?"

"Nothing," I said trying to shake my head loose from his grip.

He tightened his hold on me and stared at me intensely, his brown eyes darkening. "Bailey, I don't play that "nothing" game. I want this to work. In order for that to happen, open and honest is the only way to go."

My mind was stuck on *I want this to work* comment. What the hell did that mean exactly? What did I get myself into, and how do I get out of it? Did I want to? What? Of course, I wanted to. I couldn't be with anyone for more than one night of fun. Well, maybe a few nights or days if you want to get technical about the situation. Didn't I already give him more than I gave anyone else before?

My mind was spinning through all these thoughts that I forgot I didn't answer his question until I heard his gritted, "Bailey."

"How many girls have you called *baby*?" Yep, I just blurted that shit out. What the fuck was wrong with me? I wanted to bang my head against the window, but his hands held me in place, his eyes intent on mine.

"None," he answered causing me to suck in a sharp breath.

I didn't question the honesty in his answer. I knew he was telling the truth, and I felt the relief flow through my body. His mouth spread in a cocky smile that made me tense. He looked satisfied by my reaction, and it put me on edge. I was way too exposed to him, and I didn't like it. I had nowhere to run with his eyes pinning me in place and his fingers pressing into my scalp.

His eyes softened with his smile before he softly brushed his lips across mine. He moved back and started the truck. We headed out of the parking lot and onto the highway in silence. I looked at the passing lights and buildings as I tried to figure out what the hell was going on and where I went from there.

"What you feel like eating?" he asked.

"Can we just hit a drive-thru?" I asked looking down at my uniform.

I had splashes of food and drink on my shirt from a toddler gone wild with pasta and chocolate milk, even my socks had brown spots on them. I shook my head at the reminder of that family. The kid was doing whatever the hell he wanted while the mom and dad had their faces pressed into their phones. I had threatened the kid with a time out, and he didn't even know what that was. That was one kid that should have time outs frequently. The parents never looked up at my threats.

"Sure. How about some burgers?" he asked.

"Sounds good," I agreed.

I jumped with the sudden intrusion of loud drums and guitars blaring from the speakers. I instantly recognized the sound of *Full Moon Posse*. I loved the band. They were fucking awesome.

"Sorry," Ryker said smiling sheepishly at me as he turned the volume down.

I smiled back and nodded. "I like them."

"You do?" he asked watching the road in front of him with concentration.

"Yeah," I answered deciding maybe I could let him in a little at a time. "I actually met them before they got famous."

He quickly glanced at me before returning his attention to the road. "Really?"

I nodded leaning back into the seat with a smile. I looked out of the window and replied, "Yeah, I actually went to school with two of the members. After I left, I watched their career take off. I worked a few festivals where they performed and met up with them again. They are all crazy talented."

"Didn't they originate in Florida?" he asked.

"Yeah," I answered swallowing thickly. I never told anyone where I was from. "I grew up in a little town outside of Orlando."

Now, apparently, I told people where I was from. *What the fuck?* I tensed waiting for the telltale signs of an impending panic attack to overwhelm me. They never came. I let out a slow breath as I sorted through what I was feeling. I didn't feel anything, except maybe relief? I'm not sure what it was, but my chest felt lighter. I wanted to share some of me with Ryker, wanted him to know more. I didn't think I was ready to share everything, but I could do this. I could tell a little about a past.

"They are playing in City Park in October at a big festival," he replied. "Do you want to go?"

I smiled and shook my head. "I'm working it."

He glanced at me. "What?"

"I'm working the merchandise stand," I explained. "When I traveled from Florida, I worked at music festivals along the way. I even worked a beer stand at a NASCAR race one time. The noise in that booth was insane."

"How long ago did you leave Florida?" he asked such a simple question.

"Three years ago," I answered quietly staring out of the window.

It seemed like a lifetime ago that I was stuck in the hospital then physical therapy before Carter and I left it all behind, but sometimes it felt as though I was still stuck in hell. I wasn't constantly waiting for something to happen to end what I found here. This was the longest period that we stuck in one spot. Every other place we landed, we took off again a few months later. We lasted nine months in Biloxi, Mississippi before we moved on to Louisiana. We stayed in Slidell, Alexandria, and New Orleans before arriving in Houma. We were thinking of moving to Lafayette, but we never finalized that plan. I think we both settled without talking about it. We were comfortable here, felt a sense of home here for the first time ever.

We pulled into the closest drive thru, and he ordered a couple of burger combos. He wouldn't let me pay for any of it which if I were honest, I didn't really fight him too hard. I mean free food is free food. I learned a long time ago that some things were worth denting your pride for.

After we were handed our order, he pulled his truck into a parking space and handed me my food. The greasy smell hit me with its delicious aroma. My stomach growled loudly making Ryker chuckle.

"I didn't get a chance to really eat at work," I confessed slightly embarrassed.

"Well, it's a good thing I had this brilliant idea, huh?" he teased as he unwrapped his burger and took a huge bite.

He licked his lips catching the ketchup at the corner, and I had to tear my eyes away. Damn, he really was sexy if I was getting hot watching him eat a freaking burger!

We ate in silence, but I could feel his eyes on me. Awareness shot through my system from the heat of him watching me. The sexual energy between us was insane and put in the confines of his truck it was intensified.

I was glad he was content with silence because I wasn't too confident about my conversation skills when my whole body vibrated from being this close to him. I was sure if I tried to talk I would babble and stutter not making any sense.

"I can't eat anymore," I said groaning with a hand on my stomach. "That was a big freaking burger."

He laughed. "Alright. Are you ready to go?"

I nodded. "Yeah, it's been a long day."

He started the truck, put it in gear, and pulled out of the space. We pulled onto the highway and headed to our place. It felt weird saying our place, but we lived next to each other, so it was kind of true. I ignored the little flutter in my belly at the description. He parked in his assigned spot in front of his building and put the truck in park. He shut the ignition off and opened his door. I stared at him as got out and rounded the hood. He moved so smoothly and confidently. My eyes ate up his broad shoulders, hard chest, and lean torso covered in a tight shirt that was trying to contain the bulging biceps. That all led to his perfect ass and muscled thighs covered in faded denim. I licked my lips as he opened my door.

His mouth tipped up with amusement lighting his eyes with flashes of gold. "You good, baby?"

His deep voice combined with the name caused a shiver to race down my spine. Knowing that I was the only one that got that endearment meant something to me, something bigger than what I was ready to face. That didn't mean I wasn't going to bask in this feeling.

I nodded my head with a whispered, "Yeah."

He held his hand out to me. "I'll walk you home."

I looked at his hand for a few seconds before sliding my palm over his. His fingers wrapped around my hand as I slid out of the truck and encountered his body on my way down. He didn't back up and give me room. He was all in my space, his hard body pressed close to mine. I felt my full body shiver at the contact. His eyes held a possessive glint and arousal darkened the irises. My nipples beaded pushing further into his chest. I assumed he felt my reaction if the groan that escaped his lips was anything to go by. My core tightened when his erection pushed into my stomach.

He lowered his head until his lips hovered right above mine. "Give me a chance."

My brows knit in confusion. "What?"

"Give me a chance," he repeated cupping my face in his hands rubbing his thumb along my bottom lip. "Be with me. Date me. Hang out with me. Talk to me on the phone. Text me."

"Like what, a boyfriend/girlfriend thing?" I asked wincing at how juvenile that sounded.

It was so junior high, but it still gave me butterflies to hear him ask. Nobody had ever asked me that before. I never dated, never hung out with a guy for extended periods of time except for Carter. I didn't know if I could do a relationship. Most of the time, I struggled to maintain the friendships I loosely had because of the walls I surrounded myself with. Would I be able to do this with Ryker? Would I end up with a broken heart, or would he?

His closeness with his words clouded my brain. His warmth was all around me, and all I wanted to do was lean further into him and soak it all up. At the same time, my feet were getting ready to run and my mind was planning my escape.

"Yes," he answered seriously without hesitation.

Before I could analyze the situation further, he bent his head closer to mine and ran his tongue along my full bottom lip making it shine. I sucked in a deep breath as my eyelids started fluttering closed. With a groan that vibrated through his chest into mine, he slammed his lips on mine taking everything I had in me. He tasted so fucking good like mint with a hint of something spicy. His lips were soft but firm against mine. His tongue licked the seam of my lips until I opened for him. I couldn't contain the moan that escaped my throat at the feel of his tongue against mine.

His hand gripped my ass tighter tilting my hips up to rub against his hard dick. We both groaned when my heat hit his bulging jeans. He slid his other hand into my hair pulling slightly to change the angle, so his tongue could go further into my mouth.

I couldn't contain the moans from spilling into his mouth where he swallowed them with a groan. He slipped his hand up the back of my tee shirt and down the waistband of my shorts gripping my flesh. His strong, steady touch left a trail of fire along my skin. My hands dug into his hair as I stood on my tip toes to get closer to him, to his mouth.

I let out a gasp and dropped back down on my heels when I felt his fingers over my panties. I didn't even feel him undo my shorts much less get in them. With his eyes locked with mine, he bit my bottom lip with a groan.

"So fucking wet," he growled against my lips.

My hands grasped his shoulders trying to steady myself. I was burning up between my legs for him. My panties were soaked through, and I knew he could feel what he did to me. He increased the pressure of his fingers against my slit, and my hands slid down his chest to his abdomen where I fisted the material of his shirt on both his sides. He moved the fabric of my panties to the side and slid one finger smoothly inside of me. The walls of my pussy squeezed around him, and I could feel myself gushing with arousal.

I threw my head back with a moan when he added another finger inside of me pumping fast and hard reaching that perfect hidden spot. He pressed his thumb down hard against my clit. He took that opportunity to attack my neck using his lips and tongue. He sank his teeth into that sensitive spot right behind my ear. He wrapped his lips around the bite and swiped his tongue across my skin before he sucked hard. He changed the angle of his hand, so the heel of his hand was pressed down on my clit rocking in a perfect friction while he finger fucked me. My pussy clamped down on his fingers in an intense orgasm. I arched my back and moaned his name.

Fuck! My mind was blown, and all I could do was pant through the overwhelming sensations rolling through me. The pleasure was so fucking intense I saw spots across of my vision. My breath came back with a whoosh. My heart pounded in my chest like I had just run a marathon.

I felt his fingers slowly glide out of me as he slid his lips across mine in the gentlest and sweetest kiss I've ever had. I wanted to cry from the loss of him and the empty feeling I was left with, but I was still trying to recover. That orgasm was so fucking good, and it came from his damn fingers. The man was damn good.

My eyes shot open as the real world intruded into my brain. We were outside in a fucking parking lot, and I just got finger banged. What the hell was I letting him to do me? Fuck! I tried to push against his chest to gain some space, so I could think clearly. He wouldn't budge. I felt the panic rising. There was no way out. I couldn't get away.

"Shhh," Ryker whispered in my ear as he ran his hand up and down my back. "I've got you, Bailey."

My hands went to my shorts to find they were already zipped and buttoned. I must have really been out of it if I didn't feel him fixing my clothes. My shirt was pulled down into place, and Ryker's hand was resting lightly on my ass while he kept stroking the other hand up and down my back. My panic was still hovering, but it didn't blow into an attack.

He pulled back and tilted my face up, so I was looking in his eyes. His gaze was sharp and searching. His brows were drawn inward, his mouth pulled down in a frown. His fingertips caressed my cheek as he studied me. I could feel the panic receding, and my breathing returned to normal.

"I would never let anyone see you like that," he whispered softly and reverently. "That look on your face when you let go of everything and just feel is for me and only me. I will always protect it and you."

At his words, my body relaxed fully, the tension melting away. I felt tears prick the backs of my eyes knowing what he said was honest and sincere. I believed him, and I could only count on one person giving me the sense of security. I never expected to meet and allow someone else to be so close to me that I would feel safe with them. Now, Ryker was giving me all of that, and I wasn't sure what I was going to do with it.

"I know," I whispered, my voice cracking at the end.

I cleared my throat to get rid of the lump that lodged there. I needed to get into my apartment and think about this. The urge to run was stronger now than before, but I didn't know if I was running from him or me and my feelings. I needed to figure that out and see if I was strong enough for this.

"Bailey," he said softly.

I looked back into his eyes, and a tear escaped to slide down my cheek. He swiped it away with his thumb. If I hadn't felt so unbalanced, I would have been pissed to expose my weakness in front of him, but I didn't have it in me to care at that moment.

"Will you be my girlfriend, Bailey?" he said so seriously that I couldn't help the smile that tipped my lips even if it was probably more sad than happy.

"I'm broken," I whispered as I closed my eyes not wanting to maintain eye contact with him.

It was hard to admit a weakness, but he needed to know. He needed to know that I was fucked up. He witnessed one panic attack, but they could get so much worse. Then, the nightmares sucked ass. I hadn't had one in a long time, but that didn't mean I wouldn't. That was one of the reasons I didn't spend the night with anyone. I was afraid I would freak out in my sleep, and whoever was there would have to deal with me. I didn't want that. I didn't want someone else seeing me at a low point.

"Look at me," he commanded softly.

I shook my head. I couldn't look into his eyes and see pity. I didn't want pity from anyone, but it would have been so much worse if it came from Ryker.

"I don't know how to do this!" I was freaking out and didn't know how to stop.

"Breathe," he instructed gently. "I've got you."

I believed him. Why? I had no fucking clue. He had all the power here. I was vulnerable and exposed. I took a deep breath and kept my eyes on his. My breathing evened out, and my heart steadied its pace.

He stood there studying my eyes with the lingering question in his eyes. My air flow and heart rate returned to normal, but my mind was spinning. I had a very intense orgasm in the middle of a parking lot, and he was asking something that required thinking while his stare felt as though he could see straight through me.

Could I be someone's girlfriend? Could I open myself up enough to let Ryker in?

"Yes," I breathed right before his mouth took mine.

I guess I would find out.

Chapter Ten
Ryker

I woke up with images of Bailey running through my brain and my hand on my dick. I groaned as I stroked upward with a tight grip. My balls were already drawn up tight. I thought about the night before when Bailey came on my hand and moaned into my mouth in the parking lot, and my strokes went faster. Her lips were plumped up from my lips, and I pictured them wrapped around my dick. I put a pillow over my face to drown out the groans that came up my throat. I came all over my hand and abdomen with Bailey's name on my lips.

I threw the pillow to the side and took a deep breath. I looked down at the mess I had made and laughed when I saw my dick was still hard. Damn, I wanted Bailey. I had to see her. I needed to see her. Last night I wanted to show her that I wanted more than sex with her, but I still had to make her come. When I watched her come apart for me, my dick was so fucking hard it hurt to move.

Although we had done this relationship thing backwards, I knew I wouldn't be able to go back. I wanted to be with her and inside her as often as possible. I needed to be with her and inside her as often as possible. I should have been able to slow down and ease into a serious relationship with her, but I couldn't. I wanted it all. I needed it all.

I looked at the time and wondered if it was too early to go over to her apartment. I had to go into the gym in a few hours. I had to clean up and knew I wouldn't be going back to sleep after. I wanted to bring Bailey to the gym and see what she thought. Maybe we could go after grabbing some breakfast. With that plan in mind, I got out of bed and cleaned up.

However, when I knocked on the apartment door, I didn't expect to come face to face with a half-naked dude answering her door. Did I have the wrong apartment? I looked at the number on the door again. 13. Nope, this is the right place. I had been in this damn apartment. There was no way I would forget which one it was.

"Who are you?" I demanded because I mean, come on! I was at my girl's place and some shirtless guy answered the door.

"Who the fuck are you?" the guy demanded with an arched eyebrow.

"Ryker," I gritted out.

"Carter," he replied. "What can I do for you?"

"I'm here to see Bailey," I answered.

"What's going on?" I heard Baily ask from the other side of Carter.

I tried to look around Carter, but he moved to block me. The width of his chest blocked the doorway, but I could just make out a bare leg underneath his raised arms that were gripping the top of the doorframe. My hands clenched into tight fists, and I took a deep breath.

Bare leg? Bailey's voice? Oh, hell no!

"Move out of the way," I gritted out.

"Ryker?" Bailey said from behind Carter.

Then, her head popped up over Carter's shoulder where her hand landed to keep her balance as she stood on the tips of her toes which made me grind my back teeth. She was really touching him?

"Yeah," I cleared my throat looking away from Carter's smug face. He knew what the fuck was happening, and he was enjoying it, that motherfucker.

Bailey dropped back down onto the flats of her feet, and I glanced down to see her backing up. Hell, no. She wasn't getting away from me. She had a few questions to answer, but first, she would be fucking changing.

I pushed Carter out of my way stalking toward Bailey. Before I could reach her, I was stopped by arms strong as steel wrapping around my chest. He tightened his grip when I tried to break free. I could have probably gotten out of the hold, but I knew it would have been a fight that would result in blood with the way I was feeling. The sight of Bailey in a guy's shirt and a dude with only jeans on that were unbuttoned made my vision blur in a haze. I wasn't sure what their relationship was, and I didn't want to upset Bailey, but I was close to fucking him up.

"What the fuck do you think you are doing?" Carter growls.

"What are you wearing?" I demanded in a harsh tone.

I looked directly at Bailey. She looked scared and confused before she straightened her shoulders and tilted her head up with a glare. I needed to tone down my shit before she shut me out completely. It felt like a fucking act of congress to suppress my anger. The anger wasn't necessarily at Bailey because I honestly didn't think this was what it looked like, but that didn't mean I wanted her to walk around looking like that.

"Well, you just woke us both up," she stated giving me a glare of her own. "I didn't get the chance to get dressed."

"Why are you wearing his shirt to bed?" I gritted out between clenched teeth in a slightly more even tone.

I couldn't let this go. She was wearing boy shorts and a man's shirt that was not mine. I knew what most people would think about this situation, but I was a firm believer in not assuming anything without all the facts. I knew they weren't together. Yeah, he held me back from reaching her, but if she was his, he would be in front of her. He wouldn't let me see her like this. At least, that's what I wanted to do.

Her legs were on display all toned and tanned, and I could see the bottom of her black boy shorts. The big shirt was hanging from one shoulder showing the wing of the dragonfly reaching her collar bone and more evidence she wasn't wearing a bra along with her nipples poking through. Her hair was a sexy, tangled mess around her head. Fuck, she was fucking beautiful. I wanted to see her like that every morning, rumpled from a night in my bed. I didn't want him to see her like that, and I fought to break his hold on me.

"Let me go," I demand.

"Bai?" he questioned pissing me off further with the nickname sounding too close to *bae*.

She looked up at him over my shoulder, and I could see the debate she was having with herself in her eyes. I hated that she was looking at him. I wanted her eyes back on me. I clenched my jaw tightly as I watched her nod and lock her jaw. She came to a decision.

"Let him go," she said softly.

As soon as I was released, I reached for her and wound my arm around her waist bringing her body against mine. "Where's your room?"

"Fuck that," she snapped. "You are not getting in my room. Just tell me what you wanted from me this early on a Saturday morning. If you came here to fuck, it's not going to happen."

She may have told Carter to let me go, but I could see she wasn't happy with me. Her walls were up high, her eyes guarded as she tried to get out of my arms. She wanted to push me away, and she didn't know me enough to know I wasn't going to be pushed away. She would find out, though. Last night she said she would be my girlfriend, give me a chance. Today, she was trying to make it sound like that didn't mean anything which was bullshit. It meant everything. I knew she in defense mode, but it still stung.

"I don't want to fuck," I answered softly in direct contrast to my seething insides. I wanted to go all caveman and toss her over my shoulder to throw her in her room, but I didn't. She had to take me to her room on her own.

I took a few steps forward forcing her backwards. Her hands gripped my biceps to keep herself steady on her feet. Her eyes searched mine and her breaths became shorter.

"What are you doing?" she screamed as her back hit the wall behind her.

I had her pinned in place not allowing her to move. She wasn't running from me. I was also trying to block her body from the guy at my back. I knew she was more than likely right, and he had seen her like this before, but I didn't want to focus on that fucking fact. I was concentrating on the now, and now she was mine.

"What the hell are you doing?" Carter growled putting his hand on my shoulder attempting to pull me back from Bailey. Yeah, not happening. I pulled my shoulder roughly from his grasp pushing my body further into hers. She looked at Carter over my shoulder. They had a silent conversation which pissed me off even more.

"Carter," she stated firmly. A beat passed before he released me.

"I want you to get dressed. I don't want him seeing you like this."

She laughed a hollow laugh like she thought I was full of shit. "Yeah, right. Anyway, it doesn't matter what you want. We live together.

We've been together for years, and he's seen me in a lot of different ways."

The urge to spank her beautiful ass until it was a nice shade of pink surprised the hell out of me. I have never been into that much, but I wanted it with Bailey. I wanted to mark her and let everyone know she was mine. I wanted her to submit to me and understand that she was mine.

I wrapped a hand around the back of her neck to keep her in place as I pressed my lips against her ear and whispered, "Last night you agreed to be my girlfriend, Bailey. I don't share. I don't want to see you in another man's shirt ever. You are mine and mine alone."

She tensed at my words, but I didn't let up my hold when she jerked her head back. I slid a knee in between her legs and pulled her closer with my hand firmly on her ass. I could still feel Carter at my back, but I didn't pay any attention to him. I felt the shiver that ran through her body and smiled against the skin of her neck.

"Back up," she commanded with her hands planted firmly on my chest trying to put space between us that I wouldn't let her have.

"No," I whispered right against her lips. "Who is he, Bailey?"

"Carter," she answered swallowing thickly.

"Who is he to you?" I pushed. I needed to know what his role was here.

"My best friend," she answered causing me to scowl. "And my roommate."

I figured the last part which pissed me off since I assumed her roommate was a girl and she didn't correct me, but the first part was a little more concerning to me. How close were they? I was hoping he was her brother. That would have made this situation tolerable. As it was, I wanted to kick his ass out, but evidently this was his place, too so all I could do was stake my claim.

I wanted to ask her what kind of history they had, but I didn't want to do that in front of him. If she told me they had been together and lived together, I would have been devastated, and I didn't want him to see how affected I was. I was sure she could see the uncertainty in my eyes because I wouldn't hide from her.

"He's always been like my brother," she said softly.

I let out a breath of relief, and she ran the tip of her tongue along her bottom lip. I didn't hesitate. I kissed her. It started out slow and easy. My lips brushed softly against hers. Her eyes fluttered but stayed open. I shifted my hand into her hair to cup the back of her head and moved her back slightly fitting my lips more firmly on hers. She didn't kiss me back, but she didn't pull away either.

I ran my tongue along her bottom lip. I felt and heard her gasp as it passed through her lips giving me an opening inside of her mouth. I took it. My tongue sought out hers. I kept my movements slow and measured. I didn't want to come on too strong and scare her, but I didn't want to give her an out either. With a moan, she gave in. Her tongue tangled with mine. Her lips moved against mine harder and more urgent.

"So," Carter interrupted with what sounded like humor mixed with a cough.

Her eyes flew open, and she jerked her head back. Her whole body tensed as she pushed against me, but I wouldn't let her get far. Her eyes were swirling with emotion, her walls down, but I didn't know for how long, so I needed to move this scene to somewhere private.

"Where is your room, Bailey?" I asked.

Her eyes scanned my face before answering, "It's the one on the right."

I grabbed her behind her thighs and lifted her up. I walked quickly to the door standing open on the right side of the short hallway. I walked into her room and slammed the door shut with my foot. I set her down on her feet and lifted the shirt up and over her head within seconds. She let out a high squeak and crossed her arms over her breasts.

"What the hell are you doing?" she demanded with a glare.

"I told you," I stated evenly. "I couldn't see you in his shirt. It doesn't belong on your body. Please, don't wear it again."

I wasn't above begging her. I wanted to demand she listen to me and do as I say, but I had to keep that under wraps. That wasn't the way to keep Bailey. She would run if she thought I was going to control her in any way.

She opened her mouth to say something and from the look on her face, I knew I wouldn't like it. Fuck it! I couldn't hold back. I was pissed off because of this whole fucking scene, and she kept saying stupid shit to get me to back off. I had enough. With a growl, I slammed my lips down on hers and immediately demanded entrance with my tongue. Her lips parted, and my tongue went inside. I gathered her hair in my fist tilting her head back, my tongue delving deeper into her mouth.

She moaned and wrapped her arms around my neck, her fingers clutching my neck. Her naked breasts pressed into my chest, and I could feel her hard nipples poking me through my shirt. I groaned and tightened my hand on her ass and in her hair. My fingers dug into the flesh exposed below the hem of her boy shorts. I dragged my fingers up taking the material with me. Once her ass cheek was exposed, my hand grabbed it and squeezed.

She moaned deep into mouth as her hands reached down to the hem of my shirt drawing up my body. Her hands ran along my skin, her nails scratching. More, I needed more. Her touch left a trail of fire burning me up. I ran my finger down her ass until I met wet fabric making me moan.

"Always so wet for me," I said as I teased her slit with the tip of my finger.

Her head dropped back on a moan, and her nails dug into my back right above the waistband of my jeans. I put a little more pressure against her, pushing the fabric against her as my lips latched onto her neck. Her back arched when I nibbled on the skin behind her ear, scraping my teeth down her neck. I licked my way back up to her ear as I eased one finger under her panties to feel her bare pussy slick with her arousal.

She pushed further into my hand, and I let my finger slip inside of her wet heat. I groaned as I started stroking in and out of her body. I placed my hand in the middle of her back and pulled back from her neck. I latched my mouth on her nipple, sucking roughly at the same time I added another finger inside her and pressed my thumb against her clit.

Making her come was my one and only goal at that moment even though my dick was ready to break out of my jeans. She was close. I could feel her walls fluttering around my fingers. I increased my pace slamming my fingers in and out of her, pressed my thumb down harder on her clit, and bit down on her nipple. She screamed my name as her pussy clamped down on my fingers and her body shivered.

I kissed the tip of her nipple before pulling away and gentled my fingers before pulling out of her completely. Her eyes were slowing opening and a nice rosy color covered her cheeks. Her chest was heaving with her uneven breaths, and my eyes went to her moving breasts to see marks from my beard across her skin.

I growled at the sight, and my dick twitched for attention. I felt her hands move up my back, and my eyes shot to hers. The same fire I felt inside was reflected in her eyes, gold sparks spread throughout the emerald. I tugged my hat off my head and pulled my shirt all the way off.

"I need you," I gritted out before kissing her roughly.

"Yes," she breathed when I released her mouth.

I spun her around until she faced the bed with her back to me. I ripped her panties down her legs, and she kicked them off. I pushed her forward and guided her to her hands and knees. My hands went to her ass cheeks and gave them a squeeze.

She threw her hair back, the blonde locks trailing down her back. She looked at me over her shoulder, and I could see the hunger in her eyes. She wanted me as much as I wanted her. I grabbed a condom out of my wallet and put it between my lips before stripping myself out of my gym shorts and boxers.

She watched me intently as I rolled the condom down my length. I stroked up and down with a tight grip at the base trying to stave off the orgasm I could already feel coming. I stepped up behind her, my dick bumped against her backside. She pushed her ass out and arched her back.

I put my hand on the small of her back as I guided my dick to her entrance rubbing the head of my dick through her wetness.

"You ready for me?" I asked as I spread her moisture along my shaft.

"Yes," she gasped out.

I lined myself up and thrust myself inside of her to the hilt. We both groaned as I hit the end of her. She grabbed a pillow and buried her head in it to silence her moans as I started thrusting, holding tightly to her hips. She pushed back into me as I went forward causing me to hit so deep. Then, she started moving faster and more frantic. Her ass was bouncing. She was twerking. She was twerking on my fucking dick. I groaned and thrust harder. My balls drew tight to my body, and I knew I wouldn't last much longer. The sight of her lush ass bouncing up and down, my dick going in and out of her slick with her juices, had me on the fucking edge. I reached around her hips and zeroed in on her clit, pinching it between my thumb and forefinger. She screamed into the pillow as her pussy squeezed my dick so hard, I let go. I came hard into the condom on a strangled grunt. Fuck, she wrung me dry. I locked my knees to keep myself from falling on her and gentled my thrusts.

She let out a soft moan when I slid out of her but didn't move, ass still in the air. I removed the condom and tied the end before I tossed it into the garbage can on the side of her bed. I stretched out on the bed next to her and pulled her into my arms.

She let out a contented sigh and snuggled into my chest. I pressed a kiss against her temple and laid my head on the top of hers.

"Do you have plans today?" I asked running my fingers through her hair smiling at the sound of contentment that came out of her mouth.

"My shift starts at four today," she answered drowsily.

"Do you want to go somewhere with me?" I asked. "I'll have you back in time to get ready for work."

She looked up at me. "Where?"

"I need to go to the gym for a few hours. We could grab some breakfast on the way there," I said hoping she would agree.

"What gym?" she asked tilting her head up to look at me.

"Heavy Bags," I answered dropping a soft kiss on her lips. "My dad owns it, and I work there. I have to finish up some schedules and put in some orders."

"Okay," she answered with a smile.

Chapter Eleven
Bailey

He left the room, so I could get dressed and ready to go. After that whole encounter, I didn't know if I would ever be ready when it came to Ryker. When I had woken up to the sound of Ryker's voice, I thought I was dreaming until I replayed the last conscious moments I had and realized I heard knocking followed by two male voices. I knew the voices belonged to Carter and Ryker.

After taking in the pissed off look on his face, I had backed away. I should have told him about Carter before I agreed to be his girlfriend. I had never been a girlfriend before, but I figured that was an important detail to share. Logically, I knew I should have just explained the situation to him, but I didn't do that.

I wasn't entirely sure why I pushed him like I had. The only explanation I could come up with was I wanted to see how far I could push before he snapped, needed to see how far. I knew he would snap, and I would rather control as much of the situation as I could. I learned a long time ago to not lie to myself ever, so I wasn't going to start. He scared me, not physically, but emotionally, the way he made me feel, the way my body came alive for him, the way my brain shut down of all logical thinking.

I knew I was safe there. Carter was standing guard and was ready to strike if Ryker got rough. I didn't really believe he would hurt me, but I knew first hand that people weren't always what they seemed to be. I wanted to push him to the ugly underneath. I wanted to be able to say, "and that's why I can't do this." I could make him leave and forget all of this ever happened. I needed to push him away now before it got any further. So, I had tried to make what we had seem so much cheaper than what it was. I knew I was talking shit, but I couldn't stop myself.

I watched him prowl towards me with a fierce expression that made his face hard. My heart started pounding in my chest, and my breathing sped up as I backed away from him. He just kept stalking towards me until my back hit the wall preventing me from any further retreat. I couldn't escape, and he kept coming until we were so close I could feel the heat of his skin against my body. His fists were balled at his sides, and his jaw was ticking with anger. I had to fight to stay standing instead of cowering in fear.

I looked over his shoulder to see Carter at the ready to jump in if needed which gave me comfort in the face of Ryker's anger. Then, everything shifted. His anger was still there, but his voice softened when he spoke to me. I lost a little of my shit talking skills in my confusion. I thought for sure he would at least yell accusations at me about what was happening with Carter, but he didn't. He just begged me to change before he kissed the hell out of me. As soon as his lips landed on mine, I was done. My walls came me down, and I fell into him.

As soon as Carter's voiced penetrated my brain and Ryker pulled away, I was a hot bundle of nerves. I was turned on and embarrassed in equal measures. I didn't lie when I said Carter had always been like a brother to me. He was, and it was embarrassing to have him see me all wrapped up in Ryker.

Ryker picked me up and started carrying me down the hall; I looked at Carter to see his eyes on me. There was a knowing look in his deep blue eyes. He gave me a slight nod almost like he was encouraging me to go with Ryker. I thought he would have gone in protective brother mode, but he gave me his approval instead.

Well, then I ended up naked with Ryker in my room with Carter a wall away, and nothing else mattered. Any time he touched me, his breath blew against my skin, or he growled at me, I was done. I had no control when it came to him. There's this something about Ryker that made me want, made me need. When I was with him, I just let go. My body sank into him, and my brain took a fucking vacation every single time.

I shook off all other thoughts, and I pulled on some cotton shorts and an old concert shirt. I figured if we were headed to the gym, I should dress the part like him in his hot as hell black basketball shorts that hugged his ass perfectly and the tight white tee shirt that clung to his chest and shoulders. His tattoos looked so fierce against the white cotton. Then, he added the black, fitted hat turning it backwards looking like Channing Tatum, and I was in fucking heat, panting and drooling.

I slipped on my socks and red Converse before I threw my hair up in a messy bun. There were so many knots in my hair I knew it would be useless to try and untangle them. I slipped into the bathroom to wash my face and brush my teeth.

Oh, my God! We did all of that and I hadn't even brushed my teeth! What the fuck was wrong with me? I was Ryker high obviously. *Ryker high?* I snorted to myself, that about sums it up. I felt high when I was with him and like nothing could touch me. It was a crazy, insane, have me committed type of situation.

I grabbed my phone and stuck it in my back pocket and slipped my wristlet that held my key, ID, a card, and some cash down my arm. When I made it into the living room, I saw Ryker stretched out on the sofa and a flashback from the last time he had sat in that spot came to mind. My steps faltered slightly, and I must have made some kind of noise because he turned his head in my direction.

I cleared my throat and made my way to the front door as he stood. "Are you ready to go?"

I just had him, and I was tingling everywhere wanting more. Fuck, this was ridiculous. I needed to find some damn self-control around him. I would probably have to dig fucking deep to find the ability to tone down my want for him.

He flashed me a smile, "Yeah, baby, I'm ready." He so knew what I was thinking, and from the looks of it, he was thinking the same thing. His eyes darkened as they swept down my body and back up, stopping briefly on my chest. I knew he could see my hard nipples poking through my shirt. Damn sports bra doesn't hide anything!

After locking up the apartment, we headed down the stairs and to the parking lot. He grabbed my hand as we made our way to his truck. His fingers laced through mine, and I reveled in the feeling of being connected to him. The warmth of his palm against mine made me feel secure with him. I knew I could get used to that feeling.

"So, your dad owns this gym," I said trying to distract myself from my train of thought.

"Yeah," he smiled. "He built it from the ground up. We all pitched in when we were old enough, and I've always loved being there."

I smiled at the look on his face from talking about his family. "Are y'all close?" I wanted to know how a normal family interacted. I had been in homes with a lot more than eight people in it and it sucked. That was because everyone was out for themselves, and it was a daily struggle just to eat.

"Yes," he answered without hesitation. "We all have our own things going on, but we talk regularly and try to get together as often as possible. You know I live with Ryder, so I see him pretty much every day. He also works at Heavy Bags. Ryden and Rian own a tattoo parlor in Lockport called *Soul Ink*. Rylan is a freelance photographer. He travels a lot, but his home base is here. Riley started school this year, and she works at a dance studio."

I felt a pang at seeing how he adored his family and wondered what that felt like to have a big family. I had been in places with a lot of kids, but those were always the worst. The best you could do in those houses was keep to yourself and be as invisible as possible.

"What's wrong?" he asked.

I looked over to see him watching me intensely. "Nothing."

"Bailey," he said in warning, and I remembered his "nothing" game comment.

"I was just thinking it must have been nice growing up with a close-knit family." I shrugged like it was no big deal to expose a part of me hoping I pulled it off.

"Most of the time it was awesome. There was always someone to talk to and hang out if I wanted. Privacy was an issue since there was none, but we managed," he laughed. "Do you have any brothers or sisters?" he asked.

I looked away as I answered. "No."

"What about your parents? Are they still in Florida?"

I took a deep breath as I contemplated my choices. I could blow off his questions, or I could give him the truth. I knew I had to give him the truth. He deserved that. I felt like a coward for even thinking about blowing him off because I was scared, scared of what could happen, scared of what I was feeling for him, and scared that when he decided to walk away, I would have nothing left of me.

"Bailey, you don't have to tell me if you're not ready to," he said. "But I need to know that you will open up one day."

He was giving me an out, and I wanted to take it. I didn't want to hash out my background and the things I've dealt with my whole life, but I had to. I agreed to give him a chance. He had already witnessed one of my panic attacks, and he didn't look at me like I was a freak. I gathered my courage and spit out a bare bone highlight.

"I grew up in the foster system. I was nine when my mom overdosed on pain pills in a nasty ass bathroom of the hotel room we were staying in. I don't know if I had any relatives, but the state couldn't find any. I didn't know who my dad was, so I couldn't give them a name. I went into my first foster home six months later, but I never stayed in one place long. I moved around so much I lost count of how many homes I had been in. No one wanted to adopt me because I was labeled as a problem child. When I was sixteen, I was moved to my final placement where I met Carter."

I had to look away from him because I didn't want to see pity in his eyes. I knew my childhood didn't sound awesome, hell it was nowhere near awesome, but that didn't mean I wanted nor needed pity. I didn't. I made it through. I survived.

I looked out of the window and at our surroundings. We were on the edge of town parked outside of an older looking building with three businesses in it. Heavy Bags sat in the middle of a laundromat and a loan place.

"Bailey," Ryker said softly. "Look at me."

I slowly turned my head towards him afraid of what I would see in his eyes, but I didn't need to be. I didn't see sympathy or pity. I saw understanding and approval in his warm brown eyes. His eyes scanned my face as if he were memorizing it, his thumbs brushed along my cheekbones as his hands cupped my jaw, and his mouth was lifted in that sexy half smile he had going on.

His lips brushed across mine softly. "Come on. Let's go on in."

That's it? No questions or responses? Well, that wasn't that hard, and I felt a little lighter by telling him, by letting him in some more. I had wanted him to know more about me. I wanted to get rid of this burden I had been carrying for so long, and I wanted it to be him. I knew he would protect me. I was safe with him. I trusted him.

That realization sent a jolt through me. I've only ever trusted two people in my life, and one of those proved to be an error in judgment that I didn't see coming. Was this another mistake, or could I really trust Ryker?

He opened my door and held his hand out to me, the smile still in place with a quirk of his eyebrow. He probably knew the thoughts swirling in my head. I wasn't sure how he did it, but it seemed as though he knew what I was doing more than I even did. Could I trust him? Would I trust him?

I looked from his eyes to his hand and back to his eyes before sliding my palm across his. I guess I made up my mind. I just hoped I was strong enough to survive this.

He held the glass door open for me and slapped my ass as I passed by him. I threw a scowl over my shoulder as the bell above the door dinged. I quickly looked around and saw a girl standing behind a long counter with an eyebrow raised and a smirk on her lips staring directly at me. Not one to back down from a challenge, I raised an eyebrow back at her. She glanced back at Ryker with a softer smile that left me a little on edge. She was a beautiful girl with her long light brown hair pulled up in a high ponytail. Her hazel eyes were clear and assessing as she moved her gaze over me. My spine stiffened at her appraisal.

Ryker ran his hand up and down my spine in a soothing gesture that made me relax slightly. He always seemed to know what was going through my head even when I didn't. I didn't make friends with girls easily because most girls viewed other girls as competition, and I was never like that. Fighting over a guy was stupid and pointless, not that I had any guy in my life where fighting for him was an option. Carter was my brother in my head, and I didn't fight over him. Any of the girls who wanted to go head to head with me, Carter sent on their way saying they weren't worth it. I had to agree.

"This is Lorelei," Ryker said with his hand on the small of my back. "She runs the front desk and competes in local boxing competitions. Lorelei, this is my girlfriend, Bailey."

My head snapped in his direction at that introduction. I knew it was silly, but my stomach took off with butterflies flapping their wings furiously at the word girlfriend. His eyes were on me, a small smile on his face.

"It's nice to meet you, Bailey," Lorelei said.

I looked back at her, and she had her hand held out to me. I shook her hand squeezing a little which made her smile. She nodded in approval before looking at Ryker. "I like her."

"Me too," he answered wrapping his arms around my waist, his hard chest pressed into my back. I shivered in his arms, and he pulled me back into his embrace, making sure to press his hard on against my ass.

I held onto my composure and kept my body completely still which made Ryker laugh in my ear. With a kiss to my exposed neck, he released me and grabbed my hand pulling me around the counter. "Come on," he said. "I'll show you around."

"Come sit with me after the tour," Lorelei directed at me. She was still smiling, but her eyes were calculating.

"Maybe," I replied with a shrug. I wasn't going to take whatever shit she wanted to give me and just obey to her command. She nodded and winked at me before turning her attention back to her computer screen.

Ryker led me through the maze of heavy bags, explained the speed bags to me, and showed me all the weights they had for use. I could see the love he had for this place as he explained the equipment to me and dragged me through each section of the gym. He kept his hand on me as he introduced me to the guys spread out through the big space. He knew everyone by name, and they looked at him with respect.

When he went up to his office, I wandered around the room taking everything in. The equipment looked new, and the space was kept clean. The guys shot looks at me, but none made a move which made me somewhat grateful Ryker let it be known I was with him.

I had never been in a gym before, but I liked the feel of this one. It felt almost homey, the space cluttered with heavy bags and weights around a boxing ring. The ring had two guys in it sparring. Ryder was giving instructions while keeping his mitted hands up and moving his feet. They both had on protective gear and were circling each other.

I walked back to the front desk and stood next to Lorelei deciding to get it, whatever it was, over with. Ryker worked with her and probably saw her each day, so I figured I needed to understand the dynamic between them.

"I've never dated, kissed, or slept with him," she stated looking over at me.

"Okay," I replied like her comment didn't fill me with relief which it totally did. I knew he had been with other girls, but that didn't mean I wanted to know them or see them around him regularly.

"Look," she started turning her chair to look at me head on. "I had some issues. Ryker helped me off the streets and gave me a spot."

"Okay," I repeated not really knowing what else to say. I was fucking ecstatic they didn't hook up at some point, but relationships between girls and guys were a minefield of feelings waiting to go off. You just never knew when something would change.

"Lo," a deep voice said causing me to jump and spin around.

The voice belonged to a beast of a man. He looked to be a couple years older than me with a hard edge to him that spoke of a rough childhood. He had clear sea green eyes and sandy blonde hair cut short. He was built like the fucking Hulk and had full sleeves of tattoos on both arms. His biceps bulged as he leaned on the counter.

"Kole," she responded with an icy tone to her voice.

Hmmm, well that was interesting. I figured I wasn't needed so I walked away and left them to it. Neither one of them glanced back in my direction, clearly locked in some kind of battle with their eyes. Not knowing how long Ryker would be, I decided to get a run in on one of the treadmills placed in the corner of the room.

Ryder dropped out of the ring and stalked toward me. Yes, he stalked. I backed up which made his eyes narrow and his feet stop.

"How is Lyla?" he demanded.

"Why are you asking me?" I demanded. "You should ask her."

"She won't talk to me," he said quietly running his hand over his close cropped brown hair.

I didn't really know what to tell him. She texted back when I texted her, but she never answered the phone or her door. She only left for classes as far as I could tell. I didn't know how she was dealing or even if she was dealing at all.

Looking at Ryder, I saw the worry clouding his blue eyes. His eyebrows were dipped down, and a frown pulled down his lips. I would have felt intimidated if it weren't for concern he felt for Lyla. He was a big dude, an inch or two taller that Ryker and built, it was hard to see him like that. He wore a muscle shirt over his broad shoulders. He had tattoos on his chest and shoulders over his tanned skin.

"Don't give up on her," I told him quietly. I knew he would be so good to Lyla. I would never push anyone on her but after seeing the protective way he handled Lyla, I thought he would be able to help her. She needed a friend to get her through the abuse and aftermath of break up.

"Never," he said with such conviction I knew he meant it.

"Good," I nodded. "So, what's your role here?" I felt a little awkward standing there witnessing the pain he didn't try to hide. *Were all the Landrys so open with their feelings?* I didn't really know if I could get used to that. I have always hidden any emotion I may have had. Emotions were a weakness I couldn't afford. Once somebody found out what made you tick, it was all over, and torture was your daily, whether it was verbal or physical didn't matter. Any weakness was exploited to further somebody else. It was all about power in foster homes. The more power you had, the more essentials you had. You didn't have to fight for food, you were given food. You didn't have to fight for a bed, you were given one.

Anyway, changing the subject seemed imperative. I couldn't deal with my own emotions, I wasn't about to take on someone else's. He studied me a second before responding, "I train some of the boxers and teach self-defense classes a few times a week."

I nodded. "Have you ever boxed in competitions?"

"No," he shook his head and laughed. The smile transformed his whole face.

"Do you want to get in the ring?" he asked.

I tipped my head to the side and sized him up. I knew my weaknesses and what to avoid. A big guy coming at me in a ring didn't scream safe to me but for some reason I wasn't denying wanting to get in there as fast as I thought I would.

"Sure," I agreed surprising myself.

He lifted an eyebrow, "Yeah?"

"Yeah," I nodded decisively. "Let's do this."

His laugh boomed out to echo through the gym causing several heads to turn our way. He led the way to the ring.

Chapter Twelve
Ryker

Watching Bailey walk around my gym had struck something deep in my chest. She observed every area of the gym. She even sat in on one of Ryder's self-defense classes. She didn't talk to many of the people there, but that was the way she was. She was an observer, watching the interactions between everyone. She was a little stand offish with Lorelei when I introduced them, but after a little while I saw them laughing together. I figured she could see the way Lo watched Kole, not to mention the way Lo and I acted with each other. It was clear I thought of her as a sister. The guys in here for their workouts and training followed Bailey's movements through the gym, their eyes eating her up. She was wearing cotton shorts that hugged her perfect ass and a tee stretched across her chest, her breasts that filled my hands pushing against the fabric. She was fucking hot, and she wasn't even trying. It made me want to stand in the middle of the room and yell she was mine, but I figured it would make me look like a jackass. I just wrapped my arm around her and kissed the hell out of her in view of everyone before walking up to the office.

The gym was my future, a future I was working hard to make sure I did my dad's legacy justice. I wanted to bring the gym to the next level with some new ideas I was coming up with while maintaining my dad's integrity. He built this place with family and community in mind.

He had an after-school program set up for the kids who couldn't afford extracurricular activities to come in and off the streets. I wanted to build the program, and I was working on some ideas to make that happen.

I wanted to share this with Bailey. Would she want to be part of the gym? I know it was probably too early to think about how our futures would mesh, but I couldn't stop my brain from moving forward. I didn't even know if she had any plans for the future. The night we met, she mentioned she would like to go back to school, but she quickly changed the subject, so I didn't get any details about what she wanted to do.

Looking out the window, I saw Bailey and Ryder in the ring and had to smile. She had all the protective gear in place and was bouncing on the tips of her toes sparring with my brother. She had the most carefree beautiful smile I had ever seen on her face. He was speaking to her while she got into different stances, so I knew he was giving her beginner's instructions.

When she threw her head back and laughed at something Ryder said, I was a goner. I couldn't hear the laugh, but I knew it was beautiful just like her. Her blonde hair shimmered under the fluorescent light, and her face was lit up, a smiled stretched across her face. Her head tipped back, and she turned her head until her eyes met mine. Her smile softened and her eyes darkened. Even through the space separating us, I could feel the connection as strong as if we were standing next to each other.

She gave me a wink before she turned back to Ryder slapping her gloves together. I looked to Ryder and saw his eyes on me. He gave me a nod before turning his attention back to Bailey. I knew he understood the importance of Bailey, and he would take care of her while I did the work I went there to do.

I was so wrapped up in the work spread out before me that the knock at the door surprised me. My gaze shot to the doorway to see Bailey standing there looking uncertain nibbling on her bottom lip. I immediately got up and went straight to her, cupping her face in my hands and pulling her bottom lip out from between her teeth. I bent down and brushed my lips across hers softly. She wrapped her arms around my waist and returned the kiss.

I broke away slowly. "Are you ready to get home?" I asked looking at the watch on my wrist.

I was a little shocked to see I had been in the office for so long. She needed to be at work in a little while. Damn. I didn't mean to make her wait on me for so long.

"I'm so sorry, baby," I apologized. "I didn't realize I was up here for so long. Why didn't you come get me sooner?"

She shrugged with a soft smile on her face. "It was fine. I chilled with Lorelei, took a self-defense class, and got in the ring with Ryder which was surprisingly fun. I was fine, but I do need to get going if I want to be to work on time."

"I'm glad you had fun. If you want to come back, I'll give you the family discount," I said with a wink.

"Oh, yeah?" she replied with a sexy smirk on her lips with her head tilted.

"Yeah," I smirked squeezing her ass in my hands. "You get a free membership. You can work out here anytime you want and take whatever classes you want to."

She tried to pull back with a small frown on her face that I didn't like at all. When she came in here, she looked happy and carefree even flirting which I never saw her do, and I was enjoying it. Then, she looked mad. *What the hell?*

"What's wrong?" I asked not releasing her.

She was not running from me. I wouldn't let her. I would fix whatever I did, but I wouldn't let her go. I couldn't. I needed her.

"I can't come here for free. I'm not family. I thought you would give me like three free passes or some shit. I don't expect to use your equipment and stuff for free. I don't even know if I want to come here regularly!" she blurted in a rush, her face flushing red.

"Whoa, slow down, baby," I said sternly. "The family discount is free membership. I didn't mean to upset you. If you want to pay, we can figure it out later. All I meant was if you wanted to use the gym, you could. I liked the happy look on your face, and you said you had fun here, so I wanted to give you the option to come here as often as you wanted to keep that happy look on your face. I got caught up in the moment, and I'm sorry if I came off too strong."

I could see the anger slowly drain out of her as I talked, but she still hadn't relaxed her stiff posture which made me uneasy. I slowly drew my hands up and down her spine trying to comfort her from whatever was going on in her head. Her eyes stayed locked on mine, but I couldn't tell what she was thinking. The walls were back up, but I would wait her out.

After a few silent moments, she responded. "I don't want a handout. I do like the gym, and I want to come back. We can go over membership options and go from there. I don't want to spend a lot, so I might take a discount if I can get one, but I won't come here for free. I can't."

I nodded my head, "Okay. I'll grab some brochures, and we can get out of here."

She nodded and kissed me smacking me on the ass as I turned towards the desk. I looked back at her in surprise and saw a twinkle in her eye that made me laugh with relief. I had hit a nerve with her that I hadn't meant to, and I was worried she would keep a barrier between us. I was happy to see her back to how she was when she first walked in.

The next week went by, and I didn't see her at all. We texted everyday which she told me she wasn't much of a text person, but she made an exception for me because she kind of liked me. I laughed loudly when I read that standing in middle of the quad with people all around looking at me like I had lost my mind. I didn't care. She made me so fucking happy.

It sucked not seeing her all week, but I liked the texts. We were getting to know each other one random question at a time. I looked forward to seeing her name on my phone wondering what she came up with next to ask me. We kept the questions fun and playful, but I managed to slip in a few serious ones. Those she always took her time to respond to, but I waited her out and wasn't disappointed.

Now, I knew she was saving up her money to attend school to pursue a career in social work. She took online classes to get her GED since she dropped out when she was sixteen. I didn't know the details of what happened to her to make her leave Florida, but we were getting closer with each text.

We did manage to talk on the phone a few times which meant I got to hear her sexy, smooth voice. It turned husky when our conversation turned flirty and slightly sexual. I wanted to have phone sex with that husky tone in my ear, but she wasn't into that idea. I think I could convince her, though. She sounded intrigued even as she turned me down.

It was Friday night, and I was hoping to see her when she got off work. Every day she would go to the gym while I was in class and she'd be at work by the time I got there after football practice. I would go home and work on school work until I passed out.

"What's up, bro?" I asked Ryder as I walked into the kitchen to see him staring blankly into the refrigerator.

He looked up at me. "Nothing much. Are you hungry? I'm starving, and there's nothing in here. You want to order a pizza?"

"More like three pizzas," I laughed.

He knew I was right. One pizza would never be enough for the three of us. I didn't know if Logan was home or not, but I figured better safe than sorry. I wasn't giving up any of my pizza if I didn't have to.

He got out his phone and placed our usual order. I walked into the living room, sank down onto the sofa, and grabbed the remote from the side table. I flipped through the channels a minute before landing on an episode of *Impractical Jokers.* That show was some funny shit.

When Ryder walked in, I asked him, "How's Lyla?"

He shrugged, "I don't know. She only answers text from me, and she's not really giving me anything. She just says she's fine." He rubbed his hands through his hair and down his face in frustration.

"That sucks, man," I said not really knowing what else I could say. "Just give her time."

He balled his hands into fists on top of his thighs and clenched his jaw. "I'm fucking trying, but I want to be there with her to go through whatever that asshole did to her. I want to fucking help her, and she won't let me. It's fucking killing me."

I nodded and decided saying nothing would be better than giving him the general *she'll come around.* I didn't know if that was true, and it sounded like he was already on edge about the situation. I wasn't going to try and feed him any platitudes.

I wasn't sure what Lyla was to Ryder, but I could tell she meant something more to him than the friendship we always had with her. I wasn't sure what I would do if Bailey ever blocked me out completely, but I knew I wouldn't be able to walk away from her no matter how hard she pushed me.

Logan walked in the door with pizza boxes in hand. "I met up with the pizza guy in the hallway."

"Thanks, man," I said as he set them down on the coffee table.

We opened the boxes and grabbed slices. "What's up with you? I haven't seen you lately."

He avoided my gaze as he answered. "I've been around."

"I call bullshit," I said. "How's Riley?"

He flinched. "She's doing alright. She's been talking to that counselor on campus."

"Have you seen her lately?" I asked. "She wasn't at mom and dad's last weekend."

I texted her a few times, and she answered with short answers. She wouldn't answer my calls though, and that worried me. I didn't know what to do to help, but I wanted her to know I was there for her and always would be.

"I haven't really seen her, but I've talked to her a little. She seems to be coming back to herself," he commented with his eyes focused on the TV.

I glanced at Ryder to see him looking at Logan curiously. Logan was hiding something, but I knew from experience he wouldn't share no matter how hard we pushed him. I figured after the conversation with Ryder about Lyla and Logan about Riley, a change of topic was in order.

"What y'all got going on this weekend?" I asked.

"I think I am going to the party tomorrow night," Logan shrugged.

"I might show up, too," Ryder replied. "Are you going to go, Ryker?"

"I'll have to check to see what's up with Bailey. I think she works tomorrow night," I said taking a bite out of my pizza.

"So, it's like that, huh?" Ryder teased. "You have to ask for permission to go anywhere, now?"

"I'm not asking for permission," I said defensively. "I just want to be with her, and a party without her there is not my idea of fun."

They both laughed at me, but I didn't care. I didn't see the point in going to a party if Bailey wasn't beside me. I wondered what she would think about that, if she would even care if I went. I didn't know, but I knew I didn't want to and that was enough for me.

Sitting there with the both of them ribbing me made me smile. It felt like forever since we sat down and just hung out. We were inseparable growing up. I shared a room with Ryder at home, and Logan slept in our room more than the one he had in the house next door. We would spend hours playing on the gaming system or watching TV debating the hottest girls at school.

I walked down to the parking lot to throw the pizza boxes in the dumpster located in the corner looking down at my phone. Bailey should have texted by now, but maybe she had to work later than normal. I put my phone back in my pocket and started walking back across the lot.

When I first heard the sirens, I didn't really think much of it. I mean, our city wasn't all that bad, but bad choices were made everywhere. But when they got closer to our apartment, my stomach twisted. I looked to the road and saw two cruisers pull into the lot and screech to a halt in front of Bailey's building.

My heart raced as I took off running. As I ran past our entryway, I saw Ryder come out of our building and looked at the cop cars before he started running. I took the stairs up to the second floor two at a time. I felt like I couldn't get there fast enough, and Ryder was right behind me.

As soon as I hit the landing, I scanned the hallway seeing Lyla's door open and cops standing in the doorway. I felt horrible at the sense of relief I felt, but I pushed it back. I walked to Lyla's apartment and made my way around the cops.

Chapter Thirteen
Bailey

After working the night shift, I dragged my tired ass home. I went to the gym every day since Ryker brought me there last weekend, and my muscles felt it. It was a good kind of pain though. Ryder sparred with me in the ring, showed me some tips on the heavy bags, and had me pounding the speed bags until I felt like my arms would fall off. I felt stronger, and after taking a few of Ryder's self-defense classes, I felt safer than I ever had before.

Carter had shown me some basic self-defense moves after my shoulder healed up and my physical therapy was completed. I knew I had a chance to get away if I needed to, but after taking those classes, I had even more confidence I could handle myself.

I felt a calmness come over me at the gym I never had before. The gym gave me a deep sense of peace I craved on a daily. The smell of sweat and determination eased my mind knowing that I was stronger now. The sounds in a gym made my mind quiet as the grunts of intense workouts and the rock music blaring from the stereo competed to be heard. It was my happy place and my therapy. I worked out to get the demons to stop the torture. My mind and body concentrated on getting stronger, being able to protect myself. I never wanted to be caught without having a way to fight back again. Feeling helpless is the fucking worst feeling I could ever experience.

I hadn't seen Ryker all week, and I missed him. It was crazy how important he had become in my life. I woke up thinking about him and fell asleep with him on my mind. He even starred in a few of my dreams that had me waking up with my hand in my panties, but I would not be admitting that out loud to anyone. It was embarrassing how much I wanted him. Even hearing his voice on the phone turned me on. He tried to get me to have phone sex, but I had shut that down no matter how much I wanted to.

I wondered what he was up to tonight. He had texted me earlier asking me to let him know when I was home but hadn't mentioned any plans. I was a little disappointed he didn't say anything about coming over, but I tried to shrug it off. I could have asked him to come hang out, but something held me back.

As much as I didn't like to text, I didn't mind the texting game Ryker and I had going on. I liked the crazy questions we came up with each day. I didn't even mind answering the tough questions from him. I found it was a little easier to talk about the past through texts. I didn't want to dissect what kind of person that made me, so I didn't. I just went with it.

I was so wrapped up in my thoughts the raised voices didn't register until I was in front of my apartment door. My hand stilled on the doorknob, and my head snapped to Lyla's door knowing that's where the voices were coming from. A guy was yelling so loud I could hear every word, and none of it was good.

Cody.

I didn't stop to think or consider what I should have done. I walked to her door and turned the doorknob a lot slower than I wanted to. I still had the headspace to go in quietly, so I didn't spook anybody. I could only imagine what I was going to walk into and with the things I've seen, my imagination could pull up a lot of scenarios, none of them good.

I opened the door enough for me to see around, and I saw Cody had Lyla pinned against the wall yelling in her face. She had tears running down her face, but she was silent not letting one sound out. She stared him straight in the eye with her spine straight and head held high.

"You need to leave, Cody," she said sternly when he broke off his rant. "I will call the police."

"You fucking bitch," he said wrapping his hand around her throat.

She didn't even flinch, so I knew he wasn't hurting her, but I didn't like that hold on her at all. I wanted to end this before he decided to change her pain level. I pushed the door all the way open, the doorknob hitting the wall with a bang. Both of their eyes snapped to mine as I walked in.

"Take your hands off her," I stated with a glare.

"What the fuck are you doing here?" he demanded walking toward me. "We are in the middle of something, and I'm not done. You need to leave, bitch."

"Leave her alone," Lyla said shakily making a move towards where he stopped inches from me.

I pulled my hand back, my fingers balling into a fist like Ryder showed me and hit his nose as hard as I could. He yelled and grabbed his nose. I didn't contemplate the blood seeping in between his fingers. I lifted my knee and rammed it into his nuts making him drop to his knees.

I looked at Lyla to see her eyes wide and cell phone to her ear. I could hear someone talking on the other end, but Lyla wasn't responding. She was staring at Cody as he rocked back and forth on the floor, one hand cupping his dick, one hand cupping his nose.

"Lyla," I called.

She slowly lifted her wide-eyed gaze to mine. Her mouth was hanging open, and I was afraid she was going into shock or something. I hoped she wasn't mad I laid out her ex-boyfriend. I knew she had loved him, but damn, he deserved to get his ass beat. Obviously, he learned nothing from what Ryder did to him.

"Are you okay?" I asked walking around Cody to stand in front of her, blocking her view of him.

She nodded her head up and down slowly with her mouth still hanging open. "That was amazing," she whispered not blinking.

The voice on the other end of the phone got louder, and it seemed to have snapped Lyla out of her fog. She shook her head, took a deep breath, and squeezed her eyes shut for a second before opening them.

"Yes, he is down. He is not currently a threat," she said into the phone.

She listened to whatever the voice said before responding, "No, I don't need to stay on the phone with you. I can hear the sirens and some neighbors opening their doors. Thank you for your help."

She hung up the phone and stared at me in silence. I didn't know what she was thinking or feeling. I couldn't get a read on the situation, and it made me nervous. I liked Lyla. I considered her a friend, and I didn't want her to look at me differently because I sort of kicked her ex-boyfriend's ass. I wasn't stupid. I knew he could have hurt me if he really wanted to. He stopped moaning and groaning but made no move to get up off the floor. I could see him from the corner of my eye, and he was laying there staring at the ceiling in silence.

"Are you okay?" I asked again.

I knew she nodded her head, but I needed her to talk to me. I wanted to know she was okay physically and see where she was at mentally.

"I'm good," she said looking down before lifting her eyes back to mine. "He freaked me out, and it may sound stupid, but I don't believe he would have hurt my physically."

"I don't think he would have either," I agreed.

I could tell I surprised her. "Then, why did you hit him?"

I tilted my lips up in a small smile. "I didn't know it then. He had his hand wrapped around your neck, so I reacted. But if he wanted to really hurt you or me, he wouldn't be laying there staring at the ceiling waiting for the cops to show."

She quickly moved to look at Cody, but she didn't move toward him. I looked at him, and his eyes were on hers and filled with a sadness that matched the emotion in her eyes. They didn't say anything, just looked at each other.

The police charged into the apartment with their weapons drawn, taking in the room in one glance. They holstered their weapons and walked into the living room. One officer stood over Cody as the other stood in front of Lyla and me.

"What happened?" the officer asked.

Lyla recited the events of her evening. Luckily, Cody hadn't been there for long before I showed up. He threw around some insults and guilt trips. She kept her tone even and steady almost talking in a monotone. She was numbing herself, so she didn't feel the pain of the words he said to her. I knew that coping mechanism well. I've been using it for three years, and each day it gets harder and harder to hold onto that numbness.

Ryker.

He was changing everything for me. I wanted him in that moment. I wanted him to stand next to me and let me lean on him if I needed to. Even if I didn't allow myself to lean on him, I would know he was there if I needed him.

Blood started rushing in my ears, and my vision was hazy. I could hear the officer talking to Lyla, but I couldn't hear the words. My chest felt tight and heavy causing my breaths to come out in short pants. My hands were clammy, and I felt sweat slide down the back of my neck.

A hand on my arm made me jump backwards hitting my head on the wall. I started shaking as I tried to get out of the panic attack. I needed to get out, but the black was rising. The edges of my vision were gone, and I could feel my eyes rolling in my head, not focusing on anything.

I heard someone growl, "Back the fuck up," before I smelled him.

My head snapped up and I locked eyes with Ryker. I could feel my chest rising and falling with my unsteady breathing as I tried to force the air through my lungs. The relief I felt to see him almost brought me to the ground. He was there. He was actually there. My hands were trembling, and my eyes were watery with unshed tears. I was barely holding on, the panic attack so close to the surface.

His eyes scanned my face and body lingering on the cop's hand still on my forearm. His eyes locked on mine with a possessive glint that made me shiver. The cop turned to where I was looking over his shoulder and put his back to me. Ryker wasn't having it though. He charged through the room straight for me giving the cop no choice but to move out of the way.

He walked straight into my space and brought me into his arms. "I got you, baby. Breathe," he whispered in my ear running his hands through my hair and down my back. I inhaled the familiar clean fresh scent that was Ryker, exhaling slowly. The pressure in my chest easing, the black receded completely.

"Ryker," I whispered brokenly clutching his shirt in my fists.

"I'm here, baby," He kissed my temple.

"We still need to question Ms. Scott," a voice said to my right.

I buried my head in his neck and held him tighter. I didn't want to talk to anyone. I was too fucking shaky. The adrenaline of walking in on the scene with Cody, the aftermath, and the almost panic attack brought too much shit from the past into the now. I needed away from all these fucking people. I felt too open and exposed, everyone seeing the ugly in me.

"She'll have to do it later." I heard Ryker say above my head. His chest rumbled against my cheek as his deep, raspy voice filled my ears soothing me further. My body stopped trembling as I sank into him.

"Look I told you everything that happened. Do what y'all need to do, and if you have questions for Bailey, y'all can contact her tomorrow. I gave you her phone number," Lyla said.

Ryker wrapped his arm around my shoulders and urged me to turn, but I couldn't let him go. I needed the solid strength that oozed from him. I wanted to soak in it. I would be cold without his warmth surrounding me. I kept my face in his neck, and my hands tightened on him begging him to not let me go. He lifted me into his arms, and I circled his waist with my legs and wrapped my arms around his neck automatically.

I could feel all the people crowding the apartment as we made our way out into the hall, but I didn't lift my head. I let Ryker shield me in a way I never allowed anyone before determined to stand on my own. I allowed myself to bask in the feeling of being protected, of being safe. I heard the lock give as he twisted the key hanging out of my door. He walked us through the apartment straight to the bathroom after locking the front door and dropping the keys in the tray on the table that sat next to the front door.

He gently sat me down on the counter next to the sink unwinding my arms and legs slowly. I tipped my face up to him, and I could see the battle he was fighting in his eyes. He cupped my face and ran his thumb along my cheeks. He brought his lips to my forehead and stayed there for a minute. I closed my eyes, a heavy sigh of contentment leaving my lips. I reveled in the feeling of him holding me with such care and reverence, showing me he was there with me.

He pulled back staring intently at me. I reached up and ran my fingers along his jaw, his stubble tickling the palm of my hand making me smile. "I'm okay," I whispered as I leaned up to place my lips softly against his.

After setting the temperature for the shower, he turned his attention back to me. I sat up straight and lifted my shirt up and over my head tossing it to the floor. As I removed the rest of my clothes, he took off his. He held the shower curtain open as I climbed in. We both stayed silent as we stood under the water maintaining eye contact. I saw the way this affected him, the fear he felt when he stormed into the apartment, the relief at seeing me in one piece, the concern when I was losing it, the anguish at seeing me in pain. All of it was written all over his face, in his expressive brown eyes.

He washed my hair for me, massaging my scalp with soothing motions that had calming effects on me. I felt his arousal poke me when he rinsed my hair. I gasped as he ran the soap filled towel along skin that came alive with awareness. Droplets made trails down his skin as he kept his movements slow and steady. The comfort of his touch penetrated a place buried so deep I didn't even know it existed. Each moment spent with Ryker opened something new up within me. I was falling more and more, and instead of running, I was going to embrace it. Maybe I would run tomorrow, but today I was staying. I watched him wash his body quickly as I rinsed the suds off my body. My core clenched at the sight he made. Water dripped down his broad shoulders to his hard chest leading to the indents of his abs before stopping on his hard cock.

I couldn't resist wrapping my hand around him when he switched our positions. He hissed out a breath as the suds ran down his body and my hand tightened around him. I met his dark brown eyes filled with want. I parted my lips to allow more air and his nostrils flared.

He pulled me in for a hard kiss before he climbed out and grabbed a couple of towels from the rack above the toilet. I turned the shower off and stepped onto the mat. He wrapped a towel around his hips and held the other one up for me. I shivered walking into the plush terry cloth. He rubbed the towel over my body and hair before he wrapped it around my body. Letting him take care of me was a revelation. I liked it. I liked him in my space taking control. He led me out of the bathroom and into my room.

The shower was about comforting each other on an elemental level, and I needed that. I needed to feel his steady reassuring hands on me, feel the heat of his body there with me. Now, I needed him in a more raw and primal way. I wanted to feel alive. I wanted to know I survived and came out the victor.

I dropped my towel to the ground as soon as I heard the door click shut. I turned around to face him, my heart hammering in my chest. His eyes ran the length of my body following the trails of water falling from my hair along my chest down my torso. My nipples beaded up painfully as a growl made its way past his lips.

I locked my eyes with his and saw the same raw desire I felt radiating from him. I sucked in a deep breath as I walked toward him. I stood in front of him and dragged a finger down the middle of his chest stopping at the knot of the towel around his waist. I loosened the towel and let it fall to the floor.

"What are you doing, Bailey?" he asked curling his hands into tight fists, his forearms flexing.

I smiled at him as I dropped to my knees, his dick so close to my face it brushed against my lips when it twitched. I wrapped my hand around his shaft and stroked up and down once before swiping my tongue across the head.

"Tasting you," I said moaning as I tasted the pre-come pearling up out of the slit. I licked a line down the underneath of his shaft from the tip to his balls. I brought my tongue back to the head lapping up the moisture there. My eyes locked with his as I opened my mouth taking him in inch by inch until he reached the back of my throat. He let out a loud groan as he moved my hair away from my face, twisting it into his fist. I dug my nails into his thighs and moved my head up and down his length keeping my pace slow and steady. I wrapped my hand around the base of his dick and stroked the part I couldn't fit in my mouth.

"Bailey," he growled out as I swirled my tongue around paying special attention to the leaking slit.

As I pulled back, my tongue dragged along the throbbing vein running down the underside of his dick, and I felt his thighs flex under my hand. Saliva ran down the sides of my mouth as I sucked in a much-needed breath. I shifted my thighs together for friction when he groaned and fisted his hands in my hair as I took him down again. He pushed me a little farther, pushing past my gag reflex, and I swallowed instinctively.

"Fuck, your mouth," he cursed as our eyes locked.

He locked his jaw and parted his lips breathing heavily. His thigh under my hand was bunched. I grabbed both of his ass cheeks and pulled him further into my mouth, increasing my speed. He was close, and I wanted him to let go. I was so wet and throbbing watching the way he reacted to my mouth. I felt him swell in my mouth and, his hands tightened on my head.

"Bailey," he warned trying to pull out of my mouth. "I'm about to come."

I swallowed the head of his dick, and he started coming. I moaned moving my thighs restlessly as I took every drop. He slowly relaxed as his orgasm moved through him. He pulled out of my mouth slowly. I ran my tongue along my bottom lip to catch a stray drop I felt there, and he pulled me to my feet. He slammed his mouth down on mine and lifted me up. He laid me down on the bed covering my body with his. He devoured my mouth as his hands cupped my breasts pinching my nipples. He moved his mouth down my neck along my collarbone to my breast taking the whole thing in his mouth with one strong pull. He pulled back to glide his hands down my body.

His eyes watched his own movements before travelling to my face. His eyes were so expressive and had an intensity that caused more adrenaline to hum through my veins. I could see everything he was feeling in his eyes. He left himself open to me.

Ryker wanted me.

Ryker needed me.

He rocked back on his knees and spread my legs with a hand on each thigh. His eyes dropped down to stare intently at my core. I was wide open to his gaze. I couldn't believe how okay I was with him looking at me like this. I was never this comfortable, not even when I was by myself. I liked his eyes on me. I needed his eyes on me.

His nostrils flared when more wetness seeped out of my already leaking channel. He locked gazes with me right before he slipped two fingers inside of me quickly adding a third, working me over so fucking good. His eyes were the color of rich chocolate, intense with desire and need. I moaned and writhed as he pressed down on my clit while he massaged my pussy walls. He hit my g-spot, and I was done, coming on his fingers. He slowly removed his fingers making me moan at the loss. He brought his fingers to his mouth and sucked them clean. My eyes opened wide. That was hot!

He was looking straight up at me as his tongue took a slow slide into my core like he was savoring his favorite treat. My hips lifted trying to chase his tongue causing him to groan and lick faster, that groan, though. It sent vibrations through my pussy dragging a sharp gasp from my lips. My eyes fell shut as my back arched pushing myself closer to his mouth.

"You taste so fucking sweet," he groaned against me.

My eyes opened at his words, and I looked down at him between my legs. I moaned at the sight. His eyes had darkened to a rich chocolate color with his arousal. His nose was flared, his chest heaving with his uneven breaths. His light brown hair was tickling the inside of my thighs. His broad shoulders held my legs open. His teeth latched onto my clit while his fingers drove through my pulsating walls causing my second orgasm to erupt.

"Ryker!" I screamed.

He licked me gently as I came down. He slowly withdrew his fingers as he swiped his tongue along his bottom lip where my essence was smeared. I wrapped my hand around his neck and lifted up, so I could reach his mouth where I moaned when my taste reached me. I kissed him hard, showing my want for him. I wanted him inside me.

"Condom," he hissed breaking the kiss.

I tightened my hold on him and whispered against his lips, "I'm on the pill."

"You are?" he asked.

"After our accident, I went to the doctor," I murmured against his neck where I was running my lips.

I wanted him skin to skin with me, him bare. He took his cock in one hand to line up with my entrance and slowly sank inside of me. He stopped when he was buried to the hilt. He gritted his teeth when my pussy squeezed his naked dick.

I needed him to move. I shifted my hips urging him to move, "Ryker," I whispered.

He pulled almost completely out with only the tip of his dick inside me before he thrust back in hard, my breasts bouncing from the force. I lifted with each of his downward strokes slamming my clit against his pelvic bone. I was close. I was so fucking close I could feel my walls closing in on his length.

He growled as he bent his head pulling my nipple in between his teeth, biting and sucking the hard peak in his mouth. Two more thrusts, I was coming, clamping down on him so tight, he grunted with the power he needed to push through my quivering walls, his dick swelling.

He sat up onto his knees bringing me with him. His arms wrapped around my back, and his hands curled over my shoulders anchoring me to him. I gasped and moaned with the new position. He was as deep as he could be. We were as close as we could be to one another, and I savored it. I wrapped my arms around his neck and put my face in his neck. My hips started rocking, and he groaned as I clenched my core.

He slid his hands down and clasped my ass. We started rocking together harder and faster. He dug his fingers into my skin to the point of pain. I knew he was leaving marks, and I wanted them. I wanted to look at the marks and remember that moment I was his.

My nipples rubbed against his chest, the peaks as hard as pebbles as his course hair rubbed against my sensitive skin. I gripped his hair, my nails digging into his scalp. He slid one hand up my back to grab a fistful of my hair, the sting in my scalp when he pulled me back made me moan. His lips slammed down on mine as he thrust upward and pulled me down with his fingers on my ass, my clit crashing against him. He swallowed my scream as my pussy clamped down on his dick and started convulsing in a powerful orgasm.

"Fuck," he groaned breaking the kiss to bury his face in my neck.

His dick twitched and thickened as he thrust up harder and faster slamming me down until his orgasm took him, warm splashes against my walls. His arms banded around me keeping my body flush with his as the aftershocks of my orgasm quivered around him.

After our breathing slowed, he slowly laid me down on the bed before pulling away from me gently. We both groaned as he slid out of me. I watched him through half closed eyes walk out of the room and heard the water turn on in the bathroom. Then, I fell right to sleep.

Chapter Fourteen
Bailey

Despite the suppressive heat of the afternoon, I shivered slightly when I didn't see Carter's car in the driveway of the house we lived in together with the Baker's. Mr. Baker's rusted up Ford pickup truck was parked across the front yard, so I knew he was home. I didn't know if he had a job or not. He was coming and going at all different hours, so I never knew when he would be home or when he wouldn't.

I left work a couple of hours early because I didn't feel well. My head was pounding, and my stomach was cramping into tight knots making me want to puke. The walk from work a few miles away combined with the heat made it worse. I just wanted to curl up in my bed and sleep until it went away.

As I walked to the front door, I knew I should have just called Carter to come get me early. At the time, I didn't want to bother him when he still had an hour of work left to go. He was always there to help me with everything. I never had to be alone. He protected me. I felt like a burden most of the time which pissed him off when he heard me say that.

Walking into the house, I didn't hear or see anyone. I could hear the TV coming from the living room, but it was muted. Maybe he fell asleep in his chair while watching TV, and he won't notice I'm back.

I closed the door with a quiet click, and my eyes jerked in the direction of the living room. When I didn't hear any movement, I let out the breath I was holding, and made my way to the stairs. I went up the stairs as quickly and quietly as possible. I stepped over the step that squeaked out of habit and went straight to my room. I closed the door and fell back against it with a slight thump.

My heart was pounding, and my breathing was ragged making my head and stomach scream in protest. I made it to the garbage can in the corner of the room before I lost everything in my stomach. I was left shaking and dry heaving over the small can when I emptied everything I had which wasn't much.

Once my stomach settled and my breathing returned close to normal, my head felt slightly better. It still hurt, but it was manageable. I stood up on unsteady legs and took a deep breath. My strength was returning, but I was still sluggish. I went to my dresser and pulled out a T-shirt and some yoga pants. I tossed them on the bed, and drew my work uniform up and over my head. I dropped it in a heap on the floor beside my feet.

I was so tired. My arms felt like they were made of cement and so heavy to lift. My brain still throbbed in time with my heartbeat, the sound loud in my ears. I didn't hear my door open. I didn't hear him walk into my room when I reached down to grab my T-shirt.

The door slammed shut behind me and made me jump and scream in surprise. I whirled around and saw a fist coming toward my face. I staggered back from the blow that felt like it broke my face. I fell onto my bed and looked up at him with blurry eyes. He stalked to the bed and loomed over me with a horrifying look on his face that made me stop breathing in fear.

"I'm going to fuck that tight pussy," his voice in my ear, hot breath against my neck made me gag.

I tried to pull away from him, but he had me pinned against the bed. One hand had both my wrists pinned above my head, his whole body pushing into me. His other hand went between our bodies to grab my breast so hard I cried out. It felt like my nipple would pop off.

I tried to buck him off me, but that seemed to excite him more. He pushed his erection so hard into me my jeans dug into me so painfully it made me scream in pain. He laughed and grabbed my breast pulling my nipple. I bit my lip so hard to keep the scream inside me, I tasted blood. I let the copper taste bring me to another place where there wasn't pain. I checked out of the situation.

I didn't know how long it would take Carter to find out I was back here, so I didn't have hope he would be able to get me out of this situation. I let my body go limp and stopped fighting. Mr. Baker was a big man. He was tall with a wide chest. His shoulders and biceps bulged with muscles from doing manual labor. He was also sick and twisted which made him extra dangerous. I wouldn't be able to fight him.

He didn't seem to like my surrender though. His hands became rougher pulling my breast and squeezing until a small sound of distress escaped my lips. He sneered at me, and I turned my head away from him staring blindly at the window where sunlight peeked around the edges of the curtains that were closed.

He let go of my breast and tangled his hand in my hair pulling so hard my scalp burned and tears sprang to my eyes. He jerked my head back until I was staring in his cold and dead eyes. I shivered under the glare of those lifeless eyes.

He levered his body up enough for him to slip his hand roughly in my jeans. He grabbed my already bruised mound in hard grip. He shoved two of his thick fingers in my dry core so hard and so deep I couldn't contain the pain anymore. My hips jerked away from his touch, but he just dug his fingers deeper. The tears fell from my eyes, and I started screaming so loud my migraine came back with a vengeance.

He pulled his hand out of my pants and pulled back sharply. He back handed me across my cheek which caused my head to whip to the side and my scream to cut off abruptly. He let go of my wrists causing my arms to fall loosely at my sides where they tingled from the lack of blood flow his tight hold created.

My head turned sharply, and my eyes widened when he wrapped his strong hands around my throat pressing his fingertips into my skin so hard I knew I would have marks left behind. He squeezed until my vision became spotted with white dots.

"Shut the fuck up and take it like a good little slut," he growled so close to my face spit splayed across my face making me cringe and shut my eyes tightly.

My eyes flew open, and my hands grabbed onto his wrists trying desperately to get him to let go. My nails bit into his hand causing blood to dot his skin. I scratched up his arm just as hard causing him to let go of my throat. I gasped as much air as I possibly could which made me dizzy and light-headed.

"You stupid fucking bitch," he roared at me. He reared back and balled his massive hand into a fist.

He hit me on the temple, and I blacked out. The pain was unbelievable. My head felt like it was going to fall from my body. I felt blood trickle down the side of my face. The metallic taste in my mouth let me know I bit into the inside of my cheek when his fist met my head.

Suddenly his weight was off me and there were sounds of a struggle, but I couldn't open my eyes to see what was happening or who it involved, but I knew. Living the way I have, you learn to hone all your senses not relying so heavily on sight. I smelled the motor oil and sweat that clung to him wherever he went.

"Let's go," I heard through the fog surrounding me.

The voice sounded far away and tiny, but I could feel a hand on my shoulder.

I moaned trying to open my eyes. I managed to open them to slits, the bright overhead light making me squeeze them shut again.

I was going to be sick. The throbbing in my head getting more intense with each breath I took. My stomach rolled. There was a steady pressure on my side that felt like my lung was being squeezed. I felt something dripping over my eyebrow to the corner of my eye.

I suppressed another moan when I opened my eyes slowly adjusting to the brightness. Carter was fuzzy in my vision. His grip on my shoulder was warm and comforting. I sighed in relief when his face became clear in front of my own.

"We have to leave," he said sternly reaching for my hands. He wrapped his long fingers around my wrists and pulled me until I was standing in front of him.

"Ahhh," I tried to contain my pain, but my wrists were bruised and throbbed.

He let go of my wrists immediately, and I flopped back on the bed with a bounce that made me groan and grab my head to keep it attached to my body. I had to close my eyes and take a deep breath to settle the rolling in my stomach.

I opened my eyes and could only stare at the look on Carter's face. His strong jaw was even more chiseled than normal. He was locked so tight, his jaw twitched. He looked like he was made of stone and was so close to crumbling with the heat of his anger surrounding him. I'd never seen him like this before. He'd always been gentle and careful with me like I was made of glass, and he was afraid he would break me. I'd never seen him lose control and surrender to the intense emotions he hid from the world. I didn't know what would happen if he did let go and follow his heart instead of his head, but I did know that I loved him.

His crystal blue eyes looked like ice urging me to get up. His strong hands slid under my arms and lifted me gently to my feet. He gripped my shoulders to steady me when I swayed slightly. His eyes darkened with black clouds making his eyes look gray, and his nose flared as his gaze tracked across my face. He took a deep breath after seeing each mark and cut that covered my face and on my neck around my throat. His eyes landed on my chest before they closed tightly while he took a deep breath and held it.

I looked down and saw my breast was still uncovered pushed up with the cup of my bra holding it. I had bruises in the shape of a hand covering my flesh, and my nipple was bleeding. I let out a small whimper when I pulled my bra back into place and my nipple pushed against the fabric.

"I'm okay," I assured him as I took a deep breath through the pain and stood up on my own. "Let's go."

I reached down and grabbed the T-shirt that was still on my bed, but I froze when a low moan came from behind Carter. I turned around with the shirt held tightly to my chest and looked at the body sprawled limply on the floor. I sucked in a sharp breath, and my eyes widened at the sight before me. There was blood covering his face, and one of his arms was positioned at an odd angle. He had a big knot on his forehead with a cut in the middle that had blood flowing from his hairline and dripping down his chin to pool in the hollow of his neck.

He didn't move or open his eyes making me release the breath I was holding slowly. Carter's hand appeared in my vision, the bloody knuckles made my eyes jerk to his. I saw determination and love and fury and hate swirling in the vortex of his blue orbs. His eyes were searching mine intently just like mine were searching his. He did this for me. He protected me. I had to be strong for him like he was strong for me.

I nodded, "Let's go," I repeated.

He nodded and turned to the door that was standing open. The doorknob was stuck in the wall like it was thrown open hard. He grabbed my hand with one of his own linking our fingers together and a duffel bag with the other that was on the floor at the end of the bed. I tightened my fingers around his as I picked up my guitar case that stood on the other side of the doorway and slung it over my shoulder.

I stayed close to his back as we made our way down the hallway to the stairs. Some of my aches and pains were coming back, and I was trying to push them down. My head was a little foggy as I followed Carter down the first few steps. We both froze when I stepped on the loose board and, the stair creaked loudly.

Shit! I stopped breathing and stood there frozen. What if the noise was enough to wake him up? The memory of his harsh, mean hands on me made me shake. What would he do to me next time? What would he do to Carter? Flashes from the attack were crowding my brain trying to make a slideshow. I felt moisture sliding down my face, and my chest felt heavy.

I was jerked back to the present when Carter tugged on my hand to get me to keep moving. I shook my head to clear it and regulated my breathing until I felt the pressure in my chest ease up. I had to get free before I fell apart. Freedom and safety were what mattered right then. I could deal with everything else as soon as we were free and safe. My eyes met his and I nodded.

We made it to the front door without making another sound. Carter's hand turned the doorknob, and the door opened an inch. Then, I let out a wail of agony from the fire burning in my shoulder. My hand fell limp in Carter's, but he didn't let go. He turned us so fast my shoulder slammed into the door causing me to whimper. Carter's back was against my front, my whole body hidden by his. I pulled the strap of my guitar case over my head so that it crossed over my chest. I needed the freedom to use my hands to help escape this shit storm.

"Where the fuck y'all think y'all going?" Mr. Baker growled.

I shivered clinging to the back of Carter's shirt. Even though I couldn't see him, his voice scared the fuck out of me. It was evil. It was demented. It skittered along my already frayed nerves straining the strength I just managed to gather back.

"We are leaving," Carter stated in a calm and steady voice, but I could feel his body tense ready to spring in his direction. "And you are going to let us."

My hands fisted tighter in his shirt, my forehead pressed in between his shoulder blades, my eyes squeezed shut. I had to get my head straight and help get us out of here. Carter needed me to be strong. I couldn't keep hiding behind him. If something happened to Carter because of me, I would die.

I could feel the tension radiating from him casting an intense heat along the front of my body. His muscles in his shoulders and biceps were clenched so tightly his vein that ran down the side of his neck was throbbing wildly. He started moving forward slowly, and I followed like we were performing a well-practiced dance. We knew how to read each other's bodies to determine the steps we needed to take to survive. We'd encountered several situations that we managed to escape with no damage. This time there was so much damage, but we could survive with the way we were in sync with each other.

Carter stopped his forward motion when there was enough room for me to grab the edge of the open door. We were standing off to the side, and if I could get the door opened a few more inches, we would be able to slip through.

I held my breath and backed up a step bringing Carter with me from my fist that was twisted in his shirt. The door opened more, and I took another step back when his voice stopped me.

"Like hell y'all leaving," Mr. Baker growled followed by a click of a bullet moving to the chamber of the gun I could see when I peeked around Carter's shoulder. The sight of that gun made me remember the pain in my shoulder, and I looked down to see my shirt being soaked with the blood oozing out of the gunshot wound.

Wood splintered right above our heads as a bullet went through the door. I jumped and clutched tightly to Carter as he moved us backwards.

"We are," Carter stated firmly. "We are done here."

He moved back swiftly moving us through the door and slamming it closed before Mr. Baker could react. I turned around and started running with Carter right behind me. I could hear the front door open and heavy footsteps against dead grass following us.

Boom! I flinched from the loud sound, and my steps faltered.

I heard Carter grunt, and I didn't feel his heat at my back anymore.

I slowed down and started to turn around to see if he was hurt, but he stopped me with his hands on my hips giving me little before letting go.

"Keep going." His voice sounded tight and raw. "I'm good."

I knew he wasn't good, but there was nothing I could do about it until we were away from this house. My adrenaline was rushing through my body so hard, I could run faster and harder than I had ever ran before. It was not long until I couldn't hear Mr. Baker's heavy steps behind us. I looked over my shoulder and locked gazes with him. He was wavering on his feet before his body gave out and fell to the ground.

I snapped my gaze to the front of me and kept going. We ran for miles weaving in and out of the subdivision, my guitar a solid weighted thudding against my back with each slap of my feet against the ground. I had no idea where we were going, but I followed Carter knowing he was going to get us to safety. Even though I saw him fall, I still needed to put as much distance between us and Mr. Baker as possible. I didn't want to take any chances of him catching us. I trusted Carter to get us to a safe place. He's the only one I have ever trusted in my life. He would never hurt me. He's a protector. He's been my protector the entire time we have been together.

We finally stopped after what felt like hours of running. The sun was dipping low in the sky and the sweat on my skin was drying a little from the wind moving the stifling air around me. I think we were behind a school, but I was so mixed up in my head I couldn't focus. Once we stopped, all my pain came rushing back as the adrenaline rush wore off. I felt so weak and dizzy as painful tingles ran from my shoulder to my fingers leaving my arm hanging useless along the side of my body. My ribs hurt like a mother and trying to breathe steadily was difficult. One eye was almost swollen shut. My lip stung from where it was split, and my mouth was extremely dry. My head throbbed with an intensity that had my stomach cramping into a tight knot. I didn't have anything left in my system to come up, but I dropped to my hands and knees anyways. My guitar case was heavy against my back. I couldn't stop the dry heaves that wracked my body. My skull felt like it would break open from the pounding it was taking. My eyes watered, and I gasped for breath.

Carter dropped to his knees in front of me, his eyes full of concern and love. Unshed tears shined in his eyes, his face full of determination. Blood seeped down the sleeve of his shirt. He cupped my face, and his thumbs brushed the tears away. He gently removed the guitar case and set it to the side.

He maneuvered us to where he could hold me on his lap. He pressed his lips softly against my forehead. My eyes closed as I leaned into him further. I felt him move slightly before settling down again. I opened my eyes to see him putting his phone to his ear.

"Angie, we need you."

I closed my eyes and let his voice and warmth soothe me. It still hurt to breathe, but I inhaled deeply anyway. His scent washed over me, oil and man. That scent was my safe place. If I could smell him, I knew I would be alright and I could let my guard down because he had me.

He ran one hand soothingly down my back while whispering comforting words in my ear. Even though the temperature was still high, and Carter's heat surrounded me, my body was still shaking like crazy. My teeth chattered so loudly my head was going to blow wide open. My lungs burned, and I let go.

I was done.

I was gone.

I had no fight left.

We were safe and free.

I welcomed the black void that took the pain away.

"You will be okay, Bailey," I heard Carter whisper as I floated into nothingness.

I sat straight up in bed gasping and clutching my chest. My body was covered in sweat and tangled up in the blankets. My heart was pounding furiously. Fuck! It had been a long time since I had the nightmare that I wish was actually a nightmare and not part of my reality.

I looked over at Ryker to see him sleeping soundly, a peaceful look spread across his face. I had to get out of there. I was aware I was running away again, but what other choice did I have? I had to get away from all these feelings and uncertainties before I lost my shit completely.

Chapter Fifteen
Ryker

When I woke up, I realized right away I was alone in the bed. I reached out my arm searching for Bailey, but she was gone. The sheets were cold meaning she left a while ago. Fuck! She ran again, out of her own damn apartment.

I rubbed my hands roughly down my face before rising from the bed gathering my clothes from the chair in the corner of the room where I dropped them after watching the towel fall from Bailey's body. Shaking my head of the image, I looked at my phone to see it was a little after eight. Maybe she went on a run and would be back soon. I knew she had a lot of stuff in her head she needed to wrap herself around.

Last night was intense, the altercation with Cody's dumbass, the panic attack, and the powerful lovemaking. I wasn't surprised she ran. That was a lot of shit to deal with. I had hoped we were moving past that, but I could be patient.

It had only been basically a week since we had been together, but the need to protect was stronger than anything I've ever felt something for. I wanted her to feel safe whenever I was around. I needed to be the one to help her. I needed to be the one to bring her back to me. She was mine. I needed her to need me like I needed her, to walk, to talk, to eat, to sleep, to fucking function in daily life. If I knew she would be with me, I knew I could accomplish anything.

After locking up her place, I went to mine to change into some gym shorts and tee. I noticed Carter's truck wasn't in the lot, so I figured I would head to the gym to see if Bailey was there. If she wasn't there, I could get a workout in and see what was up in the office. I would give her a couple hours before I went searching. I would find her. I had to find her. I had to stop letting her run from me, from us.

As soon as I stepped through the door of the gym, my eyes scanned the interior until my eyes landed on Bailey running on a treadmill, and I knew something was seriously wrong. I could tell she was deep in her head. Her high ponytail was swinging back and forth with the speed she was moving. I could see the wires hanging from her ears, her arms and legs moved in sync.

I watched her turn the machine off as I started moving in her direction. She was wiping her brow with the towel hanging around on the handlebars. Before I could reach her, I saw her whole body tense up and the towel fall to the ground. Her eyes were opened wide in shock with her lips parted.

A movement to her left caught my eye, and I turned to see some guy I had never seen in here before with his hand on Bailey. He had his fucking hand on my fucking girl. She was fading into a panic attack, and he still had his fucking hand on *my* fucking girl.

"Back the fuck up," I growled as I crowded in the guy's space, getting between him and Bailey.

His arm fell to his side and his face showed pissed off confusion.

"Who the fuck are you?" he demanded.

"Her man," I answered tersely.

I didn't want to have a discussion with this motherfucker. I needed to see to Bailey. Every second I wasted with this douchebag, the more pain she would endure. Fuck that. I turned my back on him and pulled her body to mine.

"Hey," I heard douchebag start before he was interrupted.

"Back the fuck up," another voice ground out.

I turned my head back clutching Bailey to my chest and came eye to eye with Carter before turning his back on me giving Bailey privacy.

"Now, who the fuck are you?" douche demanded.

"Her brother," Carter growled out. "You do not get in her space, you do not talk to her, and you sure as fuck don't fucking touch her. Got it?"

I had to get her out of here now. Every person in the gym had stopped to watch this showdown and it was going to bring attention to her panic attack. I knew she would fucking hate to know anyone saw her weakness. I knew by the look in her eyes, she wasn't even there, but when she came back to herself, she would probably disappear in some other kind of way.

She had shut down completely. Possessive anger coursed through my veins just knowing some asshole in my fucking gym caused this. I still didn't know her past, but I did know I had to be able to bring her back. I felt like that is a major exam I had to pass. She has had a few moments where she would go somewhere I couldn't go. I always managed to get her back, but this was on a different level. She was seriously gone in that moment. Last night triggered something major for her, and the guy touching her was the final nail in the coffin.

I scanned the crowd until I locked eyes with Ryder and Logan. They both nodded and stood on either side of me and Bailey providing some protection for the curious stares. We pushed our way through the people and made it to the locker rooms. I felt Carter follow us in, and I was too worried about Bailey to be pissed about him invading our moment. He didn't say anything as I handled her. He just stayed still watching my every move, but never intervening.

I cupped her face between my hands and tipped her face up, so I could see her eyes. I sucked in a sharp breath at what I saw there, nothing. There was nothing in her beautiful green eyes, the gold flecks nonexistent. I blocked her body from Carter with mine. I was sure he had dealt with his share of her panic attacks considering how long they had been around together, but I couldn't let him see this one. This one was mine. I had to get her back. I needed to get her back.

I pressed my lips against hers gliding slowly with a gentle brush of a kiss. Her body jumped slightly at the contact, and her body tried to slide away. I sat down on the bench running through the middle of the room pulling her stiff body down with mine. I gripped her thighs positioning her stiff body until she straddled me. I pulled each of her arms and laced them behind my neck.

I ran my thumb along her jaw. "Bailey," I whispered. My lips brushed hers with each word I spoke. I could feel her breath in quick bursts against my skin. "Come back to me, baby. You're safe. I've got you."

She was still gone, and my chest felt heavy. I needed her here with me. I put my mouth next to her ear. "I'm here, baby. I've got you. Come back, Bailey."

I kissed her again, slowly brushing my lips back and forth across hers. She was so cold. I felt a pressure behind my eyes that I wouldn't be giving into. I needed her to come back to me. I licked the seam of her lips. Her nostrils flared, and she inhaled sharply. I pulled back to look at her eyes again and saw a small spark of gold filter in the emerald. I pushed my hands into her hair and pulled slightly causing her breath to stutter and her body to soften against mine. I kissed her roughly letting some of my panic and desperation seep into the way I took her mouth. I broke the kiss when I felt her body tremble and heard her soft moan.

She inhaled deeply, her chest rubbing against mine. She opened her eyes wide showing me she was back. I couldn't help nor stop the give in my body from my relief. I sagged into her giving her some of my weight, my grip on her butt and her neck tightening.

"Fuck," she groaned shaking her head. She rested her forehead against mine and took several deep breaths.

Her head lifted and took in her surroundings. I lifted my head up and scanned the room with her. Carter was still standing in front of us, but he had his back to us. I felt her body tense up again.

"I'm fine," she said shakily. She was breathing heavily. Her whole body was shaking, and her muscles were locked up tight.

"No," I answered. I couldn't let her go yet. I had to convince myself she was back. That she was going to be okay. I could see the walls come up, and I didn't want that. I pulled her down against me and just held her.

Carter turned around. "Are you okay, Bai?"

She glanced at him before looking away. "I'm fine."

"Bailey," Carter said sternly, her eyes snapping to his immediately. "Talk to me. Lay it out for me. You haven't had an attack like that in fucking forever. What the fuck happened?"

She made a move to get off my lap, but my hands tightened. She looked down at me with a glare in her eyes. "I need to talk to Carter, and I will not do that on your fucking lap. Let me up."

Logically, I understood what she was saying, but fuck it hurt to let her go. I slowly released my hold on her dragging my lips across hers one more time. She kissed me back before rising which I took as a positive sign.

She turned to face him looking him in the eye. "Last night Cody was in Lyla's apartment yelling a whole lot of bullshit. I could hear every word as I made my way up the stairs. I went in and saw his hand wrapped around her throat, and I reacted. Then, the cops and paramedics were there crowding the space. Ryker showed up and stayed at our place."

"What?!" he yelled. "Why the fuck didn't you call me?"

"You were in Baton Rouge, at least two hours away! Everything was under control. There was nothing you could have done!" she exclaimed.

"I don't give a fuck where I am or what the fuck I'm doing, you call me. You fucking call me if some shit goes down," he said keeping a tight leash on the strong emotions crossing his face.

I could see his fists balled at his sides, his forearms flexing with the motions, his face was set in stone, a muscled jumped in his cheeks, his nostrils flared, and his eyes were glassy.

She walked until she was toe to toe with him, her head tilted back to maintain eye contact with him and her hands fisted on her hips. "Carter, you are my brother and will always be my brother. You have protected me from the jump, and you've always kept me safe. Since we've been on our own, you've taught me how to protect myself. I have learned a lot from the self-defense classes I've been taking so I could handle the shit that went down with Cody. It wasn't the same as when I was fucked up by Baker."

Baker? Who the fuck was Baker? I didn't know, but I sure as fuck was going to find out.

"Where's Cody now?" Carter demanded.

"The cop that took our statements called this morning and told me Cody had bailed out this morning," she answered. "Lyla didn't drop the charges, but his parents put up the bail money, so he was released. He has a court date in a couple of weeks, and we may have to be there."

That motherfucker was out already? That was news to me. I needed to talk to Ryder and see what was up. I was sure he was more than a little concerned about Lyla and her headspace when it came to him.

"What else?" Carter gritted out making my eyes snap to Bailey.

"I had the nightmare last night," she shrugged like it was no big deal.

"What the fuck?" I asked. "What nightmare? Why didn't you wake me?"

I saw her head drop forward before turning towards me. "I had nightmares for a while, but I hadn't had one in a while until last night."

She turned back to face Carter, and I let her have that. I would know about these nightmares, but not in front of anyone. It would be a conversation for me and her, just like what happened with this Baker person. Today was the day she would let me in and have her hurts.

"Look, Carter," she said gently laying her hand on his taunt arm making me grit my teeth. "We can hash this out later. I want to go home."

"Fine," he relented. "But we will be talking."

"Let's get out of here," I said standing up. I needed to get her to her safe place. I figured her place would be where she wanted to be. I was going to stay with her though.

We left the gym and drove to the apartments in silence. She had her eyes closed and her head resting against the window during the entire ride. I let her have her time because I could not begin to imagine how she was feeling after what I witnessed.

We walked through her apartment and curled up on her bed, my body spooning behind hers, holding tightly with the knowledge she was safe and in my arms. I listened to her soft breathing even out and let the steady rise and fall of her chest under my hand lull me to sleep.

I woke up slowly to the feeling of soft flesh pushing into my hardness, and I groaned tightening my arm wrapped around her. She put one arm behind my neck as she rocked her hips against me. I became fully awake when I heard her moan and felt her shudder.

I didn't waste any time. I pulled her panties down to her knees and pulled my cock out of my boxers. I slid all the way inside of her welcoming heat and took her in an amazing love making. It was slow and unhurried despite the need pounding in my blood. I ran my hands along her skin as I kept the pace steady and deep. She thrust back into me and made my eyes cross.

I needed more. I wanted to keep it slow but every time we were together, the need became too great. Without pulling out of her, I moved her to her hands and knees and I pounded into her from behind. We both reached our climax together screaming each other's names.

I slowly pulled out of her and made my way to the bathroom to clean up and get a wet washcloth for her. I walked back in the room to see her in the same position I left her in, her eyes closed and small smile on her face.

I ran the warm cloth between her legs, and she moaned when the rough fabric met her sensitive skin making me chuckle. I placed the soft press of my lips against her temple dropping the cloth on the floor.

"Are you okay, baby?" I teased.

"I think you killed me," she giggled.

"You feel alive to me," I commented.

"You ready to talk, yet?" I asked as I settled on my back with an arm under her head.

I felt her shrug her shoulders and looked down to see her biting her bottom lip. "Seeing cops pull up in front of your apartment last night scared the fuck out of me," I admitted. "I wanted to hold you last night. I needed to hold you last night. Then, I woke up alone."

"He didn't hurt us," she reminded me, but I think she needed the reminder too.

"What all went on last night?" I asked needing to know the details.

She rolled to her back and stared at the ceiling. "I heard him yelling, and I went in. He had his hand around her throat. I didn't think he was hurting her, but I reacted anyway. I got his attention and when he came toward me, I punched him in the nose and kneed him in the nuts. That's it. That's all that happened."

"You went in without knowing what you were walking in on?" I asked tightening my hold on her hip.

She tensed and said, "It wasn't smart. I know that, but I had to get to Lyla."

"What if he had a weapon?" I demanded. "What would you have done?"

"I don't know, but I couldn't do nothing! She's my friend, and I had to help her especially after what I endured!" she flung the covers back and sprang out of bed.

"Baby," I said wrapping her in my arms. "What did you endure?"

I didn't think she would answer. She kept her eyes glued to the ceiling and I could see her body grow tense. She took a deep breath. "I grew up in foster care. I know what it is to be alone and face bad shit every day. I lived that life. Lyla is not alone. She needed to know that," she expressed with a tear falling down her cheek and her eyes glistened with unshed tears.

"Fuck," I breathed against her forehead.

"Not all the homes were bad," she said with a sad smile on her face. "There was this one couple I didn't mind too much. The mom looked like a hippie and always smelled like pot, but she was nice. The last home, though? That one was the worst. I was caught home alone with Mr. Baker. He was a dirty asshole who liked the monthly checks among other perks. I made sure I was never alone with him, but one day I miscalculated. He attacked, but Carter ended it."

I focused on keeping myself steady and tried to tamp down the anger coursing through me at what she had to endure. I held her and breathed evenly brushing my lips across her forehead in encouragement. "What did he do to you?"

"He attacked me. I fought back, but he was too fucking big and overpowered me. He knocked me around, and I passed out at one point. When I came to, Carter was there," she said quietly with a slight waver in her voice.

I felt the tear roll down my face at her admission. I knew something bad had happened to her, but I wasn't prepared for the anger and hurt I would feel at knowing the truth. I wanted to kill the motherfucker. I wanted to beat the fuck out of everyone who ever harmed her. She was the kindest, gentlest, and truest person I had ever met. Nobody would touch her ever again. I was so fucking pissed at everyone who ever harmed her mentally and physically.

It killed me to sit there and listen to her recount the horrible events of her life. I wanted to go to her and pull her against me, let my warmth soak into her trembling body. She had gotten dressed before she started talking. She had her arms wrapped around herself protectively which hurt to see, but her voice hurt was worse to hear.

Her tone was flat, monotone as she told me all her ugly truths. She stated the events of her life in a matter of fact way, her walls were stacked so high and were reinforced with steel. It hurt to keep my distance, but she needed my silent strength to get it all out. I had to keep my shit locked down. The rage tried to consume me, but she couldn't see that. She needed me to listen to all of it, so I sat there with my fists clenched, jaw tight, and face blank. At least, I hoped my face didn't show the furious turmoil racing through me. I wanted fucking blood.

My life had been fucking rainbows and unicorns compared to hers. I've always known I was lucky to have the home life I did, but Bailey's story drove that point home. My parents were strict, but fair. We never went a day without knowing we were loved. Even with six of us, my mom and dad had always given us each our own attention. Not to mention, we always knew where we would sleep at night.

"When we were escaping, he shot both of us. He got me in the shoulder and Carter in the thigh. We ran and never looked back," she pulled back to look me in the eye and said with conviction. "I didn't want it to be worse for Lyla."

She was shot?! He fucking shot her?! My finger reached out to softly brush against the scar I knew was hidden underneath her dragonfly tattoo. Her eyes flew to mine with unshed tears. I didn't know what caused the scar before that moment, but I knew it was there.

"I know, baby," I said letting out a long breath. "I understand what you wanted to do for her. I promise I do understand, but if something ever happened to you, I wouldn't survive it. Promise me you will be more cautious and continue going to classes at the gym."

I knew I couldn't stop her from wanting to help, but I could make sure she was more prepared.

She nodded and gave me a sleepy smile. "I promise."

"Was the nightmare last night about what happened to you?" I asked gently. I needed to know what I was up against, but I also needed to know what to watch for and find a way to help her that didn't cause her to run away from me.

"Yeah," she sighed snuggling into my side. "I used to have them all the time, but then I found drugs and alcohol illuminated them pretty well. For about a year, I made sure I didn't go to sleep sober. Hard liquid, pills, weed, it didn't matter what I had. If I was on a level, the nightmares stayed away."

"Are you a recovering addict?" I asked. I never saw her with a drink, and she never looked to be on anything. I'd seen her with blow pops, mints, and gum. She always tasted like candy to me.

"No," she shook her head. "I didn't get far enough to be an addict. I didn't need it to survive. I just wanted to keep the nightmares away. Carter wasn't having that shit though. He got me cleaned up. I went to some meetings and met with a therapist. I still call our last social worker, Angie, sometimes just to talk. She helps. She is the one that helped us get out of the system and on our own. She is one of the reasons I want to go into social work. The way she actually cares for those kids is inspiring."

She had been through so much, and I wanted to ease the way for her now. I wanted to show her what life could really be if she would just let me. "I'm glad you had them, baby, but I'm here now. I don't like you running from me, Bailey. If something happens, I need you to talk to me. If you have a nightmare, wake me up, and we will talk and lay together until it's gone."

"I can try," she said softly laying her head on my chest.

"That's all I ask, baby," I kissed the top of her head and curled my arm around her.

"Okay, Ryker," she said with a yawn.

"Alright," I said. "Let's get some sleep."

"Okay," she mumbled into my skin.

Sleep didn't come easy for me with all the information she had shared with me. To know that she was hurt at one point killed me. That's where the panic attacks came from, and now her nightmares made her relive that shit. I hoped like hell I could help her.

Chapter Sixteen
Bailey

Ryker: I'll pick you up at 6.

I couldn't look away from the last text Ryker sent. The one he sent thirty minutes before. I'm not sure why it raised the alarms in my head. It just felt like more of whatever we were. We never labeled it, and I was beyond grateful for that. Being close to anyone scared me to the point of wanting to run, so a label would just make my feet move faster in the other direction. I wasn't ready to run yet. I wanted to soak up whatever Ryker and I had going on.

Over the last few weeks, we had hung out almost every day. We were either at his place or mine. We would pick up food, watch Netflix, watch crazy YouTube videos, talk about random stuff, tease each other, but all of that was done in private. We didn't attend any parties except that one where we had to pick up a drunk as fuck, Logan. He'd come see me at work, but I was busy with customers and he was hanging out with his brothers and friends, so we didn't really interact with each other, but I knew he was there. He drove me home almost every night.

Bailey: Why?

That's the only thing I could think of to send back to him. It was a valid question. Maybe he was tired of staying at home. I mean in.

Maybe he was tired of staying in, not home. My home was not his home, and his home was not mine.

Fuck! My brain was tired. That's what all this babbling bullshit going through my head was. I hadn't slept a full night in over a year. Recently it had been due to a sexy man who couldn't keep his hands off me.

Ryker: Cause we're going out.

Yeah, he was tired of staying in.

Bailey: If you want to go out, you can.

I'm glad I read what I wrote before hitting send. It sounded like I was giving him permission to do something without me. I just said we didn't have a label which meant I was in no position to "let" him do anything.

I deleted the text and stared at the screen trying to figure out how to say what I wanted without revealing what I really wanted. Ugh! Since when did texting involve so much brain power?

Bailey: I'm not up for going out. I have some stuff to catch up that I've been neglecting. We can catch up over the weekend.

I hit send before I could talk myself out of it. Part of me wanted to be with him, but I couldn't do that in public. By making whatever we had public would make the fallout worse when things fell through.

Ryker: I'll be there at 6. I'll help with the neglected stuff tomorrow.

He was so bossy! Fuck that! I let anger rule over the swirling emotions rioting in my system.

Bailey: I said I'm not going out. I'll talk to you later. Bye, Ryker.

I hit send and threw my phone on the sofa. I heard the ding of a text coming through as it bounced on the cushion. I snatched my hand back that automatically reached for the phone. No, I said what I needed to say, and that would be the end of it.

I pushed myself off the sofa and looked around the living room. Now what? I had no clue. Work had been super busy that day. I made generous tips that I hid in the shoebox shoved in the back of my closet. My feet hurt, my back hurt, my head hurt. All I had wanted was to relax with Ryker, but that was a no go. That kind of pissed me off but made me sad too.

I had gotten so used to hanging out with him I didn't really know what to do if the possibility of seeing him wasn't going to happen. I wanted to throw a fucking tantrum, and that pissed me off. How did he become so important to me so fast that I didn't know what to do if he wasn't there? I'd rather hold on to the anger than let the sadness in.

"Hey," Carter said from behind me scaring the fuck out of me.

I screamed and turned around so fast I lost my balance. Carter grabbed my upper arms to save me from the hard, unforgiving floor.

"You okay?" he asked with concern.

I nodded and closed my eyes. I took a deep breath and opened my eyes taking a step back making his hands fall from my arms.

He quirked his eyebrow but didn't comment. I was grateful because I wouldn't have been able to explain why after five years I didn't want him to touch me.

"I thought you already left," I explained my mini freak out.

Nodding his head while searching my eyes, I could see he was trying to read me. I didn't want him to read anything in my expression, so I walked around him heading towards the bathroom.

"I'm going shower," I threw over my shoulder trying to escape his knowing look.

"Okay," he said slowly. "I'm about to head out. You sure you don't want to go to the bonfire?"

When I got home from work an hour ago, he asked if I wanted to go to a party that involved lots of property and some wood burning. I told him I wasn't up for it. I thought I would hang out with Ryker, but that shit wasn't happening. It didn't matter though because I told Ryker I wasn't going anywhere so I wouldn't. Frowning to myself, I decided I didn't want to decipher what that meant. I did what I wanted, when I wanted. Relationships were never my thing because I didn't want to answer to anyone. I grew up being told what to do on the daily, and I didn't want to do that ever again.

Shaking my head at myself in exasperation, I went into the bathroom to shower. I turned the water on to warm up and pulled the lever on top of the faucet until water poured from the showerhead. I stripped off my work uniform and stepped under the spray and moaned instantly. The tension I was feeling melted away as I left the water beat down on me. Of course, even showering made me think of Ryker.

The shower we shared last night ran through my mind. His intense stare of my body as he watched the water drip down my body had made me feel powerful. The way he licked his lips and ran his fingertips from my collarbone to my thigh chasing the droplets made me feel intense hunger.

I cupped my breasts and moaned with the heaviness of my flesh in my palms. I pinched my nipples and gasped. I let one hand wander down my torso over my belly and straight to my core. I pushed two fingers in my channel and smashed my thumb against my clit. I moaned as I plucked my nipple with the hand still squeezing my breast.

Ryker's face as he hoisted me against the tile of the shower and pulled me down on his hard cock flashed behind my eyes, and I came. I squeezed my eyes shut as I rode out my orgasm. Once the shudders faded, I felt hollow. There was no Ryker to rain kisses along my face until I came back to reality. There was no warm body to hold me until my legs were steady. It was fucking insane how insatiable I was with him. I never liked sex all that much until Ryker came along. Now it was all I could think about.

With a huff, I washed my body and hair quickly. It had been less than twenty-four hours since I had seen him, and I was moping like a sad little girl. I was fucking pathetic. I had so many issues that I would never be able to solve them all. I would just drive Ryker to the point of insanity. I would change the good guy he was. He was clean while I was dirty. It was best to put some space between us. We could still hang out just not every day. We could still have sex, but I would refrain from the cuddling he liked to do. That was his thing. I wasn't the cuddling type, even if his arms gave me a sense of belonging and security.

I shut the water off and ripped the curtain back roughly making one of the rungs on the shower bar crack and fall to the floor with a loud clang. I ignored it and grabbed a towel. I ran it down my body before wrapping it around me and securing it between my breasts. I ran another towel through my hair as I headed out of the bathroom to my bedroom.

As I walked in my room, I was thinking of the hours I would endure alone. I almost wanted to just go to sleep and wake up in the morning, which was alarming. I was used to being alone. Carter went into the gym early in the morning. By the time he got home, I was usually at work and came in after he was already in bed. On the rare occasions we were both home at the same time, we would bullshit with each for a couple hours. We might share a meal, watch a little TV, but I would retreat to my room. He understood I needed the time alone. All those years I spent in foster care, all I wanted was space to be alone. The group homes had so many kids, some slept on the floor.

There was never any room to be by myself. In the foster homes, other kids were there in your space talking trash and taking anything you had.

Now, alone time seemed lonely and cold. I didn't have many friends because I didn't want to be close with anyone other than Carter. I never invited anyone to my place, and I never went to any of theirs except for Lyla's. Over the last few months, we had become closer, but she had a block up that I hadn't been able to get through. I would have to keep trying. She was my friend. I needed her friendship like I thought she needed mine.

I let out a squeak and dropped the towel in my hand to the floor when I saw my bed, or rather who was on my bed. Ryker was sitting on the edge of my bed looking sexy as fuck. He had a black fitted hat on backwards. The black t-shirt he wore clung to his chest showing all the dips and valleys of his chest and abdomen. He had khaki cargo shorts on that hung past his knees and red chucks covered his feet. My eyes traveled back up his body noticing a bulge that wasn't there before.

I snapped my eyes to his and saw a fury I didn't know what to do with. I took an automatic step back clutching the towel in between my breasts, my heart hammering against my fist. His face was set in stone and his eyes blazed as they travelled the length of my towel covered body.

I closed my eyes and took a deep breath before looking back at him. "How did you get in here?"

"Carter let me in," he answered. "Do you walk around naked when Carter is here?"

My heart rate slowed as I took deep steady breaths as the fear started leaving me. I knew Ryker wouldn't physically hurt me but emotionally? Yeah, he could fucking break me. The way he was looking at me, I knew I wouldn't like what he had to say.

"You walk around like that when Carter is here?" he demanded.

My eyes narrowed on him. The urge to go bitch on him was strong so I locked my jaw, grinding my teeth together.

"I know I sound like an asshole, but I can't stop it. You are mine, and the idea of Carter seeing all of your smooth skin on display makes me a little insane," he explained.

"I'm not doing this again," I frowned and propped a hand on my hip. I could feel the towel slip, but I didn't care. "We've already established what Carter is to me and what I am to him. You don't get to come in my place and do this jealous bullshit. Either you trust what I told you, or you don't. That's up to you."

He rubbed a hand against his chest and nodded his head, "I'm sorry I overreacted. Could you please not walk around here like that? I can't stand the thought that he could have seen you. I'm the only one that can see you like this."

"You are the only one," I said softly and honestly, my eyes locked on his to show my sincerity.

I had never felt such truth in any other words I had ever spoken. I talked trash a lot to get all the crap rolling through me to disappear and to release some of the pressure the emotions had on me. I talked a lot of smack to avoid the truth. I told myself I would enjoy him but keep a distance between us. That was a lie. I couldn't do that. I wouldn't be able to. Just being in the same room as him, the distance between us was nonexistent even with the physical feet separating us.

"When I got your text about not going out tonight, I immediately responded that I would see you in a little bit which you didn't read," he growled sounding extremely aggravated with me. I must have read it about ten times letting it circle my brain, and I feel like you're pulling back. Why? We've been hanging out for weeks with no fucking issues."

"It's out in public, with other people," I blurted out slapping a hand over my mouth.

Why the fuck did I say that? Just let everything hang out, no risk in that, said no one ever. He was staring at me a calculating look in his eyes like he was trying to figure out what my words meant.

"We've been around friends and my brothers before, even Riley," he argued.

"Yeah," I answered. "At the grill, I was always working at the time. Sometimes, I would see them at the gym, but most of the time you weren't there." Why not go all in? I already said more than I should have why not let him have it all?

"We went to that party last weekend," he pointed out.

"We were there to get Logan. I stayed in the front hall while you found him in one of the rooms or something. We walked in together and left together, but that's it," I explained.

"Fuck!" he exclaimed. "How did I never take you out on a fucking proper date?" He stood up and paced a few times at the end of my bed pulling his hair. He stopped and turned his eyes to me, studying me.

"I'm that good," I shrugged with a short laugh. I knew I dodged every time he suggested we go do something. I just distracted him. It could be food, movies, or sex I would use something to make him forget about whatever he wanted to do. It wasn't often he asked for us to go out. I think he was content to chill with me, just be with me. That filled me with a warmth deep in my chest I would never be able to duplicate.

"You can't pull away from me. This isn't a game, I need you forever, Bailey," he said seriously. "You can't brush me off or shut me out. I want you with me. I need you with me. I know you are freaked at this thing between us, and I'm trying to be patient and take my time. I really am, but you have me by the balls, Bailey. The thought of you running from me sends an ice-cold dread through me."

"I'm trying really hard not to run. I want to stay. I want to hang with you on the fucking daily!" I exclaimed beyond frustrated. His words were so raw and honest. He made it clear that I could break him like he could break me. I didn't know what to do with that information. I didn't know what to do at fucking all.

"Come here," he demanded in a deep rumbling voice.

My body immediately responded to the demand. I stood about a foot in front of him with my head down. I felt too open and the pressure behind my eyes was increasing. I didn't want to fucking cry, and I knew I would have if I looked up into his eyes. I knew love would shine out at me, and I couldn't deal.

"Bailey," he said softly.

I looked up into his face and there it was, love. Fuck! He held his hand up to me. I stared at the hand for several minutes trying to figure out the right answer. The answer that would result in a way I would stay whole. I quickly realized that it didn't matter which choice I made, I would hurt. If I took his hand and he eventually left, I would break. If I didn't take his hand and let him leave, I would break. Either way, I would fucking break.

I lifted my hand and placed it in his. He closed his eyes and let out a slow breath of what sounded like relief. He opened his eyes and pulled on my hand until my knees touched the bed in between his legs. I grabbed his shoulder with my free hand when I stumbled. His free hand landed on my hip giving it a squeeze while his other hand moved to the back of my neck pulling me in until our lips met in a searing hot kiss.

"Now, get dressed. I'll be back in an hour," he said pulling away from my lips.

"Huh?" I asked confused and a little wobbly.

He smiled. "We are going on a date tonight. We will go eat, and then meet up with everyone else."

"Holy shit," I muttered. We were going out. We were going public.

"Don't freak out," he said gently as he stood up. "We have been together for a few months now, and I've never taken you out. My momma would bust my ass if she knew this. I don't like disappointing my momma. I'll be back in an hour."

I nodded stupidly as he walked around me and out the door. A few minutes later I heard the soft thud of the front door closing. That snapped me out of my confused daze, and I jumped into action except I didn't know where to fucking start. I'd never been on a fucking date. I didn't even know if I owned anything date worthy. What the fuck? I mean, sure I've thought about dating, just never actually did.

Sometimes my mind wandered to a place where I was normal. I was just a girl working at a temporary job working towards a bigger goal. I could like a boy, and I had a great group of friends that I was super close to. I could call anyone up for impromptu lunches and shopping. I could go to the coffee shop and meet up with my study group.

That normal world sounded amazing. It was so close I could almost see it in 3D clarity. Of course, it was all an illusion. Ryker would get tired of my shit and realize I wasn't worth the trouble. He would find some nice, attractive, stable girl he could settle down with and have a nice, normal life. It was going to happen. I knew it would, but it didn't stop me from picturing a different outcome. The outcome where we were in a normal world, and I was the nice, attractive, stable girl in his life.

I stood in the middle of my room surrounded by clothes thrown all over the floor and furniture. What the fuck was I supposed to wear? All of these clothes and I had no fucking clue what to pick! Lyla! Lyla would know.

I ran out of my bedroom, down the hall, straight to the front door. I yanked it open and slammed it closed when I crossed the threshold into the hall. I knocked loudly on her apartment door. After a few minutes of nothing, I raised it to knock again when I heard the locks being turned. I dropped my hand and waited until the door inched open. Lyla looked a hot mess. Even in the middle of a freak out, I knew she wasn't doing well. I gave her time, and it sucked big time. I wanted the girl I met that first day on the stairs to come back. I didn't do attachments, but I made them with Lyla. I wondered if that was what Carter felt when we first left that house. Did Ryker feel like this with me now? This situation definitely sucked, but I knew from personal experience, she had to work this out herself.

So, I pushed forward and demanded, "What do I wear on a date?"

I sounded damn near hysterical because I was, and I couldn't help it. I was freaking the fuck out. I was going on a date with Ryker Landry where we would be seated together in the middle of other tables filled with couples and families. Then, if that wasn't enough, we were going to a spot with all his friends, probably his brothers or some of them, as a fucking couple out in the fucking open.

"Depends on where you're going," she broke me out of my internal war. "Wear a sundress or something."

"Um, do I look like I own a fucking sundress?" I demanded.

She giggled, and it sounded so close to wind chimes a small smile spread across my lips. Her eyes were twinkling with humor at me. I didn't find anything funny in this situation, I was happy she had a smile on her face.

I groaned in frustration. "I can't do this shit. Look at me. I'm a fucking mess!"

She smiled slightly and shrugged a shoulder. That moved caused the oversized sweatshirt to slip down. The bones were more noticeable than before. Shit! She obviously had lost weight, and she had dark circles under her eyes.

"Come on," I said grabbing her wrist and dragging her across the hall. "You have to help me!" I dragged her straight to my room. She gasped and laughed a full body laugh when she saw my clothes strewn everywhere.

"You really are freaking out, aren't you?" she asked walking slowly through all the debris.

"Yes," I stated digging through a pile of shorts and discarding them. I couldn't wear shorts on a date. It seemed wrong, I think. Fuck, I was going with my gut. I didn't own any sundresses, so jeans would have to do. I found a pair of skinny jeans that were fairly new. They were a dark wash that wrapped all my curves in the right place. I slid them on.

"This tank," Lyla called from the pile of tanks I had thrown to the side of the bed. "With this top over it."

I looked at her to see she had a black ribbed tank dangling from a finger and an off the shoulder white blouse hanging from the other. I walked to her and grabbed both items. I yanked both shirts on and walked to my closet for shoes. I picked some high-top red converse.

I looked in the full-length mirror hanging on the back of my door and nodded my head. It would do. I smiled at Lyla as she made her way out of my apartment. I left my hair down in natural waves and put on some light eye make-up and a little gloss on my lips. I was ready.

There was a knock on the door, and my eyes widened. I wasn't ready! Fuck, that! Yes, I was. Here we go. I blew out a heavy breath and headed to the door.

Chapter Seventeen
Ryker

My breath caught in my lungs when the door swung open revealing my beautiful Bailey. "Wow," I breathed. Her blonde hair cascaded down her back in waves. Her green eyes widened as she looked me up and down before locking eyes with me, the gold flecks in her eyes shone brighter. Her tongue slipped out of her mouth to glide across her bottom lip. My hand wrapped around her neck hauling her to me. My lips crashed down on hers with an urgency I couldn't explain.

This would be our first official date, but we had been together for months. I was anxious to show her off, to have her on my arm, and to let everyone know she was mine. Her arms wound around my neck, her hands delved into my hair, her nails bit into my scalp. This kiss wasn't a "hello" kiss. It was a "you're mine" kiss. She needed to know this information. I wasn't letting her go.

"You're beautiful," I said softly while running my gaze from her head to the tips of her red converse shoes. Her eyes were dazed and unfocused as she looked at me with plump lips that I just abused. "Damn," I breathed adjusting the front on my jeans. Possessive pride spread through me knowing I made her lose her mind a little. "Grab your stuff. Let's head out or we won't leave at all."

"That doesn't sound so bad," she murmured. I knew she was nervous about tonight, but I wouldn't back down. We were going out.

"We are going," I said taking a step back into the hallway taking her with me.

We made small talk on the way to the Italian place I was taking her to. I wanted to get her comfortable and relaxed like she was when we were holed up in her place. I didn't want anything heavy that night. I wanted her happy, and I knew I could be the one to make her happy.

"Am I dressed okay for this place?" she asked uncertainly as I pulled into a parking spot.

"Bailey, you look great," I assured her. The place may have looked fancy, but we were in Houma. People dressed how they wanted wherever they went. It didn't matter though. She could wear a paper bag and still be the most gorgeous one in the crowd.

She loosened up sometime over the appetizers and started smiling her real Bailey smile I loved so fucking much. I kept hold of her hand throughout most of our meal just needing to touch her. She rubbed little circles with her thumb on my palm. She opened up more to me about her past, and she didn't shut down.

She told me about a girl her age that had lived with her and Carter. The three of them were really close. They went everywhere together and talked about everything from every day things to hopes and dreams. She felt as though that girl was her true sister until she was gone. Bailey said they went to the house after school, and all her stuff was just gone. There was no note or anything. I could tell that cut her deep. She didn't let many people in and to have someone disappear on her like that was the biggest betrayal for her.

She changed the subject when it got to her, and I let her have that. Seeing her reveal some dark part of her past and move on from it instead of running, lit me up inside. I was fucking ecstatic. She had finally let me in behind those walls and stayed with me.

Walking out into that field crowded with people I knew gathered around the bonfire with my girl next to me made me puff up my chest in pride. I could tell she was still guarded to be around this many people, but she was pushing through it for me. That hit me deep in the chest.

I laced my fingers through hers as we walked around the bonfire toward where I saw Ryder standing with Lyla. I felt her pull on my hand and turned to her in confusion. Then, I saw the fear reflect in her eyes as she stared at me.

"You are always safe with me Bailey," I murmured low enough she was the only one to hear me. "I would never let anyone hurt you or make you uncomfortable. Lyla is standing with Ryder and them."

"Lyla is here?" she asked surprised as she looked over my shoulder in the direction we were headed.

"Yeah," I answered.

She nodded, "Okay."

When I got a close look at Lyla, I frowned. She looked miserable and slightly drunk if the way her cup was hanging dangerously from her loose grip and her body slightly tilted to the side was any indication. Ryder placed a hand on her arm to steady her, but it did the opposite.

She jerked back from his touch and almost landed on her ass. Her cup dropped to the ground. A little liquid leaked out of the cup meaning she was almost done with that drink anyway. She looked to have lost a lot of weight and her eyes were too wide in her face.

Ryder put both of his hands on her shoulders and turned them, so his back was facing the crowd and blocked her from view. He bent his head down, and I could hear him talking in a low rumble. He backed away after a minute, and she was in a defensive stance, her arms crossed over her chest and her eyes narrowed.

"Lyla," Bailey called quietly.

Lyla turned to Bailey and smiled. They started talking, and I could see the tension leak out of Lyla. Ryder, on the other hand, was stiff as a board as he stared at Lyla. I approached him and slapped a hand on his shoulder.

Logan, Rian, and Ryden joined us with a lot of back slaps and handshakes. I glanced over at Bailey to see her and Lyla expand their huddle to include Kenzi and Riley. The rest of the night went off without a hitch. The girls laughed and danced around. Lyla stopped drinking and looked a hell of a lot better than when we first got there. The guys ribbed on me relentlessly every time I looked over at Bailey, but I didn't care. They called me pussy whipped, and I didn't argue. I couldn't. I knew I was. I owned that shit.

I was so ready to head home. I was getting harder by the second. Every time she laughed, she threw her head back and her hair trailed down her back brushing the top of her perfect ass that I wanted to grab onto. The smile on her face and the happiness in her eyes shot straight to my dick. She looked over at me catching me staring at her and shot me a wink. Fuck this! I was done. It was time to go.

I walked to her and slid an arm around her waist. "Come home with me," I breathed against her lips.

She nodded her head and that's all the agreement I needed. We yelled out hasty goodbyes. I could hear the laughter and the taunts, but none of it mattered. I was taking Bailey home with me, just the thought of her naked body made me practically run to my truck. We made it to the apartment in record time and inside my apartment where we were all alone.

I knew I couldn't make it to the bedroom before tasting her. I shoved her roughly against the wall and slammed my lips down on hers. She tasted like the candy she sucked on all night, so sweet. She moaned into my mouth and pulled me closer.

"Baby, I need you," I groaned as I squeezed her ass lifting her off her feet.

Her legs immediately wrapped around my waist, and she tilted her hips rubbing harder on my erection. My erection? Ha. That was putting it mildly. I was rocked the fuck up. I could feel her heat through the denim covering her pussy. I gripped her hips holding her still against my throbbing cock. Her head hit the wall as she arched into me. Her tits thrust out, and I licked the tops of her breasts and dipped my tongue in her cleavage.

I moved until she was straddling my leg, my knee holding her up. My hands ran up her sides taking both of her shirts with them. I licked up her ribs until I reached her bra. I lifted the shirts over her head and dropped them to the floor. My hands curled around her shoulder just drinking in the sight of her. She had on a black lacy bra that barely contained her perky breasts. One of her nipples was peeking out from one of the cups. My lips latched onto it, and I groaned on impact. Her back bowed up pushing her soft flesh into my mouth further. She tasted so good, I could lick and suck her every day and I still wouldn't get enough. I wanted to drown in her. Keeping one hand curled around her shoulder, I drifted my other hand down her back until I gripped her ass. Her ass was a thing of beauty. It was more than a handful, so plump and firm.

I groaned against her breast as I felt her moving up and down my leg. She gasped and thrust her hips faster. Her breaths were getting choppy and her chest started heaving making her tits jiggle in their cups. I moved my head back, so I could watch her come for me. She was so fucking beautiful every day all day, but when she came, she was the hottest girl I'd ever seen. Her skin was flushed leaving a pink tint from her chest up her throat to her cheeks. A light sweat made her skin glisten. Her full lips were parted as she tried to control her breathing. Her eyes were a deep green that darkened to the most amazing emerald color with her arousal. They shone so bright with so many emotions as she stared into mine. My breath caught in my throat. I loved her.

I loved her!

I thrust my leg higher while rocking her body down, putting enough pressure on her clit to make her go off. I needed her to come at least once before I pulled my dick out, and I needed that to happen soon, like real fucking soon. My dick hurt throbbing against my zipper.

She threw back her head and yelled, "Ryker!" Her body trembled in my arms.

I held her until her orgasmic haze lifted. When her eye lids lifted, she was wide open to me. The love, the fear, the uncertainty, the confusion, and the acceptance filtered through her eyes. I could help her get rid of the negative emotions while I soaked up the positive ones.

I gently let her legs slip from my waist. When she stood up tall, I stepped into her until her back was against the wall and my body was flush with hers. I cupped my hands around her jaw, my fingertips reaching her hairline behind her ears and my thumbs tilted her chin up until her eyes met mine. Then, I brushed the softest kiss I've ever given against her lips. Her hands wrapped around my wrists.

"Bailey, I love you," I whispered hoarsely staring intently in her eyes.

She had to see the sincerity in my gaze because I didn't hold anything back. Her grip tightened on my wrists as she gasped in surprise. I know it may seem too fast, but I didn't care. Once I realized I was in love with her, I knew I had to tell her. I needed her to know that I was in this with her. I was staying. Her eyes were wide as she searched my gaze.

I didn't need her to give the words back to me. She had to sort through her feelings on her own, but I knew what I saw when she looked at me. I knew she loved me even if she didn't yet. I kissed her deeply. She was stiff at first, not kissing me back. I worked my lips back and forth across hers. Then, I ran my tongue along the seam of her lips making her gasp. My tongue slipped through her parted lips to lick along her tongue. I kept the kiss slow and controlled. I savored the taste of her, memorizing every contour of her mouth.

She moaned and started kissing me back as our tongues moved against each other. Her hands delved into my hair pulling me closer. The kiss turned hungry, and my dick started pulsing. I reached under her ass picking her up again and walked to my room. I needed her under me. I kicked the door shut with my foot and went straight to the bed. I laid her down, my mouth never leaving hers. My hands went behind her back to unhook her bra. I trailed the straps down her arms. She let go of my head removing her bra and throwing it to the floor.

Her hands went back to my head pulling my hair hard enough to leave a sting in my scalp that caused me to grind my hard on against her pussy. She arched off the bed in response. I put more of my weight on her making her lay flat on bed. She submitted to me as her body went soft under my own. Fuck! I was losing my mind. I had to get her naked. I went back on my knees and looked at her body laid out before me. Her breasts were jiggling softly with her rapid breathing. Her flat, toned torso was quivering slightly from her anticipation. I ripped the button free on her jeans and dragged the zipper down. I grabbed the waistband and pulled her jeans off along with her panties.

Standing at the edge of the bed, I just stared at the perfection laid bare for me. Her eyes were glassy with emotion, emotion for me, emotion for herself, emotion for us. She was mine, and I was hers. She would see it, know it, and believe it.

I removed my own clothes as I watched her watch me. When I was completely naked, I ran my tongue from her ankle to her core where I licked her once from bottom to top. I made my way up her body, my tongue swiping circles around each of her nipples before my teeth bit down gently on the hard peaks. She was twisting and writhing under me as I licked around her collarbone and behind her ear.

As my lips met hers, I slid inside of her welcoming body. I put my forehead against hers when I was buried fully inside of her, taking a moment to feel the rightness of us connected. Her skin broke out with goose bumps from the soft brush of my fingertips. I put my lips on hers softly as I rocked slowly against her swallowing her gasp. My hands in her hair tightened the pull making her pussy clench around me. When she moaned, I slipped my tongue in her mouth.

I kept the pace slow and lazy. I had lost count on how many times we had sex. We tried every position on different surfaces, like we couldn't get enough of each other. It was always animalistic. I wanted to mark her and remind her of me with each encounter. I liked looking at the physical reminders on her, hickeys in random spots from my lips, bruises from my fingers on her hips or ass, beard burn on her inner thighs from the stubble on my face. This right here was different than any of the other of our encounters. This was leaving a mental reminder she would always have.

Our lovemaking that night was so much more than anything we had ever shared before. We were connected physically and mentally as we maintained eye contact, our bodies shifting against each other. We breathed in each other's moans and groans. Our hands held each other in a light touch. Our climaxes reached us at the same time building slowly until they crested drowning us in pleasure.

"I love you," I whispered against her temple falling to the side of her and pulling her body into mine with an arm around her. I buried my head in her hair and fell fast asleep with a smile on my face.

Opening my eyes the next morning, I immediately sought out Bailey. She was there. She was still asleep next to me in my bed. She didn't run. She stayed. She fucking stayed. Watching her sleep next to me, I felt a deep sense of peace settle within me. Her blonde hair was spread out across the pillow under her head. The blanket and sheet slipped down to her waist showing me the delicate line of her spine and all her smooth, silky skin.

Fuck, that was a sight I could get used to waking up to. I had spent many nights at her place, but she was always gone by the time I woke up. I never said anything to her about it. I wanted to move slowly so I didn't startle her enough to run forever. But after last night, there was no more moving slowly.

I moved the sheet lower until it pooled around her ankles taking in her beautiful ass. Her legs were slightly parted giving me a prime view. I licked my lips and lowered my head between her legs deciding she would make the best breakfast I ever had.

Chapter Eighteen
Bailey

I woke with a gasp as my eyes flew open. Ryker's head was between my legs, his hair brushing against my thighs making goose bumps form all along my skin. He ran his tongue from bottom to top in a slow lick. His tongue dipped in my center before continuing up to circle my clit. My back arched. My hands fisted in the sheet covering the bed. My forehead pressed into the pillows, and my thighs tightened around his head.

"Ryker," I breathed so low and muffled by the pillow I wasn't sure he heard me.

I assumed he did when I heard and felt his groan before he started eating me in earnest. His tongue dipped deep in my channel and spread my moisture around my folds before his lips sucked it all up. I was so fucking worked up, I was trembling. I pushed my ass further in his face. I would be so mortified when I replayed this scene, my ass on his face, but I didn't care. I was so close to the edge.

His teeth locked on my clit as he thrust two fingers in me roughly, and I came. I screamed his name into the pillow and moaned like a fucking porn star as I rode out the orgasm. I came to with the feel of fingertips running up and down my spine. I turned my head to look at Ryker.

He had a smug look on his face and a sexy smirk tilting his lips. "Good morning, beautiful." Even his voice was sexy. It was deep and raspy, very masculine.

Well, I did it. I spent the entire night in Ryker's bed, in his arms. Waking up in the middle of the night all wrapped up made that foreign feeling in my belly spread through my body making my arms and legs tingle. I should care about the depth of feeling I felt for Ryker, but I couldn't get my badass mother trucking self to show. Throw in an orgasm before coffee, and I was done for this boy.

"Do you want some coffee?" he asked placing a soft kiss on my temple.

I nodded my head blinking owlishly at him. I needed a caffeine fix to make sense of what was happening. Something monumental changed between us last night, and I didn't have any brain power to understand it. Coffee, I needed coffee. Maybe it would help me navigate this morning after. Although, I didn't feel fear like I thought I would. I was mostly content. I felt relaxed and there was no panic waking up in his bed.

I watched him get out of bed and pull on some sweats covering his morning wood, and I involuntarily licked my lips. I looked up at the sound of his growl. He placed a hard kiss against my forehead before leaving the room, closing the door softly behind him.

I was a little slow getting out of the bed and dragging my clothes on. My body felt used and abused in the best way possible. I had a dopey smile on my face because everything felt so right. I ran my fingers through my hair trying to calm the bed head down. I made a stop in the bathroom and took care of business. I found an unopened toothbrush I used and washed my face.

I made my way into the kitchen where Ryker was filling the coffee pot, his back to me. I didn't think about my actions. I walked straight up to him and slid my arms around his waist pressing my face in between his naked shoulder blades. His hands glided over my arms before he turned around and brought my body to his in a hug.

"Hey, baby," he mumbled against my forehead.

"Hey," I smiled.

His eyes scanned my face as his fingers ran over my cheekbones into my hair. His smile was soft and happy. "Coffee should almost be done. I'm going to the bathroom. Be right back."

I nodded and let him go turning to the coffee pot. I fixed my cup and had taken the first sip when I was interrupted.

"Hey," a deep voice not belonging to Ryker said directly behind me.

I jumped causing the coffee to splash over the edge of the cup onto my skin. I cursed myself while switching the coffee to my left hand and running my right hand under cold water in the sink to ease the slight burn.

"Give her some space," Ryker growled coming to stand next me.

"I'm fine," I said quickly when he reached for my hand.

I shut the water off and dried my hand on the towel by the sink. I slowly turned to face an intimidating Ryder. I knew he would never hurt me. I took his self-defense class at the gym. He was always in control of his strength. I knew this, but I couldn't control my reaction. I backed up until my back hit the kitchen counter, waiting for the blackness to come, but it didn't. I was truly okay.

"Hey," I said to Ryder with a reassuring smile.

I smiled up at Ryker and could see the relief on his face along with his happiness. He brought me in close and inhaled deeply. We stayed that way, locked tight around each other, until Ryder demanded coffee. We broke apart laughing. I trusted these guys. I didn't have a panic attack. My brain didn't shut down.

After we ate breakfast, I headed back to my place. He wanted me to stay with him all day, but I had stuff to do before work. I wasn't lying the night before when I told him I had been neglecting stuff. I needed to catch up on laundry and pay some bills, maybe hit up the grocery store.

Carter had left a note stating he would be back late. I hadn't really seen him in so long. He was at the bonfire last night, but we didn't talk much. He was with a bunch of other guys I didn't know, and I was wrapped up in Ryker. I needed to corner him and find out what his problem was real fucking soon. I didn't like the distance I felt between us.

I spent the next few hours cleaning and running errands. By the time I was getting ready for work, I realized I had had a smile on my face the entire day. Last night was amazing. Ryker and I connected on a level I thought I would never have with anyone. I was happy, truly happy. I was confident in our relationship, and I believed in us.

I made it to work with thoughts of Ryker still on my brain. The last few months had been the best months of my life, and I knew it was all because of Ryker. I hadn't had a panic attack since the day at the gym weeks before. I still had the demons in the back of my mind, but they didn't take over anymore. I was more open with Ryker than I'd been with anyone including Carter. He knew all there was about me and he was still there. Ryker took my pain and turned it to pleasure. When I was sinking into my own mind, he took me out into our little world. I never saw myself in a committed relationship, but I had to admit it was working.

It was Saturday night, and I was working the bar with Jax. The first few hours were spent filling drink orders for the dining room. I avoided Crystal as much as possible, making Jax fill her drink orders. She kept making snide comments about Ryker and me, but I ignored her. I had been putting up with her shit for a few months, and I didn't want anything to fuck up my Ryker high. I wanted to bask in my newfound happiness.

"Hey, baby," I looked up into the warmest brown eyes and felt the smile spread across my face.

I leaned over the bar and pressed my lips against his, "Hey."

The crowd grew around the bar, and I was so busy I didn't get to talk to him much after that hello. Jax and I worked well together, making drinks, delivering drinks, cashing out tabs, restocking when needed. He did all the heavy lifting while I kept the bar top clean removing any empties. After making a scan of any needed refills, my eyes found Ryker and my teeth locked together.

Crystal.

Crystal's bitch ass had her hand on Ryker's arm, and he was squirming in his seat. I could clearly see he wanted away from her, but he was too nice of a guy to get physical with her. That's Ryker, nice guy. I wasn't a nice girl, and he deserved much more than the chaos in my head, but I was holding on to him with everything I had.

Seeing her touch him, physically hurt. I knew he didn't want her, but jealously didn't care. My throat clogged with emotion, and my eyes stung from pissed off, frustrated tears. I wouldn't let them drop though. She would not see a single tear fall. I straightened my spine and squared my shoulders walking around the bar until I stood in front of them yelling at Jax that I was taking a break. He nodded his head as he saw where I was headed.

"Crystal," I said in the calmest voice I could manage. I was quite impressed with myself. "Get your hand off him."

She looked at me and rolled her eyes before turning back to Ryker. She fucking rolled her eyes at me and turned her back on me! The nerve of this stupid bitch thinking I would just let this happen. Ryker had his eyes locked on my own, and I took a few deep breaths to calm the anger and jealously rioting in me.

I was at work.

I was at work.

I was at work.

I had to remember that before I tore this bitch up. I grew up rough, rough neighborhoods, gangs on the streets, bullies in the houses I stayed at and at school. I didn't deal well with disrespect, and that was what she was doing. She dismissed me as though as I was nothing.

Maybe at one point I would have believed that, but things changed. What Ryker and I had was real, and no one would diminish it. After a few more deep breaths, I felt as though I would be able to talk to her without pulling out all her bleached blonde hair.

I maneuvered myself until I was settled in between Ryker's legs where he sat on the bar stool, my back against his chest. His arms wrapped around my waist as he put his chin on my shoulder. Crystal dropped her hand from his arm with a look of disgust on her face.

"Do not touch my man," I snapped leaning into her space. Ryker's hand tightened on my waist.

She laughed. She actually fucking laughed in my fucking face. Of course, it lacked any humor. It sounded more like a wicked witch kind of laugh, but it was still a fucking laugh. Logically, I knew she didn't have anything to say so she was trying to belittle me like I was nothing. Fuck that!

"Look, bitch, I'm really not in the mood for your high school bullshit games right now," I said standing up straight giving her a glare. "I have let this go on too long, and it stops now. I found amusement in your plays, and since they didn't directly affect me in any way, I blew it off, but you just crossed a line by putting your hand on him."

I felt Ryker's body go stiff behind me as both of his hands tightened around my hips. "What are you talking about?" he growled in my ear.

Oh yeah, I forgot I never mentioned Crystal's antics to him. I didn't see the point. I didn't want to talk about her especially to him. He told me their history, how short that history actually was, and we moved on. I knew all I needed to, and we didn't need to bring her up ever.

"I don't know what the fuck you are talking about?" Crystal snarled with a warning glare in her eyes.

"Own your shit! If you are going to do something, at least fucking own it. You are fucking pathetic," I snapped. I could not stand people who never owned the choices they made. Call it a pet peeve if you want, but that shit pissed me off. Own your shit. That's it. Just own your shit. *I should hash tag that shit!*

"Fuck you," Crystal spat snapping me out of my mental ramblings.

"Fuck with me," I snapped.

"Tell me what the fuck is going on, Bailey," Ryker demanded sending shivers down my spine with his commanding tone.

"Bitch," Crystal started to say.

I put my hand up to stop her, and I started ticking off her ploys on my fingers. "First, the time you told Drew in front of me that Ryker texted you. That was a lie. Second, the time you followed him from the back hallway of that frat house with your lipstick smeared and hair a tangled mess like you were just worked over. A look at Ryker's face told me that was a lie, but the frat boy that walked out after you still buckling his pants with red lipstick on his collar proved that to be a lie. And my personal favorite, your phone number written on a napkin shoved in his jeans pocket. If y'all have known each other so fucking long and hooked up at some point, shouldn't he have your fucking number by now? Not to mention, who the fuck writes their numbers down anymore? Technology is a thing of fucking beauty."

Ryker's arms were like steel bands around my waist anchoring me to him or maybe to anchor him to me. I could feel the tension in him and knew he was pissed. He didn't like it when someone fucked with me. I loved that about him, his protectiveness, but this was a girl to girl thing, and I was going to fucking handle it. The crowd around the bar had grown quiet, but I heard a few giggles and chuckles. Crystal's face though, priceless. Her heavily lined eyes were opened wide and her mouth was agape in shock. She didn't think anyone would call her on her shit. Well, I fucking would and did.

"Now," I continued in an even tone. "It is not my fault you don't have Ryker. He didn't want you before I stepped on the scene, and he sure as fuck doesn't want you now that I am here. It's time to stop with this bullshit. You understand me?"

Her cheeks were flushed red, her teeth clenched shut, her eyes were narrowed to slits, and her hands were balled into fists. Her nostrils flared a few times before she turned around and stormed out of the bar area.

There were a few claps and "hell yeahs" shouted as Ryker turned me to face him. In his normal hold on me, one hand on my ass and one hand tangled in my hair, he took my lips in a possessive kiss that I felt in my core. Our tongues dueled as our teeth clashed against each other. We were taking possession of each other. Jealously was a new thing for me. I didn't like the way it made me feel, but if it ended in a kiss like that, I would not complain.

We pulled back breathless and stared at one another until our surroundings filtered in. Cat calls and whistles went through the room, and I could hear his brothers talking smack. We just smiled at each other. I placed a soft kiss against his lips before pulling away and getting back to work.

"Bailey," a voice said behind me, and all my past rushed in.

I froze. I had my head down considering the open chest full of ice cold beer. My hand was wrapped around the neck of a Bud Light. My breath stilled in my chest. My heart started thumping wildly in my chest. My breathing sped up making my head lighter. That voice. I hadn't heard it in so long. I tried to forget about the person that voice belonged to. I tried to erase that voice and that person from my brain. I squeezed my eyes shut tight. I took a deep breath and slowly let it out. I opened my eyes and lifted the beer out of the chest. I turned around and went directly to the waiting customer. I gave him his beer, and he gave me a five-dollar bill.

"Thanks, sweetheart," he said with a wink before he turned away.

I went to the register and rang up his beer, putting the change in the tip jar working on autopilot. Why was she here? Where had she been all these years? Why did she disappear? Why the fuck she left me? No, I didn't care. It didn't matter anymore. It is what it is. It happened. I've moved on. I had a good life. I wouldn't let her ruin it for me.

I should know that all good things come to an end. I'm like the poster board child of that saying. The past always comes to bite you in the ass.

I could feel the heavy gaze on my back, but I tried to block it out. I failed, but I kept trying. I wanted to pretend she wasn't there. I was at work. I had to keep my shit in check. I could do this. I needed to do this. I wouldn't let her affect me. I would do my job and go home with Ryker.

Fuck this!

I turned around and locked eyes with eyes I hadn't seen in four years, eyes that I trusted, and eyes that I let see everything, eyes that I needed, eyes that fucking left me. "Taryn," I said walking towards her. I was surprised my voice came out calm and steady while inside I was seething.

How dare she just show at my fucking job! I mean, how the fuck did she find me anyway?

"Bailey," I looked over my shoulder to see Carter walk up to the bar on the other side. My back was to him blocking Taryn from view.

I could tell the minute he saw her because his body locked up. He put a hand on the bar and got in her face. "Taryn, didn't I tell you not to fucking come here?" he growled out.

Her face paled, but her eyes were flashing fire. Wait, what? Back up. Rewind. "You knew she was in the area?" I leaned towards Carter.

His eyes flashed to mine, and the guilt on his face said it all. He knew she was here and didn't say shit to me. He knew what her leaving did to me. Fuck, he felt it too. We were inseparable. We were family. Then, she took off and it was Carter and me. I knew I always had him to count on just like he had me, but did I really have him to count on? This betrayal cut fucking deep and I took staggering step back with a gasp.

It was too much, too fucking much. I couldn't deal with all of this shit. The black was at the edge, but I wasn't giving in to it, yet. I wanted to be stronger than the black. I let rage take hold of me. The red was stronger than the black. I was fucking pissed.

"Fuck you," I spat at Carter before bolting, a ball forming in my gut. Carter was my go to person. He was my rock. He stood with me. He moved from state to state, city to city with me. He was my fucking brother, and to be this fucking angry with him killed a piece of me.

I heard Ryker yell, "Let me go!" but I didn't turn to look. I needed out. I couldn't breathe, my chest too heavy. I ran through the back door and didn't look back. I stopped a few feet in the alley and put my hands on my knees, my back hunched. I counted my breaths in and out. I had to beat back the need to fade in the darkness. I was stronger now. I didn't have to bow down to the panic rising in me.

"Bailey," Ryker's voice was soft behind me.

I straightened but didn't turn around. My mind was a mess, my emotions battling for dominance inside me, and I didn't know which one would win. I was so confused and scared and mad and sad. I was on shaky ground, feeling as though the world rocked out from under my feet.

"Bailey, look at me," he commanded in a harsh tone I had never heard from him before.

I slowly turned around to face him, scared of what I would find on his face. His eyes were blazing, and his breathing was unsteady. He had compassion in his gaze along with determination. He thought I was running again. I could see it written on his face. He thought I was blocking him out.

The look on his face was the most serious one I had ever seen him wear. He stepped into my space and cupped his hands on either side of my head cupping my jaw and neck, his thumbs tilting my chin up forcing my eyes to his. I saw the anguish in his eyes as he stared into mine and it gutted me. He saw the walls and recognized what it was, me retreating into myself. I froze as the sadness seeped into his brown irises. My eyes were wide open, and my breath caught in my throat, but I didn't look away from the unshed tears in his eyes. I deserved this. I deserved to see the devastation I caused him. I was scared, and I knew I was going to bolt. He did too.

"Don't run."

He whispered the words, but it sounded like he screamed them at me. It hurt. His face was pleading with me to stay, but I couldn't. It was too much. I got too comfortable in us and let my guard down. I was so fucking happy, and then tonight happened. The slut had me lash out in a jealous rage, the one who left me showed up out of the fucking blue, and the one person who was supposed to have my back always betrayed me. I couldn't risk Ryker hurting me. He had the ability to destroy me. I would be nothing. I would be a shell of a person. I just couldn't do it. I felt the guarded look on my face, building the walls back up brick by brick.

"Bailey, I love you. I need you," he said hoarsely, his harsh breathing fanning across my face. "Don't shut me out. Don't leave me."

The lump in my throat prevented me from responding. I ran my eyes over his face, a face I was afraid I would never see again. I memorized all the planes and lines, his thick eyelashes, and the color of his eyes. I would never look at chocolate the same again.

"I fucking need you, Bailey," he said as a tear fell from his eye to trail down his cheek.

I closed my eyes. I couldn't watch anymore. I felt my own tears fall from my eyes as he lips pressed against mine. He didn't persuade my mouth to open for his. He didn't brush his mouth against mine. He didn't move at all. He just kept his lips pressed to mine before pulling away. I opened my eyes and saw the resolution in his eyes. It was a goodbye kiss. He was saying goodbye.

I wanted to yell and scream at him as I watched him walk away. I wanted to demand him to stay and fight for me, to make me stay his. I dropped to my knees as the sobs rose up in my chest. He had fought for me from the beginning, but he wasn't anymore. I knew there would come a time he would decide I wasn't worth it anymore and leave. I also knew it would hurt like a mother fucker. I tried to keep a piece of me to myself, but in the end I had given him all of me.

I had to let him go. I pushed him away, so I had to deal with the consequences. I made him leave. I couldn't make him stay. I was the only one I could count on. I would always be alone. It was the only way to survive. Trusting yourself was a hell of lot better than trusting someone else.

I didn't know how long I stayed on my knees, the sobs rocking my body, the tears falling faster and faster down my face before I felt strong arms lift me up. My blurry gaze found Jax looking at me in concern, his strong arms holding my weight.

"Take me home please," I croaked out through a scratchy throat just wanting to escape.

The following days, my avoidance of Carter became an art form. It was difficult considering we lived together and every time we were in the same vicinity he tried to get in my space, but I did it. I considered moving, finding my own place, but knew I couldn't do it. Yeah, I was pissed at him, but he was still my brother. I would forgive him. I would move on from this. With that being said, I knew myself well enough to know that I would let this put a wedge between. I wouldn't be able to fully trust him again, and the sadness would swallow me at that thought.

On day four, Carter cornered me and wouldn't let me move past him. I knew my time was up. He wouldn't let me keep ducking him, and I couldn't really blame him. The tension in the apartment was smothering and not talking with him every day hurt.

"I forgive you," I blurted out just wanting to be done with this confrontation.

"I should have told you she was here. There is no excuse for me not telling you," he said blowing out a big breath. "You were so fucking happy with Ryker. You finally let go and just let yourself be with him. I didn't want to fuck with that. I saw a light in you I had never seen before. I wanted you to have that, to keep that. I know that doesn't diminish the fact I kept something important from you. I know that, but I wanted to see that lightness in you stay. I wanted you to keep that."

Tears gathered in my eyes at his explanation. I knew he was coming from a good place, but he was right. It didn't take away the hurt he caused. But at the end of the day, he was still my brother. "I understand where you're coming from but for future reference, don't do that shit again."

His lips tilted up on one side of his mouth, his eyes still sad. "Got it."

I walked into his familiar embrace, his arms wrapping around me. A few tears escaped as I let some of the anger and hurt go. I couldn't stay mad at Carter. I never could. "We're good."

"What about Ryker?" he asked quietly.

I stiffened and backed out of his arms. "I'm not talking about it."

He nodded solemnly. "I get it, but you need to deal with it. You can't just forget everything you two had together."

"It's done," I said firmly with only a slight wobble in my voice. I didn't stick around to hear anything else he had to say.

I couldn't think about Ryker. I could barely function as it was and knew if I dwelled on the fact Ryker was gone, I wouldn't get out of bed. I would hide under the covers and pretend nothing else existed.

By day seven, I was ready to crawl out of my skin. I missed Ryker so fucking much. I missed his soft smiles, his sexy smirks, his flirty winks, his warm brown eyes looking at me like I was his world, his stubble rubbing against my skin, his face flushed with arousal for me. I missed every fucking thing about him.

Taryn fucked with my head, and I lost Ryker because of it. Was I going to let her ruin the best thing that ever happened to me? How was I letting her ruin my happiness? She's the one that left and didn't say a fucking word. She was the one that fucked with my sense of security. She had been gone for years, fucking years! Why the hell was I letting what she did affect the one thing I ever craved, the one thing I needed, to belong.

I belonged with Ryker. Ryker belonged with me. I knew I was fucked up in the head most of the time, but he got me. He let me stay in my head when I needed to. He pulled me back when I was retreating too far. He cherished me. He took care of me. He felt with me, felt my emotions with me. He was constant. He loved me. He needed me.

I loved him.

I needed him.

Fuck! I loved him and needed him to fucking breathe, to fucking live.

I couldn't let what happened in the past with a girl I used to know to mess up my future. I wouldn't let it. I had remade myself into someone stronger. Ryker helped me climb on top of my walls and crush them to rumble. I needed him to be complete.

There was only one thing left to do.

I had to go get my man.

Holy shit!

Chapter Nineteen
Ryker

Eight days. It had been eight fucking days since I left my heart in that fucking alley. Eight days since I walked away from my soul. Eight days of going through the motions of living. It fucking sucked. I went to classes, worked my shifts at the gym, went home, ate, studied, and went to sleep. I woke and hit repeat. I even managed to show up at the football practices and games. Coach kept me benched because he knew I couldn't play, but I was still present. That had to count for something.

I didn't talk to anyone. There was nothing anyone could say that would take this pain away. I wasn't good company anyway. Everyone gave me a wide berth. My mom even let me skip out of Sunday family time without much more than a few words that I didn't hear. Unfortunately, it was Sunday again, and I knew there was no way she would let me get out of going to their house two weeks in a row.

I did have a sit down with Ryder and Logan a few days into the aftermath. They were worried about me, and I owed them something. I let them see the pain I was going through, and they understood I needed the time to process it and move on. Move on? Yeah, right. Move on from Bailey? Like that was going to fucking happen.

But they let it go and gave me the space I needed. I knew they were watching me, and I was okay with that. They had always had my back, and this time was no different. They thought I should talk to her, but I couldn't do it. The look in her eyes in that alley haunted me daily. I almost dropped to my knees when I saw her walls built back up against me. Sure, it started with that girl and Carter, but they were there for me too, and that fucking hurt too damn much.

I rolled out of bed with a pounding headache, tripping over an empty bottle of bourbon. Oh, yeah. Did I mention I developed a taste for hard liquor? Not my finest confession, but there it was. I felt guilty when I thought of Bailey's confession of the time she sought solace in a bottle and drugs, but I pushed it aside. I didn't have to feel guilty. Besides, I didn't drown myself in alcohol every night. I only got drunk twice in the last eight days.

The night before, I needed the alcohol to stop myself from storming to Bailey's apartment. I had pulled into my parking space after closing the gym, and I saw Bailey walking across the lawn toward her place. She looked beautiful under the streetlamp, her blonde hair glowing and blowing freely in the wind. Her body covered in sweats and a baggy shirt that was clearly too big for her. Then, I recognized the shirt and my heart damn near stopped. It was mine. It was an old gym shirt I had left at her place.

Fuck, that hurt to see. My shirt on her body when she wasn't even mine anymore did something to me. I was surprised at my anger. All I had felt was sadness and despair since I walked away, so the rage caught me off guard.

I was tempted to go to her and demand her to give it back. I didn't want to see it on her. She didn't deserve it. I had given her everything I had, and she still ran from me. She didn't have the fucking right to wear my shit.

I had stormed into my apartment, grabbed the bottle of liquor from the kitchen, and locked myself in my room where I proceeded to drink myself into oblivion. I was feeling the effects of that stupid ass choice. Hangovers suck, and I had to go see my parents like this. I could smell the alcohol seeping through my pores making me gag.

I scrubbed myself raw in the hottest shower I had ever taken disgusted with myself. I had never let myself get this low before, and it was depressing as fuck. Once I didn't smell the bourbon on my skin anymore, I got out wrapping a towel around my hips. Next up was the funk ass breath I had going on. It tasted like something had died in mouth. I brushed my teeth three times before I was satisfied. I swallowed three pills to take the edge off the massive headache I had going on.

I went back in my room and had to dig for clean clothes. Looking around at all the clothes thrown everywhere and the over flowing garbage, I realized I let myself go a little too much. The room had a smell that almost had me puking. This was fucking ridiculous. I put my clothes on and got to work.

It took hours and multiple trips to the dumpster, but my room looked a hell of a lot better after I was done. Lysol hung so heavy in the air, it was hard to breathe, but it was better than the BO smell it had before. I felt almost human by the time I was finished getting everything back in order.

"Hey, bro," Ryder called out as I made my way into the living room. "Do you want to ride to Mom and Dad's together?"

"Yeah, sounds good." I knew I wasn't really fit to drive. I wasn't necessarily drunk anymore, but I sure as hell wasn't steady.

We rode in silence listening to his play list at a high volume as I gazed out the window thinking of nothing. I just watched the trees sway and the leaves take flight in the wind. I watched kids playing in front yards and dads washing vehicles. I blanked my mind and concentrated on the world still revolving.

My mom gave me a big mom hug when I walked through the door. She stepped back and patted my cheek. She gave me a sad smile as she brushed the hair off my forehead. She didn't say anything. Then again, words weren't really needed, were they? I was sure Ryder had told her what had happened anyway. I was sure she knew I was heartbroken, and I was grateful I didn't have to get into it. If I had to talk about Bailey, I would probably turn into a blubbering mess, looking like the pussy I was.

I walked into the living room and gave my dad a nod as I passed his chair. He nodded back and watched me sink down onto the sofa. He didn't say anything either, just studied my face for a minute before turning back to the game playing on TV.

I stared down at the brown carpet between my feet and let out a sigh of relief. I just wanted to be left alone, and I was once again reminded how lucky I was to have the family I did. They didn't push and prod me for information. They knew I needed time and space. They were probably happy and shocked I showed up.

I could feel movement and hear voices around me, but I didn't lift my head. I didn't have the energy or brain power to participate in anything. I just stared at the floor and dissected the fibers of the carpet in my head.

I didn't know how long I stayed like that, my head bent to the floor, my mind blank. I faintly heard the doorbell ring and someone express, "Thank God." But I didn't lift my head. I didn't care who else showed up. I didn't even know who all was there in the first place. If I would have been in the right head space, I may have wandered who would ring the doorbell since we all walked in the house like it still was ours.

I felt a tingle of awareness down my spine, a shift in the air, but I still didn't lift my head. I couldn't. I could be wrong. The electricity I felt could be a lie. I wanted it to be real so much I knew I would crumble if I looked up and she wasn't there.

My breathing grew heavy, and I could feel my shoulders tremble. My hands gripped my knees until my knuckles turned white. A pressure developed behind my eyes, and my nose twitched. I was stuck in place. I couldn't move. Then, red converse covered the carpet my eyes were still locked on, and I let out a gasp. My arms reached out to wrap around her upper thighs pulling her to me. I pressed my forehead into her stomach not looking up. The tear fell, and a sob built in my throat.

Fingers gripped my hair pulling up, but I resisted. I didn't want to look up and find this an illusion. I didn't want to let go. Her coconut smell invaded my nostrils and I breathed deeply for the first time in eight days.

"Ryker," her sweet voice said softly.

I tightened my hold on her and rubbed my head back and forth on her abdomen. The sting in my scalp had my head rising without my permission. My first look at Bailey's face after so long had me dragging her down to straddle me. I buried my head in her neck and let my emotions free. My body was shaking against her and she held me tighter.

"I'm so sorry," I heard as I felt wetness hit my neck. I pulled back to look at her. My thumbs caught her tears as I studied her eyes. Her vulnerability and uncertainty clouded the gold sparks, but love shone through, too.

"I love you," she told me staring directly in my eyes letting me see her truths. "I need you, Ryker. I fucking need you."

I pulled her head down to me and crashed my lips against hers. I kissed her with all the desperation I felt. I kissed her with all the anguish I felt during the days we were apart. I kissed her with all the passion I felt at being connected to her again.

A throat clearing finally broke us apart. We were both breathing heavily as we stared at one another not loosening the holds we kept around each other. She was here. She was fucking here, in my lap, in my parents' living room, on my parents' sofa.

Oh, shit! I was at my parents' house and I was making out on their sofa like a fucking teenager. I didn't even do that shit as a teenager. I rested my head on her shoulder until I had my breathing under control.

I looked over her shoulder to see everyone standing there, and I mean every fucking one of them standing there staring at us. Ryder and Logan had smirks on their faces. Rian's face was turning red from holding back his laughter. Ryden and Rylan had big smiles spread across their faces. Riley had silent tears falling down her face as she hugged herself with both arms wrapped around her body. My dad had his own smirk tilting his lips with his arms crossed across his chest. My mom, though, my mom had her hands on her hips, her mouth pinched tight, her eyes narrowed in the stern mom look, but I could see the unshed tears she was trying to hide.

"How many are there?" Bailey asked her voice muffled in my neck.

I laughed as I ran a hand down her spine. "Um, all of them?" I was nervous what her reaction would be at knowing how big our audience was.

She surprised me though. She sat straight up and cupped my face looking in my eyes intently. "I'm so sorry for running. I should know better than to run from you. I can't run from you, Ryker. You always catch me. Even when we think it's over, you catch me and pull me back to you. I love you. I need you, baby." Her eyes were wide open and unguarded. The walls were gone and all that was left was my Bailey.

I smiled the first real smile in eight days and lifted my girl in my arms as I stood and spun us in a circle. A laugh rang out through the room in the most beautiful sound I found down to my soul. I set her down on her feet next to me, an arm around her waist to steady her. Her arm snaked around my waist as she rested her head against my chest, her eyes taking in everyone in the room.

I introduced her to Rylan since they never officially met because he had been travelling the last few months. He knew who Bailey was though. We talked often so he knew how much Bailey meant to me. He understood the monumental moment for what it was. It meant everything. It meant fucking everything to me. He smiled at her and placed a kiss on her cheek.

My dad cupped her cheek and placed a gentle kiss against the crown of her head. With a pat to my shoulder he made room for my mom. My mom greeted my girl with her traditional hug. My mom was a hugger. She believed hugs were good for you. They could cure people. She said it made a stronger connection right away. A handshake was boring and cold.

From the look, I saw on Bailey's face, I would have to say my mom connected with my girl. She probably had never received a mom hug, and I knew my mom's hugs were the best. Her eyes filled with tears as she let my mom wrap her up in her arms. I wanted to take the tears and make her smile. I wanted to give her this every day until she expects and knows she deserves the hugs. I wanted so much from her, for her, with her. I'd never felt anything like it. I just needed her with me and happy.

She looked back at me over her shoulder and I nodded my head smiling at her in encouragement. She smiled at my mom as she stepped back into my embrace. Her eyes turned to mine.

"I love you," I whispered to her.

"I love you," she said back with a smile.

"I need you," I smirked.

"I need you, too," she smirked back.

"Okay," my mom clapped loudly. "Let's eat."

Everyone filed out of the room toward the kitchen, and I pulled Bailey against me. "Welcome to the family, baby," I said against her lips.

"I'm a part of your family now?" she teased with a quirk of her eyebrow.

"Hell, yeah, you are," I said squeezing her ass in my hands. "You're stuck with me now."

"You promise?" she whispered.

"I promise," I said running my hand through her hair. "You are Landry."

"You are Ass Man," she mocked my caveman tone.

"Just your Ass Man," I said laughing.

"Damn straight!" she exclaimed pulling my head down to hers. Our lips came together in a hot searing kiss that held all the emotions we held for each other and all the promises of our future.

Everything was right in the world. I had my girl back in my arms ready to stop running. She was there to stay. She let the walls go and gave me her everything. She let me all the way in. I already knew she was my always, now she knew it, too.

She loved me.

I loved her.

She needed me.

I fucking needed her.

The End

Violet

I was an awkward hot mess all day every day. I wasn't good at peopling. I kept my interactions with others to a minimum, but sometimes it was unavoidable like the time I met him. He made me feel like I wasn't as weird as I've always felt I was. I came alive around him. A simple touch and I was shivering in the best possible way with intense, unfamiliar feelings. He demanded truth from me, but I was afraid to reveal that much of myself.

Need

Rian

I owned my own tattoo shop with one of my brothers, leaving my mark on people's skin daily. I've encountered diverse types of people. I met her, and she was by far my favorite brand of different. I was mesmerized by her. Her honesty and innocence called to me. When I was with her, I couldn't stop myself from touching her. I wanted her, all of her. I gave her my truth and asked for hers in return. The question was, would she give it to me?

Chapter One
Violet

"Son of a biscuit!" I exclaimed as the glass door caught the back of my ankle. I winced at the sharp pain as I stumbled my way into the shop.

Fuck, that hurt! I was going to have another bruise and will probably be missing some skin. Dammit!

I was clumsy and uncoordinated. I had a new bruise every day from bumping into things or tripping or even just fucking walking. Whatever I was doing, if I was moving, I was going to bruise or possibly break something. I was seen in the ER more times than I would like to think about much less admit. I've had so many stitches I lost count, a few broken bones, and even a concussion. My dad had the biggest first aid kit I had ever seen. He invested in it when I was about four, and he realized the normal sized kit just wasn't going to cut it for his accident-prone daughter.

I couldn't even walk through a flipping door without causing a ruckus. *Shoosh.* The bell over the shop's door was still ringing erratically from my rough entrance as I made my way fully inside. I didn't even want to be there. I hated going to places I had never been to before. I couldn't prepare myself accurately if I didn't know what the place looked like, what the layout was, or knew the people working at the business, which was what scared me the most. People freaked me the fuck out. You could never know how they would act or what they would say.

Need

It took everything in me to walk through that door, and the place was most definitely out of my comfort zone. I couldn't believe I actually made it in there in the first damn place. Soul Ink was located within the same shopping center as Spine Broke, the bookstore I worked at. They were separated by a jewelry store and a dry-cleaning business. I've walked by the tattoo parlor every day to and from my car in the parking lot, but I couldn't see inside because of the tinted windows.

Each time I passed by those tinted windows, I kept my head down. I wanted to know what was on the other side so bad, but I held back. I was curious to see the tattooing process and to find out if the artists were as scary looking as they were in my mind. I had a wild imagination, so those images I projected in my head kept me out of the shop. That and my awkwardness. I wished I was brave enough to go assuage my curiosity, but I wasn't brave. I tended to stay in the safe lane to avoid embarrassment.

It didn't matter, though. I needed to do this. My migraines were getting worse each month. They didn't come every day, but it was damn close. They put me out of commission for a few days, and it fucking sucked. I was willing to try almost anything to make them more bearable. Puking and sleeping for days at a time sucked. I was lucky I had a pretty kick ass boss who understood the time I had to take off, but I needed the money to pay my bills. If I didn't work, I didn't get paid.

Shaking my head at myself in exasperation, I looked around the lobby sucking in a deep breath of surprise at the beautiful art covering all the available wall space. The walls were painted this deep gray color that contrasted greatly with the bold colored paintings and portraits hanging in black frames creating a beautiful display. Even the gray and black pieces stood out in their complexities.

Whoever drew those was extremely talented. Some of the portraits seemed to want to jump right out of the glass encasing them. It was unlike anything I had ever seen. One of the frames held a portrait of an actual tattoo on the arm of a man. It was a dragon breathing fire. The fire looked so real it had a shimmering quality to it. I wanted to touch it to see if it was hot to the touch, which was incredibly stupid knowing it was a drawing, but the desire to find out was too strong.

I walked closer to the frame and put my hand out when a deep chuckle made me jump back from the art covered walls knowing I was just caught trying to touch something I probably shouldn't have. I whirled around so fast I wobbled slightly but managed to stay upright. I brought my hand up to my galloping heart and looked to the long counter separating the lobby from the workstations in the back where I could hear machines lightly humming.

My eyes collided with the warmest brown eyes I had ever seen, and I felt a shiver of awareness ripple down my spine. I had never felt that before. His eyebrows were furrowed making me wonder if the laugh I heard came from him at all because I didn't see any humor on his face.

"Are you okay?" he asked with concern.

I nodded mutely, my tongue too thick in my mouth and my throat too tight to force any words out. I stood frozen in the middle of the room staring at the hottest man I had ever seen. I was literally struck stupid at the sight of him. He was tall, well over six feet, and built like one of the guys in my romance books. His faded black t-shirt clung to his body emphasizing broad shoulders, bulging biceps, a hard chest, and defined abdomen.

My tongue ran along my bottom lip as my eyes took in all of him. The tattoos that covered his arms were colorful. The tattoo on his neck made me want to lick him which caused me to blush. I had never had those thoughts before. I had never wanted to lick another person, but I so wanted to lick him like the best ice cream cone ever created. His hands were splayed on the counter, and I wanted to inspect the black and gray ink covering them.

This man was way out of my league, but I couldn't stop ogling him. I loved men with tattoos. Tattoos were fucking sexy especially on this guy. What would a hot, tatted up man want with an insecure, awkward, hot mess of a girl? Nothing. He would want nothing with me. I looked at the polo wearing, straight-laced, boring guys. Not that I ever dated, but if I did, that would be the type of guy I would date.

"Can I help you?" he asked in a deep, warm and slightly amused voice.

I jerked my eyes away from his body to meet his eyes. My cheeks were on fire with the blush I could feel rising from my chest and up to my neck. I wasn't sure if it was from embarrassment or lust. I didn't recognize the look he was giving me, but I couldn't hold his gaze for long.

His eyes dipped downward slowly almost like he was checking me out, but that couldn't be right. I was imagining that. He was probably checking to see if I injured myself or something. When his eyes made their way back to mine, my body was on fire. I could feel my nipples pebble up against my undershirt.

I didn't wear bras because my boobs were small, and bras were uncomfortable. I didn't even fill out the whole cup so I didn't see the point in wearing one. The undershirts I wore had the top shelf bra thing in them so it wasn't noticeable that I wasn't wearing a real bra. I never had a problem before, but I had never been in this position before, either. I had never reacted so strongly to a man, and I wasn't quite sure what to do with it.

"Excuse me," a female voice said from behind me causing me to jump in surprise for the second time that day. I couldn't tell if the voice was mad, aggravated, or neutral, but my heart started beating faster at the thought of receiving negative reactions from the people in this shop. I fell forward and caught myself by slapping a hand on the glass counter, inches away from his hand.

That was until his hand moved on top of mine. The electricity of the touch shot through me, and I couldn't control the jerk of my hand under his. He immediately removed his hand from mine leaving behind a trace of heat. I balled my hand into a fist and pushed myself from the counter standing up straight.

I didn't even hear those damn bells, but I don't know if they ever stopped ringing from when I came in. I was so caught up in eye fucking this man, I didn't know anything. I looked over my shoulder to see a petite girl with straight, black hair trying to get around me. I quickly stepped to the side and watched her walk through the opening in the counter space and around to the other side. She dropped her large bag on the floor and glanced at me before looking at the man.

"What's up?" she asked Hot Boy.

Hot Boy? Really? Sheesh.

Well, he was hot, but still. I wasn't calling him that even if it was just in my head. Did people even say that anymore? It was probably considered old school. I knew words written in books. I didn't interact with people to know what was common slang.

"Nothing much," he answered with a smile.

That smile was so yummy. *Yummy?* My gosh, I really should get out of that bookstore more often. I didn't even know how to talk in my flipping head. I was annoying myself. My mind was a jumbled mess. I didn't do well with people on a normal basis, but this was so much more than that. The zing I felt from the simple skin to skin contact had me so twisted up, I didn't know what the hell was happening.

"Is Rian helping you?" The girl asked snapping me out of the internal battle I was having with myself.

Rian. Sounds a lot better than Hot Boy.

Shut the fuck up, brain!

I shook my head pushing my square, black rimmed glasses back up my nose where they had slipped down. I tried to swallow down my nerves that had a hold of my tongue. I had not said one single word since I had walked in that shop. I probably looked like a mute dolt. I needed to get my shit together.

I glanced quickly at Rian before looking the girl in the eye. "I need a piercing."

My voice shook slightly, but I managed to not stutter, so I counted that as a win. This girl was intimidating and seeing that smirk on Rian's face, yes, I caught that in the quick glance, and feeling his eyes staring at me made me want to run out the door and forget this whole thing.

She narrowed her eyes at me and tilted her head like she was studying me, assessing me. Her lips twitched, and there was humor dancing in her eyes. She was laughing at me. I internally sighed. I was used to people laughing at me so it wasn't surprising this girl found me amusing, but I was hoping I could have escaped the silent judgement.

I straightened my shoulders and stiffened my spine. I was grown now. I didn't have to put up with bullies or ridicule anymore. I tilted my head in defiance when she let the grin she was holding in spread across her face. Her eyes flashed bright blue with her amusement. I grew up surrounded by people laughing at me. My clumsiness and social issues caused multiple scenes that served to entertain many. It took a long time for me to be able to hold my head up when faced with a difficult social situation, but I made it. Through blood, sweat, and tears, I was happy about who I was with all my quirkiness.

"Is Star here, yet?" she turned to ask Rian.

I let out a slow breath when her assessing gaze left me. I hated being on the spot. Nothing was ever a simple transaction with me. It was always a story. I couldn't just walk in and get what I needed. I had to make a spectacle and bring more attention to my weirdness than necessary.

"No," he answered shaking his head before he looked at me. "I got it."

She quirked an eyebrow at Rian. "Really?"

"Yeah," he shrugged.

I shifted my feet nervously. The look that passed between them made me think I was missing something. I also thought it probably had to do with me.

That thought was confirmed when she turned to me with a calculating stare. "What kind of piercing do you want?" Her tone was a little harsher than before.

"Don't mind Tiff. She doesn't know how to act appropriately," Rian shot Tiff a disapproving frown.

Tiff elbowed him in the ribs which had him grunting and slightly slumping. I narrowed my eyes at her in anger. The anger took me by surprise, but in that moment, I didn't stop to analyze the feeling. I didn't want her hurting him even if she didn't do any real damage. I didn't want her touching him at all. I wanted to touch him.

Her smile fell from her lips as she took in my expression and stance. She held her hands up in surrender. "I'm just playing."

He looked back and forth between Tiff and I, confusion clouding his eyes. I was confused, too. I didn't understand the anger and possessiveness I was feeling. I didn't know these people at all. I probably looked like an idiot. I really needed to get control of myself.

His eyes returned to mine, and I couldn't read everything in them. That didn't surprise me since I was not a people person so figuring them out would never happen. His grin returned to his face as though he wanted to laugh, and I resisted the urge to drop my head in defeat.

Flip a duck!

I could feel sweat slide in between my shoulder blades as my embarrassment increased. I quickly looked back at the girl figuring I was better off talking with her. I needed to steer this back to where it should be so I could go home.

I cleared my throat. "I would like to get a Daith piercing, please." There. I said it all without stuttering. Success! Go me!

She raised a finely shaped eyebrow and asked, "Why?"

"Why?" I repeated a little taken back by her question.

"Yeah," she answered leaning her hip against the glass counter crossing her arms across her chest. "Why do you want to get that piercing?"

"I suffer from bad migraines," I explained honestly. "I read the piercing could help."

"Thought so," she nodded and stood up straight. "That's not a proven fact, so you shouldn't make a decision to get a needle stuck through your ear based on what the internet has to say about it."

"I know," I agreed. "But I'm willing to give it a try. Any relief would be fucking great. There are some days I can't make it out of bed, the pain is so intense. I can't even sit up without vomiting. It's horrible."

Everything I had read stated it possibly helped with migraines and anxiety because of pressure points. Professionals stated the piercing was not a proven cure or aid. It didn't matter to me. I had suffered with migraines since I was a kid. Sometimes I was out for a week because of a migraine that wouldn't quit. It sucked. If the piercing could just give me a little relief, I was in.

Tiff lifted that damn eyebrow again as she studied me. I was incredibly uncomfortable with the scrutiny. I was used to the stares and whispered conversations around me. I was weird. People stared. People talked. I got it, but that didn't mean I liked it.

My hand gripped the strap of my messenger bag, and I bit the corner of my lip in nervousness. I was hoping by biting my lip I wouldn't start babbling like I normally did when I was feeling extra awkward.

Then, I heard a growl and turned my head sharply to see Rian staring at me, or maybe he was staring at my lip. I parted my lips instinctively, releasing the trapped flesh, and I watched his eyes flare in what looked like approval.

I shook my head denying those thoughts. He wasn't staring at my lip, and he didn't have anything to approve of. What the fuck is wrong with me? I read entirely too many romance novels. That was the only explanation I could come up with for my crazy thoughts and reactions to Rian.

I took a few steps back as my heart started pounding and my breathing sped up. I could feel sweat slide down my back. I was on the verge of a panic attack. I never actually had a panic attack, but I was sure that was what was happening to me.

"We won't hurt you," Tiff snapped.

"What?" I asked confused.

"I said," she annunciated each word like she was talking to a child. "We won't hurt you."

"I know," I answered honestly.

"Then, what's wrong with you?" She asked with narrowed eyes and hands on her hips.

My eyes darted to Rian seeing the concern in his eyes. I could feel my cheeks heat in embarrassment. I didn't want them to think it was them making me behave so erratically. I was going to have to put myself out there to reassure them. *Fuck it.*

"People make me nervous," I stammered squeezing my eyes shut.

It was so embarrassing trying to explain my issues to people. I didn't even try for most people I encountered because it wasn't worth the effort, but I thought Tiff and Rian were worth it.

I rubbed my temples where a headache was forming. Anxiety sucked.

"I'm awkward," I said blowing out a heavy breath. "I'm not trying to offend anyone. I just want the piercing, please."

I placed my hands on the counter as I waited for her response. I knew it wasn't the best explanation in the world and was lacking a lot of information, but it was as much of the truth as I willing to give.

The two bars through her eyebrow pressed into her skin as her eyes widened in surprise. She wasn't expecting that response. I held back a snort knowing they probably didn't encounter freaks like me often.

"All right," Tiff said. "Did you pick out the jewelry you wanted?"

My eyes went to the glass case under my hands. "Which one do you normally use?"

"This one," she indicated an all silver ring.

It almost made a full circle with a ball on either end. It was simple and looked cool. Good enough. "That one is fine."

"Are you sure?" she asked.

I shrugged as I pulled my wavy hair into a low ponytail making sure it wasn't too tight. "Yeah, it doesn't really matter. I don't want a colored stone or anything. I just want a basic ring."

"Okay," she said taking the package out of the case and handed it to Rian. "Let's get you set up."

"You can come on back," Rian said surprising me and catching me off guard.

I forgot he was there for a second. I was so focused on the case and the sweat going down my back, I blocked him out. I wasn't sure how I managed to forget him, but it was one of my many defense mechanisms in uncomfortable situations. If I blocked someone out, I could convince myself they couldn't see me anymore. It sounded stupid and unrealistic, but it was effective in calming me down.

"Um, well," I stuttered when I heard the bells behind me ring.

"Hey, Vi," a voice said from right behind me.

A voice I knew. A voice I wanted to not hear at that moment or any moment in the future. Okay, that was a lie. I was just hurt and angry at the moment and wanted space from him. The voice belonged to a man I used to consider my best friend. A voice I had trusted since I was a little girl. A voice that used to comfort me. A voice that used to console me when I felt like I was too weird and different.

He slid an arm around my shoulders, and I stiffened at the contact. It was a familiar embrace, one that I have had since forever, but I didn't want it right then. I still needed time away from him. I couldn't just let his words go, and I wasn't ready for his explanations or platitudes.

I moved out of his hold, and my eyes automatically sought out Rian. His jaw was clenched tight, and his eyes were narrowed into slits as he looked at Caleb. I wasn't sure what that look meant, but I knew I would not get into anything with Caleb in front of anyone much less Rian. I had to get Caleb to leave. What should have been an in and out trip to get this damn piercing sure turned into a flipping excursion.

"Violet," Caleb started but I cut him off.

"Not now, Caleb," I gritted out scowling at him.

"Will you at least call me later?" he asked, remorse and sadness evident in his eyes.

"Give me a few days," I said blowing out a heavy breath.

I wasn't trying to hurt him, but I was hurt, dammit. I needed time to come to terms with what he said and try to put them with the guy I knew forever and a fucking day. He was talking about me behind my back to another person, and it pissed me off. He could suffer for a little while longer before I listened to what he had to say.

I could tell by the angry glint in his eyes that was not the answer he wanted or was even expecting. He was going to push this thing right here and now. He was a stubborn shit head like that.

"No," he said stubbornly. "Four flat tires."

Damn, the man!

I stomped my foot and growled. "That's not fair!"

"It's true and you fucking know it," he returned.

When we were fifteen, we found his dad's stashed bourbon and got drunk, really drunk. We were babbling fools, and I told him we were down like four flat tires. Caleb thought it was the funniest shit he'd ever heard and laughed until he puked, literally. Seeing him throwing up caused a chain reaction, and I found myself puking right alongside him. It was horrible. The next day we decided to forget drinking forever, but the saying stuck. Now, he decided to throw it out there while I was pissed off, and that was not fucking fair.

I scowled at him with my hands fisted on my hips. He fucking knew that would get to me, and I didn't want it to. I wanted to stay mad. I hated to admit it, but I probably overreacted and would look like a jackass in the end. I didn't want to look like a jackass, dammit.

I felt bad and a little selfish for not hearing him out. It had been a week since I heard his side of that phone conversation where he said he had to handle me, and I haven't let him explain anything to me. I tripped over my own damn feet, and he saw me standing there like a deer caught in headlights.

I proceeded to go the fuck off on him without allowing him to speak a word. I was afraid to hear his side. My adrenaline was pumping and flashbacks of high school were bouncing around my brain. I couldn't hear what he had to say, so I kicked him out and haven't talked to him since.

My show of anger didn't faze Caleb. He grabbed my wrist and dragged me out of the shop. I went willingly because I knew Caleb wasn't letting this go, and I did not want to have an audience for this impending embarrassing situation.

He lifted his eyebrow as he folded his arms across his chest. "Claire was being a bitch."

I snorted at that. Claire was always a bitch. I didn't know why he kept her around. He didn't even like her. I tried to tell him the mistake he was making, but he laughed and said he knew what he was doing. He didn't.

"What does she have to do with this?" I asked furrowing my brow.

"That's who I was on the phone with the night you misunderstood a conversation. She called and invited me to the bar. I told her I would ask you if you wanted to go since I was at your house, and she started going on this stupid ass fucking rant," he said as he ran a hand through his hair in agitation. "When I said I would handle you in the crowd, I didn't mean it like you took it, and if you really fucking thought about it, you would know that."

I sighed in defeat. "I know. I'm sorry, but you know how I feel about people talking about me."

He nodded. "Yeah, but it's me, and you should have a little more faith in me than that."

"I do," I said looking over his shoulder to avoid his gaze. "It just sucked to hear that."

"I would never say anything negative about you, Vi," he said sincerely. "I love you just the way you are."

"I love you, too," I said honestly.

"BFF?" he asked.

I laughed and walked into his open arms. "Yeah. BFF."

"Do you want me to go in with you?" he asked pulling back to nod at the front door of the shop.

"No," I said determinedly. "I got this."

"Yeah, you do," he smiled and kissed my forehead. "I'll talk to you later."

"Later," I said watching him walk away.

I took a deep breath, and the heavy pressure on my chest lifted. I missed him this past week. It sucked not being able to talk to him. I knew I misunderstood the conversation as soon as I confronted him. I just couldn't admit I was wrong, and that was fucking stupid.

I went back into the shop to see Rian and Tiff still in the same places looking towards me. I was guessing they witnessed the scene on the sidewalk. I didn't give myself time to think about it. I walked up to the counter with a courage that was so fucking fake, but I made it.

"I'm ready," I told Rian in a strong, clear voice.

He nodded his head slightly and told me, "Follow me."

I walked behind the counter and passed Rian without making eye contact with him, but my body made contact with his. My shoulder brushed his chest when he didn't move fully out of the way. I held in a gasp and controlled the shiver that wanted to take over my body at the feeling of hard muscles under soft cotton.

Since I didn't know where to go, I glanced back at Rian to see him standing tall with his arms crossed across his chest making his muscles strain against the sleeves of his shirt, but his head was down as though he was studying his shoes.

"Go in that door there," Tiff broke the weird tension I could feel in the air. "Rian will be right in."

I hurriedly turned around and walked into the room Tiff pointed me to. The room had a long silver counter with several clear containers holding cotton balls, swabs, and other things needed for the work done in here. The chair in the middle of the room looked like the chair at the dentist's office. There was even a metal rolling stand next to the chair that a dentist would use.

I sat down and tried to shake the anxiety crawling over my skin. I felt wide open and tender. I just wanted what I went there for and to get out. I was determined to get the damn piercing. I felt like a raw, exposed wire, with all my insecurities out in the open. I felt way too vulnerable, and I was afraid I would lose my shit soon. I groaned and dropped my head until my chin touched my chest. I closed my eyes and took deep breaths to gain some semblance of normalcy.

Normalcy? Yeah, believe that partner.

I snorted out loud at that thought.

Chapter Two
Rian

I didn't usually handle the piercings in the shop. That was Star's job, but I wanted to do this piercing for this girl. I wanted my hands on her, and I wanted to give something to her she wanted. I wanted her to know I was the one who gave the piercing to her every time she saw it. It sounded ridiculous, but it was the truth.

First, I had to get myself under control. I couldn't go into that room until I calmed down. Having her so close to me, smelling the sweet scent of coconut, and feeling her brush up against me had me rock hard.

Anger mixed with the desire. I wanted to know who that guy was. Was it her boyfriend? Was he competition? Listen to me. I was in high school all over again. I was a responsible business owner. It shouldn't fucking matter who that guy was. Violet was a client in the shop. That was it. I needed to get my ass in there, pierce her ear, and get her out of the shop.

"Are you okay, boss man?" Tiff asked, laughter evident in her voice.

I scowled at her. "Shut it."

She laughed a full-out belly laugh. My lips twitched because I agreed with her. I was being ridiculous, and I fucking knew it. It was all Violet's fault. She was fucking beautiful. She was a natural beauty who didn't hide her issues. She was up front about it which I fucking loved. It was refreshing compared to the ink candies that came into the shop hoping to get more than just ink from me.

"What's up?" Ryden asked with a raised eyebrow.

Tiff's laughter masked Ryden's approach. I cursed inwardly.

"Nothing," I mumbled walking around the two of them.

I didn't want to listen to my little brother give me shit. We were co-owners of Soul Ink and saw each other damn near every day. We were a few years apart, but we were close. We both had the same interest in tattooing. I waited until Ryden was eighteen before opening the shop. We both saved from the odd jobs we each had through high school and beyond. I attended the local community college taking basic business classes. It was enough to know what I was doing in running a business, and Ryden took some college courses while still in high school. By the time Ryden was eighteen, between the both of us, we were ready to open the shop.

It was a struggle in the beginning. The first year we scrambled to turn a profit, but we stuck it out together. It was just the two of us doing all the work, and we busted our asses. The past year had been a hell of a lot better. We hired a receptionist, piercer, and three other tattoo artists. We weren't rolling in the money, but we were on our way. We had a good, solid clientele that spread our name bringing more people in. We were building a reputation, and I was proud of everything we accomplished so far.

I walked into the private piercing room steeling myself. Violet jumped and her eyes snapped to mine. She looked so innocent with her big, blue eyes shining up at me. I wanted to know how far that innocence went by getting her naked and under me.

She was in the shop to get a piercing, and I was picturing her naked. I've seen her on the sidewalk before but up close and personal was enlightening. She was fucking hot, fucking beautiful. Her nervous, determined energy pulled me in further.

The closer I got to her, the more nervous she seemed. She was clearly uncomfortable, but she was soldiering on. I admired that, but I wanted to know what made her so nervous about me. I saw a hint of fear in her big, blue eyes. The source of that fear was unknown. I didn't think it was from me, but I could be wrong. I needed to proceed with caution.

She was beautiful. I felt like I had gotten sucker punched in the gut when she lifted those beautiful, shining eyes up to mine. The square, black framed glasses perched on her nose couldn't hide the deep blue of her irises that sucked me in.

Watching the dark blonde-haired beauty squirm was quite entertaining. It would have been even more entertaining if she was naked. I bit back a groan at the thought of her small breasts swaying back and forth as she rubbed her thighs together. Fuck! My thought process went down the gutter fucking fast.

I was drawn to her like I had never been drawn to anyone before. Her bright eyes opened wide conveying her every feeling. Her innocence screamed at me to make her mine, but her honest nature had me wanting to take a subtle route there. She would be mine, but I had to watch my step with her. I couldn't move too fast or risk scaring her away for real.

She tracked my movements through the room warily but interested. I saw the hint of desire in her eyes, but her stiff posture told me she wouldn't act on it. That had me wondering if that Caleb guy was, in fact, her boyfriend. Would I look desperate if I asked her who he was?

What the fuck was wrong with me? I'm a grown ass man. Why was I questioning myself? I think I already had handed her my balls, and that was not a good indication of how things would be going forward, if it went further.

"Was he your boyfriend?" I asked breaking the silence just now realizing neither one of us had said anything since I walked into the room.

Her eyes widened before she looked down at her lap where she was twisting a solid silver ring with triangles engraved into the metal around her finger in agitation or nervousness. She was silent so long I didn't think she would answer me, but she surprised me.

"No," she said softly before clearing her throat and speaking louder and stronger. "No, we've been best friends since we were little."

"That's good," I stated with a smile she didn't see because she was still looking down.

I was so pleased with her answer but cautious. They had a history, but at least, there was nothing romantic. I put my finger under her chin lifting until her eyes met mine. There was a spark there that gave me hope. That spark told me that maybe her timid reaction to me was because I made her nervous in an enjoyable way. Her chest raised with a heavy breath, and it took everything in me not to look at her breasts.

She licked her bottom lip, and I had to take a step back. Fuck! Just like that my dick throbbed behind my zipper, and all she did was lick her own fucking lip. She was dangerous, and she had no fucking clue.

I had to turn my back on her so she didn't see exactly how she affected me. I didn't want to fucking chase her away, and I was afraid my big, tatted up self with a fucking hard-on would do exactly that. I tried distracting myself by gathering all the tools I needed for her piercing. I slipped my hands into the latex gloves and opened the needle package preparing the piercing gun.

"He was my best friend growing up. My mom left when I was young, so my dad raised me. He's a cop that alternates hours, so I spent a lot of time at Caleb's house. His parents babysat me," she rambled on as though she were uncomfortable with the stretched silence in the room. "Last week I overheard him on the phone telling whoever it was he needed to handle me, and I overreacted. I tend to do that."

A scowl formed on my face at her admission. I didn't know the entire story, but she shouldn't discount her own feelings.

"Did he say that?" I snapped anger in my voice.

"No," she denied immediately finally making eye contact. "He apologized for the misunderstanding and explained what really happened. He's a good guy and a good friend. I just get touchy when I hear people talking about me. I knew I overreacted almost immediately but was too stubborn to admit it."

I gave a soft chuckle at the look of consternation on her face. She really didn't like to be wrong, good to know. I liked the fact she didn't make excuses and owned up to her mistake.

"Everything good now?" I asked as I continued gathering my stuff.

"Yeah," she muttered.

I glanced at her over my shoulder to see her eyes on my ass. With a smirk, I turned back to my task at hand before she realized she had been caught checking me out.

After I had everything set up on the tray next to the chair, I stepped closer to her. She jumped in the seat as my fingertips brushed against her neck moving the hair that escaped her ponytail behind her ear. I felt the shiver run through her, and goose bumps popped up along her skin down the column of her neck. I smiled. I was glad I affected her because I sure as hell was affected by her.

"You good?" I asked her when she wrapped her arms around her middle.

She swallowed nervously looking up at me. "Yes," she whispered nodding.

I grabbed the clamps and needle. "You ready?"

She took a deep breath looking straight ahead of her giving me a perfect view of her profile. Her chin was held high and her jaw was locked in determination. Her creamy, pale skin was dusted with a pink rose hue. She was scared but strong.

I positioned the clamps and needle in the cartilage of her ear keeping my voice low and soothing. "Take a deep breath and release slowly." Once she inhaled and began exhaling, I pushed the needle through releasing the clamps and slipping the ring through, all in one fluid motion. "All done."

I stepped back taking my gloves off and throwing them in the trash can set in the corner of the room. I took one of the wet wipes out of a cannister on the counter and wiped my hands off. Latex gloves left a nasty feeling on my hands. I should have come to terms with it since I have to use them every damn day, but I still hated the feeling.

Her eyes shot to mine in surprise. "Really?"

I smiled. "Really. Not too bad, right?"

"Not at all," she said smiling. "All I felt was pressure, but it didn't hurt. Can I see?"

I nodded incapable of words at that moment handing her a handheld mirror. Her smile. Her smile had me at a loss. It lit up her whole face. Her eyes fucking sparkled, deep blue shining brightly. Her full lips stretched across her face had me thinking of other ways to stretch her full, pink lips.

"I love it!" she exclaimed.

A smile took over my face at her excitement over the piercing. Then, she did a little shimmy in the chair causing her unbound breasts to bounce lightly. I knew she didn't have a bra on because her nipples were pressed against the fabric of her shirt and had been since she walked into the shop.

I quickly looked away and cleaned up my area. When I was sure my dick would behave, I grabbed the aftercare instructions off of the counter. I handed her the paper, our fingertips brushing. Her eyes shot to mine, and I swear to all that was holy, I knew she was mine. I knew it like I knew my name was Rian James Landry.

She hastily stood up and almost fell. I caught her with a grip on her hips that put our bodies so close together. I felt the curve of her ass under my fingertips, the thickness of her thighs against my muscular ones, and her soft breasts against my hard chest. I had to physically restrain myself from moving. I could easily picture her naked and bent over the chair she just vacated.

At the flash of panic in her eyes, I stepped back, releasing my hold on her. I saw the heat in her gaze, but I also recognized the fear. I did not want to scare her, ever. I wanted that heat to expand, though. I wanted her to heat up for me.

She paid Tiff for her piercing and hauled ass out of the shop without another word spoken. She did glance back at me once before she was fully out of the shop. She seemed surprised to find me staring back at her, and I had to smile. I honestly did not think she knew I was interested in her in a serious way, but she would know, soon, if I had anything to say about it.

"What's up with that?" Blake asked coming up from the back.

Blake was one of the tattoo artists we took on as soon as we could afford it, and he was a beast, not just in tattooing but in size, also. He was very quiet and only said what needed to be said, so when he spoke you better fucking listen.

"I'm not sure," I answered honestly as I watched Violet walk towards her car in the parking lot.

I had no fucking clue what was up with that. I couldn't decipher the connection I felt with her, but I knew it was something to take seriously. She was beautiful, but I had met many beautiful women. I worked in a shop where ink candies were the norm coming in to catch my attention. It was more than her looks. It was the different shades of blue her eyes turned with each of her emotions, her expressive face not hiding anything. She was truer than anyone I had ever met before. There was no pretense or fake bullshit from her.

I was all about truth. I had a steady girlfriend in high school and a little beyond that proved to me how manipulative people could really be. I hadn't thought about Ashley in a long fucking time, but she was the only serious relationship I had as a reference. Well, as serious as a horny high school boy and girl could have. It was great for a while until it wasn't.

It was all good and fun when we were in high school. It was missed curfews and naked time. It wasn't fun anymore when high school ended and real life came into play. I knew I had wanted to open the shop, but I wanted to apprentice at another shop while I waited for my brother to turn eighteen. I needed the experience and guidance of someone with the knowledge to help me.

I knew I could draw and sketch beautiful work. I loved art from early on. I would draw on everything I could get my hands on. I loved to space out and put all my emotions into a piece. My parents were super supportive. They paid for art classes so I could learn the different mediums artists used. Then, I watched a tattoo reality show, and I was hooked. I knew drawing and tattooing were different and I needed to understand the differences. So, I got a job with a good dude named Bo at a shop in Houma.

He showed me everything he knew. I learned the different pigments of skin, what colors worked best, the perfect placement of the piece, and how to gauge a person to see if the piece fit them or not. I did not want anyone who came into my shop to regret the work I had done. I knew how to talk to my clients so they could receive something they would love for the rest of their lives.

Ashley wanted to be with someone who owned their own business, who made bank while making their own hours. She didn't or wouldn't understand the time I had to spend to perfect my craft. We went our separate ways within a year of me learning under Bo. Soon after that, Bo offered me a position. He knew all about my plan to open my own shop with Ryden. I was honest about my goals with him because I had mad respect for the man. He understood what I was about because he had had the same goals when he started out.

After that, I had started working on real clients. I started making pretty good money that I saved as much as possible. For the next two years, I had built up a steady clientele who eventually followed me to my own shop.

I was teaching Ryden on the side while he was still in high school and brought him into the shop to learn from Bo, too. He was eager to learn as much as possible so when the time came, he would be ready to tattoo people. It all worked out for us in the end. We had a successful shop that we could be proud of.

"Wasn't that the chick from the bookstore?" Harvey asked shaking me out of my wayward thoughts.

"How do you know her?" I demanded glaring at him.

I knew my tone was harsh as his eyes snapped to mine. I ignored Blake's quiet chuckle as I kept my glare on Harvey.

"Kendra works there, remember?" Harvey said slowly studying my face. "I've talked to Violet a few times."

Shit! I knew that. Kendra was Harvey's younger sister. She brought lunch to the shop a couple times a week and hung out with us more than that. From what I gathered, her home life wasn't that great, so she avoided going home. Harvey could not wait until she turned eighteen so she could move in with him. Luckily, for the both of them, they only had another few months to go.

"Yeah," I grunted watching Violet walk to her car. "I remember."

She had a nice sway to her hips as she walked, and I couldn't help but think I hated to see her go but loved watching her walk away. It was fucking corny, but damn, that ass was fine. I heard a low whistle and snapped my head in Harvey's direction. He was watching the same show I was, and I slapped him on the back of the head only feeling slightly bad.

Harvey was a good dude, a good friend, and a better employee. I did not employ assholes, but I did not like the way he said Violet's name like he knew her, which was fucking ridiculous. Logically, I knew that. Emotionally, however, was a different story. I wanted to beat on my chest and declare her mine, but I wasn't a fucking caveman. I really needed to get my shit in check.

By the way Harvey was looking at me while rubbing the back of his head, he thought the same. "What the fuck?" he asked with a scowl on his face.

I shrugged my shoulders without answering. An answer wasn't needed. His scowl turned to a smirk telling me he would have fun fucking with me. He was the clown of the shop. He always had a smile on his face and a joke on his tongue. He liked to rib people and make others laugh. I did not think he had a lot of laughter in his life before he struck out on his own that he was making up for lost time by laughing every day.

"Don't start," I warned glaring at the fucker.

"I don't know what you're talking about," he said holding his hands up.

"Sure, you don't," I grumbled walking to my office in the back.

"Boss man has a crush," I heard Harvey say laughing.

I slammed my door harder than I should have making the frames shake on the wall knowing he was right. I did have a fucking crush. I was a grown ass man who dealt with women on the regular, and I was infatuated with a girl I spent less than an hour with.

What the fuck was I going to do about it?

Enjoy it, I thought with a smile spreading across my face. I hadn't felt that level of interest for a woman in a long fucking time, so I was going to fucking enjoy it.

To continue reading Truth please purchase at your preferred retailer.

Acknowledgments

There are several people I want to give a shout out to that made this book possible. Everybody played a role in moving me forward with living my dream.

My mom and dad encourage me to follow my heart. They are super proud with what I have accomplished and that makes me ecstatic.

Melissa rocks as my side kick. I love her knowledge of books and her willingness to help me with researches. I would be left floundering if she didn't show me the digital way.

My betas, Stacy, Jessica, and Angie, made me realize how right my path as an author is. Their love for my book and the characters I brought to life makes me so flipping happy. I swear I have been doing a happy every day since they expressed their love for the Landrys.

Tina and Victoria took the task of editing while giving feedback. I appreciate their willingness to help and excitement over my success with this book.

About the Author

I was born and raised in Houma, Louisiana with a little time done in Texas when I was little. I'm an oilfield wife mother of three, one girl and two boys. Never a dull moment in my house. My mind creates another world. I love writing and creating, meeting characters along the way. I've written for a while as a hobby. As my kids get older, I let them know they can be anything they want to if they put the work in. I decided I needed to take my own advice and here I am. I'm an author. I want to share the words in my mind to the rest the world. I love adventures and this is an amazing adventure.

Connect with me

FaceBook https://www.facebook.com/MandyLWoodallAuthor/

Instagram https://www.instagram.com/mandylwoodall/

Twitter https://twitter.com/MandyWoodall

Goodreads
https://www.goodreads.com/author/show/16392593.Mandy_L_Woodall

Newsletter sign up http://eepurl.com/cx1Civ

Made in the USA
Columbia, SC
25 May 2019